10/4/18

To Tom Deebel Jr.

Best of luck m...

and the best years

ahead of you stay strong

and keep the iron awake.

ISBN: 978-1-942500-43-8

www.BoulevardBooks.org
Boulevard Books
The New Face of Publishing

BONDS

by John Curley

I cannot begin to thank everyone who helped me write this book. Here's my attempt.

I cannot properly thank Andrew Vachss for everything he's done since we crossed paths. To meet one of the few people whom I regard as a hero and having the interaction with him confirm, rather than subvert that sentiment, is refreshing. His actions speak for themselves, Res Ipsa Loquitor. I>

Ian Hogan, my friend, I hope you find time with everything going on now, to read the book. Thanks pal, many years from now when I join you, lower me down a cold drink once in a while. For many years my dear friend Bruce Walsh encouraged me to write. Although I sent him an early draft I don't know if he got to read it before he moved on. I'm sure Ian will save you a seat at the table pal. I'm sure Paul Scano will be waiting there as well. Thanks for your encouragement Paul, I am sure the three of you are in a better place because here is less good without you.

Thanks to Walter Hertman, who so many years ago introduced me to a love of reading and writing by extension, by chance.

Thanks, Mary, for the encouragement and the crew at Manor, except for Alan … okay, him too.

Thanks to all The MoM's Clint, Terry, Edwin, Brownie, Sparky, Pedro, Oleg, Deebs, Sgt. Grizz, Don, Josh, Muhlenkamp, Morrie, Seth, Kevin M, The Alcortas, Paolo, Jose, Alain, Doug, Maija, Tim S, Romi, the whole extended family.

Thanks to Maria Mia Maniatakos, wouldn't be here if not for you.

Thanks to Jeff Ostrie, he is as he appears in the book. Thanks to Doc Testa and Doc Dasaro for medical advice. Thanks to Chief Marino for advice and input, it is an honor Chief. Thanks to Billy Hayes and Jams. For the encouragement and the real cop info.

I'm honored to thank Wayne D. Dundee who, like our mutual friend, spent a lot of time to help out a new writer. Will Graham, thanks for the summary. Dream much, Will? Marc MacYoung, my older brother from another mother. Jeff Harrell, you the man. Thanks to Sensei George Smith for everything he did to help get me here. Steve, and Brogan, and Rob S., my brothers from across the pond. Nadine, sister from halfway around the world.

Thanks Jo. Coach Hinbern, and papa Dinosaur, Brooks Kubik,. Kilpat, aka Sandman. Freddi thanks for all the encouragement.

Sgt. Rock victory is the goal but the honor is always in the battle.

Thanks, Mom, I love you.

Ana C, now we shall see.

I wish my brothers could read.

Thanks to Darthvatore when you are sane, you are quite helpful. Breacher, you remain one of the best guys I've ever known. Thanks to Kathleen Hansen and Doc Bhatia for advice along the way. Thanks Lady Di (P) and Lady Di (M). Young Theodore Jeffrey Lawrence G.

Thanks to AV, Yan K, Brackley, High-Val, Mike Cirigliano, Joe Mure, Papa Brackley, The Bionic Lawyer, Tim Parlatore, Jim Lambert, ALDP, Pam Roth, for the advice on the law.

Jimmy Hannan, Joe Lavelle, and anyone else with those last names, the Merillo's for being our neighbors. Pop and Molly Hatchet. RHJ aka the Mole and evil Deb, Linda. Felice and Dawn who appear as themselves. Thanks, Commissioner Kerik. Larry DeV.

Bruce Walsh who always told me I had it in me.

So many others helped me along the way, and if I missed you, please forgive me, you'll be in the next one. The deadline looms as I write.

Thanks to Lance J Rhea and Jyl Anais Ion for the Photos and design.

Thanks to Jack Strandburg for the edits. Thanks Mandy.

My homage to Andrew Vachss and the late Robert B. Parker two enormous influences, is evident in the writing.

So many people were encouraging along the way if I missed you I apologize. Tim B, Abbs, Patrick Birkel who from the first post wanted a copy.

Jess E. Again my friends if I miss you it doesn't mean you were not important, the gray matter has its good days and its bad days. Thanks Avi Gvili. Modo ☺
For you that fought to save your child and paid the price l>

For every Transcender, you are the very best of our race and for those the system fails.

"Bonds"

by John A Curley

Prologue

I backed out from the bedroom, tears rolling down my face. I needed to check the rest of the house. In another second, I'd be in a chasm. In my mind, I slammed the steel door shut again, a habit I developed as a kid, around nine. When I needed to stop everything and suppress my feelings, I imagined a massive steel door slamming shut. The memories, the tears, the pain, everything other than the task at hand, lie behind that door. For now.

I searched the other bedrooms upstairs. Like the basement door, the attic door was locked. Nothing. It took ten minutes, yet felt like ten years.

I reached into my pocket and shut the video off on the phone. I called 9-1-1 and reported what I found. I told them I would wait at the house, and was armed, but would leave my weapon on the steps.

I went outside and sat on the steps. I removed my holster, un-chambered the round, ejected the magazine, and put the round, the magazine, the gun, the extra magazines, and the holster on the top step. I sat on the bottom step. It felt cold. She hated the cold.

Under my jacket and turtleneck, sweat dripped over my torso. Sitting outside, with painful grief taking over adrenaline, the cold was exacerbated. The heat inside the house felt stifling. The stress of finding someone I cared about murdered, searching inside an unfamiliar home, with the risk of confronting the killer, raised my internal temperatures to a boil.

Now, I felt cold, weakened by my grief, and powerless over a situation. She was gone. I wanted her back, wanted her breathing and happy, wanted to help her. I heard sirens.

I realized I was breathing too fast, feeling the initial panic of loss. I can't deal with this right now. I inhaled slowly to gain control. Somebody would pay. Somebody would fucking pay. The relief of anger removed the cold and the grief. He better hope the cops got him before I did.

Part 1

Components

1

I watched the back of my secretary's head as she swiveled her chair to look at the small bulletin board on the wall behind her. This was a different view, and considerably different surroundings than fourteen hours ago. We hired her six months ago. She quickly picked up our system, and developed a rapport with our clients. One of the main problems was, our clients felt lost if my partner or I weren't around. She was striking, confident, and refined.

I liked her from the moment I met her. She was beautiful, no question. The world is full of beautiful women, but she was also smart and strong. She demonstrated loyalty, always an important point with me. We became friends, and often ate lunch together in the office, and had a drink after work with other staff. We celebrated with Christmas Parties, St. Patrick's Day parties, etcetera. I made a conscious effort not to dwell on her, to ignore the attraction. Then, yesterday, she called me.

She swiveled back and opened a folder. Intent on her work, she had no idea I was staring. I thought about the complications this would raise, and at the same time remember what she did and said, how she felt, and how it felt to be with her. Her beauty complicated matters, and I almost didn't hire her for that reason, but her experience and skills surpassed her looks.

Today would be busy. My appointment book was open on my desk. No appointments until the DA's office at three, but a potential client called, and I had three or four people out in the field. Of course, there were pending problems on the various cases, and at least a dozen items demanding my attention. My attempts to forget what transpired the evening before failed.

The lights on the telephone board for all four lines lit up almost simultaneously. The receptionist and Mandy each answered one, and then the other, while two remained on hold. Mandy spoke with Mary the receptionist on the intercom, and came in shortly thereafter. Our eyes met. The connection between us was real, palpable.

"Tim DiBella is on one, four is the D.A.'s office asking if you could be there at a quarter to two instead of three."

I nodded. She smiled briefly, and her visage softened. I inhaled then said, "Quarter to is good, tell Tim I'll be with him in a minute."

"Okay, coffee?"

"Only if you're getting some yourself."

As I watched her walk away, I observed her tastefully short skirt and reflected, although the back of her head was nice; she had many things going for her.

I reached for the phone. "Good morning, counselor."

"Jimmy boy, I have a problem."

What else is new? "How can I help?"

"I have papers, an income execution order that needs to be served on St. Bart's by end of business. I have the original with the raised seal from the judge that needs to be served. The payroll department isn't cooperating, and hasn't responded to my faxes or mailings."

I didn't like Tim or the way he ran his practice. He didn't give a fuck about his clients. I didn't like how long he took to pay his bills, and most of all, I didn't like the way he used my nickname. Profit, however, superseded liking him.

"We have only six hours to make the service."

"I know," he said. "I'm sorry. We dropped the ball on this one."

He dropped the ball on all of them. "I'll pick them up myself within the hour."

"How much?"

"Three hundred."

"Jesus!"

"Tim, I have everyone out, and I'm jammed."

"Your fee schedule says next day service on a business in Richmond County is two hundred."

I smiled. "This is half day. I have to do it myself, and it's a major difficulty today. I'll need to reschedule two consults as well." The last part was a lie.

"Aw c'mon, I'm a good client. Aren't I?"

If by "good client," you mean you always pay late, you only call when you have a problem, and you never use investigators, sure. Same as you are with your clients, Timmy. A woman came into my office once and told me he charged her a thousand dollars for going to court himself and filing her divorce papers. I also knew I wasn't likely his first call.

"Sure, but there's nothing I can do. Jeff sets the prices."

After a bit of grumbling, he agreed. It would have been two hundred for anyone else, but I knew I wouldn't get paid for two months; and then only after I sent second, third, and fourth requests for payment.

"See you in a bit."

Mandy brought in the coffee. Coffee was meant for ceramic cups. The warmth of the cup in your hand, and the warm feel of ceramic mattered. I nodded to one of the client chairs, and she smiled and sat down.

"Any plans for this evening after work?"

"No," she said, and smiled.

"If I take you out to dinner, will you eat like a normal person, and not like a woman on a first date?"

She smiled wider. "I'll do my best not to embarrass you."

I smiled back. "I can't imagine you doing anything but classing me up. Please tell me you don't have an aversion to meat."

"None whatsoever."

"I'm heading out. Why don't you call Alex at Luger, mention my name, and tell him we'd like 6:30 reservations. He'll tell you either 6:15 or 6:45.

Choose whichever time is better for you, eat a light lunch, and make sure there's a least a couple hundred in petty cash. If not, withdraw that much when you make the deposit later."

"Will do," she said, then smiled, got up, and returned to her desk.

I watched her walk, which she obviously knew, because she turned and smiled before she sat down. I smiled back. Jesus Christ, she *was* beautiful. This would be complicated, *very* complicated, but apparently I didn't mind, because I couldn't stop thinking about her. It wasn't as though I hadn't thought about her before; I did, but promised myself I wouldn't act on it, and seldom broke promises. But I did, and knew I would, two seconds into that phone call. Actually being with her was better than anything I previously imagined, and I have a good imagination. What the hell. Complications make life interesting.

I got in my car and drove to DiBella's office. Robert Plant made it tolerable. I had, of course, taken seven or eight second, third, and fourth request for payments on bills with me. When I got there, of course Tim had a client. His secretary rolled her eyes and said, "I'll be sure to give them to him," then mouthed the words to me, "we got a lot in today. I'll put your bills on top. You should get something by the end of the week."

We dated a few times before she got serious with another guy. She was kind and sweet, pleasing to the eye, and considerably improved the drab seventies style of the office. I was happy that she was happy.

Any faint misgivings I felt about charging too high of a fee disintegrated after my arrival at St. Bartholomews.

2

When I got in, I asked one of the security guards where payroll was. He directed me to the other side of the hospital, and one of the many smaller buildings. I knew he assumed I was someone important that worked for or with the hospital. A good suit often acted as an ID card. I walked the five minutes to the building where payroll was located.

I nodded to the security guard seated at the desk in the foyer of the small building. He smiled, and I continued on my way. Irritation crept into my psyche. The meeting at the District Attorney's Office was important. The irritation worsened when I knocked on the payroll door and no one answered.

A fat, mean looking man walked out of the door, down the hall, and to the left. I think the door had ARCHITECT stenciled on it, but I couldn't be sure. He came out, and I noticed from the corner of my eye he was standing with his hands on his hips, staring at me. Imposing. I ignored him, which I thought might irritate him, and continued knocking.

"Can I help you?" He asked after a long pause, his voice thick with condescension.

"Are you from payroll?" I asked.

"No," he replied with a harsh squint and tight jaw.

"Then you can't help me," I replied, with what I hoped was infuriating politeness.

"Who are you?" he asked. Apparently, my plan worked, as his tone indicated anger.

"I'm the guy looking for payroll," I responded. Although I meant to be sarcastic, I smiled and appeared affable.

"Hey, do you work for the hospital?" Irritated and angry, he was irascible by nature. I thought it didn't take much poking. Mission accomplished.

"No, actually, I'm just delivering something to your payroll department."

"You're not supposed to be in here, Jack."

I love it when people call me by names other than my own. "I imagine that's a matter of perspective," I said, and smiled again.

"You shouldn't have gotten past our security. It won't happen again."

"You know, by sheer coincidence about five years ago, I actually did a security survey at your hospital. It sucked then, and it sucks now."

"Well, I'm in charge of security now, and rest assured, it won't happen again."

"I'm sure you'll see to that," I said, with a smile. "I'm sorry if I took you off the Stairmaster."

He cursed under his breath as I walked away, and I heard his office door slam. No doubt he would get on the phone with someone and heads would surely roll.

When I walked back downstairs, I asked the guard where RISK Management might be, since experience dictated that department would likely be proper for service as well. He was a nice man, and I felt bad. He nodded his head in front and to the left toward another small building. I walked quickly across to the building he indicated. An unmanned security desk sat in the lobby. I walked to the second floor and found an attractive young woman just closing the door to RISK management.

"Hi," I said with a smile. My face was getting tired. "I have a delivery for payroll, but there's no one there. I was hoping RISK Management could take it."

"I'm sorry," she said. "I'm from a different department. I was just leaving something on someone's desk. They're all in a meeting with payroll."

I almost laughed. "Would you know where that is?"

"Somewhere in the main building."

I smiled again, thanked her, and as an afterthought, said, "May I ask which department you work for?"

"Human resources," she replied, as her eyes lit up.

"I hope I have a delivery for human resources ... *soon.*"

"I'm Jenna," she said.

"See you soon I hope."

"I hope so too," she said with a smile, and then walked away. I admire the female form, and watched her walk, but was surprised to think of Mandy. I looked at my watch. At an accelerated pace, I walked outside the building and past the guard, who was returning with a cup of coffee.

I walked back into the main entrance of the hospital. The young security guard who helped me initially walked toward me and asked if I found payroll.

"I was told that payroll and risk management are in a meeting. It's urgent I get there."

"Follow me," he said. We walked through a maze of corridors, but I've been in the hospital many times before and had a general idea where we were.

He took me to a conference room. I thanked him, and was happy he walked away without bringing me into the room. I had a job to do, but he was a nice kid, and I didn't want to get him in trouble. If he worked for me I'd have reprimanded him, but he was a nice kid all the same. I walked through the door. Seven or eight people were gathered around a conference table, in the process of getting up, closing planners, folders, etc. A studious looking woman with short gray hair and glasses looked at me with raised eyebrows.

"I need to speak with someone from payroll."

"That would be me," said a heavyset woman with short brown hair, closing a briefcase. She wore rings on almost every finger.

I smiled. My face was sore. "I'm sorry. I believe we met, but I forgot your name."

"Ellen."

"You're the head of the department, right?"

"Yes, what do you need?"

"I have an income execution order your department hasn't responded to." I withdrew the order from my suit coat pocket and held it out. She squinted and cocked her head. "I'm not accepting it."

I sighed. This was *really* getting old. "Allow me to educate you in regard to the rules and regulations governing service of process within the state of New York. Acceptance of papers is not voluntary. If that were the case, no one would ever get served. Your department was faxed and mailed this order on numerous occasions. In addition to serving these papers, my office has determined that," I paused, looking at the papers in my hand, "Dr. Riley happens to be dating someone from your department."

She pressed her lips together and narrowed her eyes. "That's not …"

"Allow me to finish, Madam. As acceptance is not an issue, I'm informing you, which I don't have to do, you're now formally served with this income execution order for Dr. Riley. He's eighteen months behind in his child support," I said, with a genuine grin. "Knowing Judge DiNapoli, if I testify before her that I personally served you with these papers, and you still didn't comply, she won't view that action in a positive manner. If I were you, I'd speak to RISK Management and your in-house counsel, then prepare for a contempt proceeding."

As I walked out the door, nothing but silence followed me. I walked back the way I followed the guard, and winked and thanked him as I passed. I looked at my watch on my way to the car. I had twelve minutes to get to the D.A.'s office. As I turned on the ignition, Warren Zevon greeted me. I turned the volume way up as he sang the line "and his hair was perfect," then looked in the rearview mirror, and saw mine wasn't.

It's a short drive to St. George from the hospital. St. George is the political and business center of Staten Island. Government offices, Supreme Court, the Chamber of Commerce, a number of good restaurants, and the beautiful old St. George Theatre were scattered throughout the area. I was on good terms with the parking lot attendant in the open-air lot down the block from the courthouse. I pulled into the lot and took my usual spot. Reuben was giving directions to the courthouse to an older couple.

"So just walk down the street," he pointed. "On the left side, right after the only intersection, is the courthouse." The couple walked away, and he turned to me.

"Hey, boss, how you been?"

"All is well, my friend," I said, as I handed him a twenty, ten more than the usual fee. As always, he started to make change, and as usual, I waved him off. He smiled and thanked me, then turned to help the next customer.

I walked the short distance to the courthouse, across the street from the County Clerk. The District Attorney's Office in some courtrooms is temporarily housed there while the new courthouse is being built. I entered the courthouse, and one of the officers I knew nodded.

"How goes it?" I asked.

"One year from today. Retirement."

"Be sure to look me up if you're interested," I said.

"Well, I can't very well stay home with the wife all day."

"No, we can't have that. I need to relinquish la pistola."

"Not much going on today. If it's only a stop or two, no one's going to notice."

"Appreciated, however, I have business across the street." The company providing security for the County Clerk had no facilities for people armed with weapons, and it was common practice to bring the weapons across the street to the courthouse. Bob nodded. I went to the room where the firearms were checked, and left mine.

A few minutes later, after a delay at the metal detector and the disapproving looks of some of Bridgeview Security's personnel, I sat upstairs in the waiting room for the district attorney's office. I said, "Hi" to some of the ADAs and detectives I knew. When I reached the reception area, I greeted the pleasant looking woman, who on previous visits appeared invulnerable to charm … at least *my* charm.

I flashed my warmest and most sincere smile. "Jonathan Creed to see Mr. Doyle."

"You can go right in, Mr. Creed. He's expecting you." She smiled briefly and professionally then went right back to work.

I was in Bob Doyle's office a number of times. It was well decorated with rich dark oak, thick carpet, diplomas and a few tasteful paintings on the wall. On his huge oak desk sat a picture of his wife, children, and two Golden Retrievers. A marginally toned down refugee from Saturday Night Fever occupied one of the chairs.

Bob was a big man, at least six inches taller than my five foot ten, and built like I was, but for a man his height, I'd put him at almost three hundred. He had short brown hair and a high forehead, with a pleasant face that could be serious or mirthful, depending upon the circumstances. He was a politician, but I liked him anyway. He was clean-shaven, and wore expensive cologne.

He rose from his chair as I came in, and seemed genuinely pleased to see me. We shook hands over his desk. Less enthusiastic and much slower, the Guido stood to my right.

"Good to see you, Jimmy," he said, as he shook my hand. His family came over from Ireland when he was a kid, so he still spoke with a slight brogue.

"Same here, Bob."

He gestured to one of the open chairs, and I sat. I'm good at sitting. "How's business?" he asked me.

"Booming, thanks in part to your office," I said with a wink.

"I must be doing my job if you're busy," he replied. "Good that you're still keeping in shape."

"I can say the same for you. In a parallel world, I know you under different circumstances, and you got me season tickets for the Giants before you retired as All-Pro defensive end."

We both laughed. "The wife is on top of me to exercise," he said. "For some reason unknown to me, she'd like to keep me around for a while."

We had a good relationship, which bordered on friendship. That relationship was strong, because, at least so far, each of us always did what he promised. Our relationship was also strengthened because I contributed twenty-five hundred the last time he campaigned.

We continued to exchange pleasantries for a few minutes, when I felt the Guido stirring. Probably late for his afternoon cannoli. I was as much Italian as Irish, so felt no politically correct generated guilt due to my ethnic musings. Actually, I *never* recalled any politically correct generated guilt.

"Before we get down to our business, I wanted to introduce you to Tony Giordano. He'll be heading up the investigation squad when Mark retires."

"We've actually met before," I said, as I extended my hand.

"You seem familiar," he said, without emotion.

"I was just telling Tony how you've been of service to our office on occasion," Bob said.

"Surprising," Giordano said. "I wouldn't think a private investigator would be helpful to a district attorney. Don't you usually work for the other side?"

"I come across information on occasion," I said, with a quick smile.

"Don't you usually work to get those scumbags off?"

"Not all of my work is criminal cases. You may want to remember, everyone is actually entitled to a defense. And there are occasions, albeit not too frequently, where the police are wrong."

"I could never understand why cops put perps away, then turn around and try to get them off."

"Well, it should be easy for you. I wasn't a cop."

"I didn't think it was possible to do something like this without being a cop first."

"Don't feel bad. I didn't think it was possible for someone who spent their career primarily kissing ass and driving bosses, and advancing through political connections, to become the person in charge of the district attorney's investigation squad."

The Guido's face darkened, and he opened his mouth to reply. I still smiled warmly, then Bob got up from his chair and said firmly, "Anthony. Jim is a good friend, and has worked with Chris in the past. I expect you'll develop a good relationship with him as well." Giordano nodded.

"I got a few things to do. I'll see you tomorrow, Bob."

The Gindaloon looked at me. "See ya around."

"Nice seeing you again," I said, and smiled warmly and falsely for about the thousandth time that day. Dickhead.

"You must owe someone something."

"You know politics; debts have to be repaid, Jimmy."

I smiled. "Must be a large debt."

He smiled back. "They all are, at least as far as the secured party is concerned."

"How does re-election look?"

"Odds are we don't have to worry about a job anytime soon."

"That's good. I would hate to have to establish contacts," I said, after searching for a proper word. "If the guard changed, that is."

"Now, that would be a shame," he said with a wry smile.

I paused then added a genuine sentiment. "You also manage to do some good."

His smile changed to more warm than wry. "Did you want coffee?"

I looked at my watch. "It's still early enough in the day, I'd love one."

He pressed the button on his intercom for one of the interns. A young man barely out of college or law school came in. We chatted idly but sincerely until the intern returned with our coffee. I sipped the coffee, and found it to be worthy of another immediate sip, then took a longer sip and nodded my head in approval. Bob's was almost gone.

"So, how can I help you, my friend?"

"Actually, today I'm going to help you. I have information on a low level but very successful drug dealer who's laundering his money within a stone's throw of your office."

Bob's head shot up, his eyebrows raised. He put down the coffee cup on the desk. "Do tell."

"I would appreciate something out of this."

"And that would be?"

"Said drug dealer employs people he trusts. His sister, who works for him in the sales department, is in a custody battle with my client. I'd like to ensure your investigation includes her, that she's arrested and serves time. I'm attempting to assist my client to see his child isn't raised by addicts and dealers, and gets to live in a stable environment."

"Does she have a prior record?" he asked. "What kind of drugs are we talking?"

"A misdemeanor and a few juveniles. It's likely you'll catch her with a considerable amount in her possession, at her apartment, and while the child is there. Even thirty days would be helpful. Their inventory is primarily ganja and pills. However, we're talking several hundred pounds of weed a month. I need to move on this quickly. We have a court date next month. She makes a habit of keeping the kid around while they conduct business."

He looked me in the eye. "How reliable is this?"

I met his gaze and smiled, making a mental note to watch a sad movie at home later to prevent me from smiling.

"I verified the operation with a couple of weeks of surveillance."

"Based on my experience with you, that's more than sufficient."

"Please tell me I can still speak with Mark."

"Tony isn't that bad," Bob said with a laugh. "But Mark will be around for a few more weeks. You should come to the retirement party. He's in his office. I'll call down and tell them you're stopping by."

I stood and shook the big man's hand. As I headed for his door, I heard him tell Mark on the intercom I was on my way down. I walked through the reception area and into the hall, past the elevator, and walked the stairs two flights down. Just after I walked over to the cop at the security desk and asked for Mark, he walked through the door. A few seconds later, we were in his office.

I liked Bob, and felt I could trust him. I also liked Mark, and knew I could trust him. His suit was ill-fitting and hanging off him. He was about my height and had a pleasant face. His close cut gray hair was spreading. We walked into his office after getting coffee.

The surroundings here were significantly less aesthetically pleasing than two floors up. The coffee didn't taste like the beans were hand-selected by a barista the way it did two floors up. The D.A.'s investigators mulled around the office, including Joni Moore, who was previously a second-grade detective with the NYPD, and for a short time, more than a friend. She noticed me when I walked, and smiled and waved. I waved back and winked as Mark, then walked toward his office. Tony, the Guido, was walking toward Mark's office as well.

Once we sat down, I sipped the coffee, then grimaced. "I'm fairly certain I have no more enamel on my teeth."

Mark laughed, "This ain't Starbucks."

"I'm not asking for Starbucks, just something besides coffee colored sulfuric acid."

Mark said, "Bob tells me you have something important." The Guido observed silently.

I told him the information I had, and the name of the business. He shook his head. I provided all the details, out of state delivery dates, the sales associates, and delivery methods. I gave him several license plates and addresses of the principals. Both he and Giordano jotted notes while I spoke.

"Bob said you'd need something on this," Mark asked.

I told him about my clients soon to be ex-wife, and what I needed. I told him I needed it quickly, and I brought it here instead of other agencies so they wouldn't get caught with their pants down. Mark assured me he'd do his best to get it done, and I trusted him. I also told him about the fix-it man.

"Their cousin is an ex-cop, responsible for my client being arrested on a bullshit Order of Protection. The charges were dropped, but he's been a general thorn in everyone's side. He doesn't have many friends, but has some. He's not completely stupid and gets around enough. Be aware of that when you set up the tail."

I gave them his name and address, and what kind of car he drove. Half an hour later, I gave them every detail I knew. Mark and I set up a tentative lunch date for early next week. I shook hands with him and the Guido, who seemed a little more amiable this time, although appearances are often deceiving. It might not be entirely out of the question that I, myself, could rub someone the wrong way. I rode the elevator down, then walked across the street, claimed my gun, walked to my car, and drove back to the office.

My last appointment, a referral from a woman I knew, was waiting for me.

3

His eyes darted back and forth. Not nervous, but hyper aware. He was shorter than I was by a couple of inches, and weighed about the same. Hard fat, with a lot of muscle underneath, probably built over a number of years while a guest of the state or the government. His nose was off center.

Vicky brought him in to see me then she waited outside. I felt sad to see her this way: a couple of almost healed bruises, and high as a kite. She did well as a successful mortgage broker before the economic collapse, now she was Anthony Luca's kept mistress. The Gumada, as he would likely refer to her.

Back when we were exploring the limits of her orgasmic endurance, she smoked a little weed now and again, but no coke. She managed to accomplish a lot with average intelligence, and a kick ass body. Now, she was a shell, emaciated and worn. I saw her about a month ago, after I heard she was with a wise guy who used her as a punching bag. These days I rarely gave a fuck about anyone, but the memory of her, the laughs we shared and the smell of her hair, rushed through me. She looked as if she hadn't slept or eaten for days. She was a wreck.

Years of playing poker well enabled me to keep my jaw from dropping. She almost walked past me before she realized it was me. When I hugged her, she felt like skin and bones. Her face was drawn, and she looked like she suffered from combat fatigue. Not once, but several times I offered her help when we talked. I told her I could get her away from him, make a few calls, get him off her, but she insisted she was in love.

We met a few years ago when she hired me; first to find out who owned property a client of hers wanted, then for security work after she had trouble with someone. We dated after I finished the job. I still had an open retainer with her for security work.

"He's the first one I fell in love with since you," she said. Her eyes lowered and she walked back outside, which was good, because I had no response.

I told her at the time she wasn't in love with me. Apparently, the men she was didn't care whether she felt good. She knew ahead of time, like any other woman I'd been with, I wasn't looking for a relationship, but I was rarely honest enough to say I didn't think I'd ever be looking for one.

Now, she walked in and out of the building while I talked with Luca. When he walked in, I saw he'd been worked over. I could tell by the way he walked, and the way he eased himself into the chair. I'd been worked over and worked people over in my time, so knew what it looked like and how it felt.

"A car accident," he said. "So, Vick says you know who's a good lawyer and who ain't."

"It's rare for the general public to know a good lawyer from a bad one," I said. "I work with them. Maybe seventy-five percent of my business is from attorneys. I think we've both been around enough to know, reputations are rarely earned properly."

Vicky came in to get a cigarette from him again, her hands shaking. I smiled at Luca while we talked and felt even sadder for her. I thought about the last time we were together. Her head was resting on my chest, and I felt her tears on my skin as she told me she didn't think it was possible to feel good like that.

"I think I came more times tonight with you than I did in my entire life."

"Well, it's a tradeoff, see? Sexism and the pain of childbirth in exchange for multiple orgasms." I tried to lighten things a little but it didn't work, one of the many times I realized I wasn't always as funny as I thought.

"So tell me the situation, Anthony," I said. "That way I'll know who to send you to."

He rambled on about how his wife convinced their two daughters to lie, and they all had O.P.'s against him.

"Are they temporary orders of protection?" I asked. "You have a court date for the judge to decide if it's going to be a permanent order of protection? And are there criminal charges pending for assault?"

He nodded. I tapped my fingers on the desk. Some time ago I removed my hand from my gun, which I put on a small shelf under the desk. I had by no coincidence faced my consult.

"... and dat fuckin lawyer, Rizzo, she's just gonna lie like dey all do..."

Yes, I'm sure your wife's lawyer is the bad guy in this. I'm sure you did nothing wrong. You wouldn't hit your wife and kids. I winced as he continued to butcher the English language. I didn't have extensive language schooling myself, nor was Locust Valley Lockjaw an effect of mine. I use profanity on occasion to make a point, but it felt as though my ears were bleeding.

"I spent 10 years wit da feds, because I picked da wrong lawyer," he continued. His voice sounded like gravel swirled in his throat and crowded his voice box. His speech was a caricature, but he would be far from pleasant to deal with if he crossed the average person's path.

Then I remembered. It's a small world after all. I once worked for an attorney who represented one of Luca's co-defendants. I dealt with the lawyers, but had a limited role in that production, and never met any of the accused. I remember that, although at that point my eyes didn't widen much anymore, they still did on occasion, and that was one of those times. Mike Barone was the lawyer I worked for, and it was one of his last cases before he retired.

They were all guilty, but Luca was sold out in more ways than one. Not only had his "friends," sold him out, his lawyer did too. He took a bad deal for his client. Barone explained it to my satisfaction. He was considered one of the best around by those of us in the know. Luca should have received a much better deal. My employer never explained why he thought Luca was sold out. Backroom deal? His mouthpiece had better things to do? I didn't know, and for the most part, other than out of sheer curiosity, I didn't care.

Luca droned on. Yeah, yeah, yeah. My mind wandered back to Vicky, chain-smoking in the parking lot. Back to business, a large part of which was referrals. I gave him the name and number of the attorney who could handle both the family court O.P.s, and the criminal court complaint against him. Vicky came in and he told her they were leaving. I walked them to the door. He shook my hand, complimented me on my grip, and told me with a short laugh that was how he knew he could trust me. She hugged me goodbye, and judging by the look on his face, held on just long enough to get a rap in the mouth later.

I refused the gratuity he offered, something I rarely do. I didn't like owing people, and liked the idea of owing him even less. After they left I found I'd been staring at the door a long time. It's a small world after all.

4

Peter Luger is the place where the cooks in heaven secretly get their steaks. Mandy and I arrived early and stayed at the bar for a few minutes. Alex, the day manager, had left, and Tom, the night manager, greeted me as we walked through the door. After we shook hands, he smiled and talked with us for a few minutes. I loved Tom, and Luger wasn't just a place I loved; it was a great investment.

I landed more clients from there than I could count. Tom asked me how soon we'd like to eat, and I told him, "Yesterday." He smiled and walked into one of the dining rooms, came out shortly, and then we were seated, much to the disappointment of a few grumbling people already waiting in line.

"How do you like your steak?" I asked.

"Rare to medium rare."

"Honest? And for true?"

"Honest and for true."

I resisted the urge to say we should get married. My offbeat sense of humor sometimes elicited a non-humorous response, and that particular line once elicited a let-me-get-the-hell-out-of-here response.

The waiter came. Some of the wait staff acted a little gruff, but all were characters. In the 80's, when I first started coming, they were mostly German, now they're mostly Russian or Eastern European. I knew this one.

"Do we need a menu?" he asked. "Not that I would serve you if you asked for one," he snorted.

"I believe I told you what was on the menu your first day, Vladimir."

"I have grown emotionally since then, Jonathan." Vlad replied.

I laughed and Mandy smiled. "Steak for two, rare, German fried potatoes, creamed spinach, tomato and onion salad, shrimp cocktail, and two slices of the bacon."

"Very good, I will bring you two more drinks?"

"Please, and some water."

I looked at her as she looked around. Luger in Williamsburg is rustic with wooden tables. The building is over 200 years old, with hardwood floors, plaster walls, and an ornate metal ceiling. The neighborhood had changed a dozen times.

The restaurant opened in 1887. I heard the menu offered prime rib as well as steak, but in truth, never actually saw the menu.

She had a curiosity about her. She appeared comfortable, but excited that she'd never been there.

I gazed at her, and like every other time before, detected no flaws. She was tall, five seven. Her curious eyes, like hazel but more blue, were now fixed on me. She was stunning. Raven hair a few inches past her shoulders. Her face was fresh and delicately sculptured. Her striking eyes were kind and bright at the same time. Her skin was lightly tanned, her build between medium and slim. She was toned and strong, curved in the right places. I never really had a type per se; I found most women beautiful in one way or another, and she was beautiful in too many ways. She was bright, with a strength to her, and was maddeningly sensual.

"Can I ask..." she started, then trailed off as we gazed at each other.

"Ask away."

"How old are you?"

"Forty five."

Vlad brought the bacon, shrimp, tomato, onion, and rolls. The shrimp were the size of small dogs, and the bacon, cooked for just a minute in the 1200-degree oven, was more than a quarter inch thick. The tomatoes and onions was what you put the steak sauce on. The staff might smack you if it went anywhere near the steak with the sauce, and they would, in fact, be justified.

"Oh my God," she said, as she tried the bacon.

"Amazing isn't it?" I said.

"I'm sure this will mean an extra hour in the gym all week long, but it's worth it."

We made small talk but not idle conversation while we ate. She asked me things in a charming and patternless way, and I did the same of her. I knew some things since I hired her three weeks ago. She was thirty and had a son, who wasn't at her apartment last night.

I felt restless and was trying to decide whether to go for a walk or a ride, when she called my cell. I heard fear in her voice. She apologized and asked if I could see her, then apologized again.

When I got there I asked if she was hungry. She said she'd eaten. I asked if she wanted to go for a drink or coffee. She brought me a cold Blue Moon in a glass, and one for herself, and we sat on her couch. Pink Floyd played in the background. She drew her legs underneath her on the couch and looked at the television, which was off.

"Are you okay?" I asked.

She nodded, "Yes," then looked at me and smiled, and moved closer. Shortly after, she moved even closer and pressed her lips to mine. I was never one to be impolite, so naturally pressed mine to hers. We kissed for a while, and then she laid her head on my shoulder.

"Would you like to ..." she began to say, and softly kissed my neck. I stood, scooped her up in my arms, and carried her to the bedroom. A man of action am I.

Her hair smelled faintly of lavender, and the clean natural smell of her skin was intoxicating. She was sensitive to my touch. I couldn't quite be sure, but I thought she climaxed before her clothes were off. The things she said, the way she felt, the way she tasted, and the warmth of her skin, intoxicated me. She was erotic, and her actions, sensual. She was bold yet vulnerable at the same time.

We were at it for a long time. As sensitive as she was, how easily she reached orgasm, as intense as her body rocked, moved, and shuddered. We didn't pause; we didn't rest. Forever later, we lay there. The room was quiet.

Her head, again rested on my shoulder, and her fingers moved across me. Her hand ran across my shoulders and chest, then rested on my leg.

"Strong," she murmured.

We repeated the exercise program again and then slept. We said about a dozen words each. Sometimes, conversation is overrated. *Most times.*

The steak and accoutrements arrived. As you can count on the sun rising in the east and setting in the west, you can count on the steak at Luger cooked perfect every time. Vlad put steak and juice on each of our plates, followed by spinach and potatoes, then left without a word, as we had half our drinks left.

"Is your son with you tonight?" I asked.

"No, he's with my mom."

We talked more and learned more. We both ordered coffee. I ordered strudel, which she sampled. Without requesting it, Vladimir brought Schlag, German whipped cream, which went on the strudel and in the coffee; one of the few times I didn't drink it black. I rarely eat dessert during the week, but when I came here, which wasn't often enough, that rule went out the window.

"In a rush to go home?" I asked her.

She shook her head, "No" and smiled.

"My place?"

"Sure," she said.

We were silent during the drive back, but it wasn't an uncomfortable silence. Her hand rested on mine. I turned on the radio, and Carol Miller was just about to get the Led Out. Things progressed far better than I expected. We talked for a while. Before I could say I was in a non-commitment place, she told me about her divorce. She was lonely and want became need. Right after the divorce, she made the common mistake of jumping into a too serious relationship too fast. She was on her own, with her son half the time. She was getting herself together, and wasn't ready to date seriously. At first, she felt a little bad at how fast things happened between us. I told her what I genuinely felt. Intimacy can be as necessary as breathing or eating; and no reason to feel ashamed.

We both agreed this type of relationship could be difficult, but both agreed to chance it. It was a first for me to be with someone that worked for me. We both agreed, if either of us felt uncomfortable, it would be an easy out.

I was honest with her, and told her my sex drive was like Le Mans. She said she didn't mind that. I thought I made it to heaven when she said how hot she found a few of the ladies that stopped by to see me, although to my credit, I managed not to drool. After a few more drinks, we repeated some of the activities from the previous evening. We spoke a little before she drifted off.

"Your name is Irish?"

"Ah sure, now," I said, in a badly manufactured brogue.

"Why do people call you Jim?"

"My initials."

"That doesn't help, sweetie," she said.

I laughed. "My full name is Jonathan Michael Creed. My uncle, who was a State Supreme Court Judge, took to calling me JMC, or sometimes JM. With his voice, JM sounded like Jim."

She laughed. "Are you Irish?"

"I'm a mutt, father was Irish and Italian. Mom is Polish, Dutch, and American Indian." I paused. "Forgive me, *Native* American."

She fell asleep with her head on my chest and her hand across my shoulder. The room felt cool. My left hand rested lightly on her back. The pale light from the alarm clock read one-thirty. I never slept with a woman unless I felt genuinely attracted. I also cared about every single woman I'd ever been with, and never considered any woman a trophy. But after that first major one, where the four-letter word came into play, there hadn't been another one, at least not to that level. The pain was long lasting, haunting, and searing. I was never in a rush to risk that again.

I was wide awake. My phone started flashing. Jeff and I split the weeks, and this was mine. We signed contracts, and sometimes were needed in emergencies after business hours. I managed to get the phone without disturbing her.

It was Vicky. I was a little concerned, or I wouldn't have risked waking Mandy. I answered and said hello as softly as possible, but heard nothing, then it disconnected. When I called back, it rang once before going to voicemail. I sent a text, asking if she was okay. Nothing.

"Everything okay?" Mandy asked me softly.

"It was Vicky. No answer, didn't pick up when I called back."

"The woman from today?"

"Yeah."

"Are you worried?"

"A little," I said. "She was a wreck. I don't like Luca."

"Do you need to call her back?"

"I tried, sent her a text, too. Maybe I shouldn't have."

"Why?"

"Maybe Luca will object to her trying to call me. I'm betting he'd be free with his hands."

She rolled over. "Why not call the cops?"

"And tell them what?" I shook my head. "It could have been a misdial."

"But you don't think so."

"No."

I kissed her forehead and got out of bed. I went into the bathroom, washed my face, and then got dressed. I reached into the nightstand and took the Glock .45 and two extra magazines of ammunition. New York's latest governor, in response to a tragic shooting, had pushed legislation through to reduce the number of carried magazines to seven rounds. The kind of thing a politician would do to make it look like they were actually accomplishing something. Knee jerk reactions were often worthless. Like my going over to Luca's house.

I put on jeans and a black turtleneck, with heavy solid black shoes and a brown leather jacket. I had most of my outer coats altered, to allow me to reach the gun on my hip through a hole in my right jacket pocket. Not a big deal as most of the clothes that fit me around the chest had sleeves that ended past my fingers, so there were alterations anyway.

"What are you going to do?" she asked, concern evident in her voice.

"I'm not sure, baby girl. I'll look and see, but they're probably both asleep by now."

"Please be careful."

"I will. I promise. I'll do my best to get back quickly to a warm bed and a beautiful woman."

She smiled. "Somehow when you say it, it doesn't sound like a line."

"Well for one, I already nailed the hot babe."

She threw a pillow at me.

"And for two, it's not a line if I speak the truth. You *are* beautiful. I'll set the alarm. Try and sleep."

"No chance. I'll turn the TV on."

I told her again I'd be careful, then went outside. It was raw, giving the sky a clean and clear look, with stars showing as white pinholes of light in a dark valance. I got in my car. I started remembering things about Vicky and pushed them away, reminding myself to stay clear for the task at hand. I thought for a few seconds about the many possibilities. I took my cell phone out and put it in blocking mode, then turned the recorder on and put on 1010 Wins, the twenty-four hour news station. I left it recording on the seat and pulled away.

5

I was at Luca's, a small mother-daughter at the end of a dead-end street, on the South Shore, in less than fifteen minutes. I hoped the lights were off, but of course, the lights were on. I parked at the top of the block, cell phone still recording in my pocket.

I was down the block in less than a minute. I startled a cat exploring a garbage can. I was quiet, and as I approached the house, I saw two cars in the driveway. On the first floor, all the lights were lit.

My stomach dropped as I looked through the window, and I knew this would be bad. Luca was lying face down on the floor. Blood showed on the back of his head, on his back, and on the floor around him. My first thought was, I hoped she shot him, then she'd probably be alive. We can work with that.

The front door was unlocked. Gun in hand, I pushed open the door. I'm not interested in being a hero or a cop, and wouldn't be here if it weren't for Vicky. After passing the prostate exam and colonoscopy included in the NYPD regulations for obtaining carry permits for myself and some of the people working for me, I spent considerable time learning how to use it and what to do. I spent several weeks training with a good friend who was a retired Navy SEAL for just that purpose. There were also a lot of good-looking women in the bars down in Virginia Beach.

I searched the house room by room. I couldn't help Luca; he was dead, but honestly, I wouldn't have cared in either case. I was there for Vicky.

Drug machinery and product sat on the kitchen table, along with coffee in a cup at room temperature. I was quiet enough that someone else in the house wouldn't know I was there. I knew I shouldn't be, because I had no idea of the situation. I called out her name after I searched the first floor. The idea of her afraid and hiding somewhere in the house, maybe armed, stuck with me. That's what I hoped.

I called out her name a few times. Silence. I kept my breathing under control and listened. Nothing but house sounds. I continued moving through the house. If there was someone in the house with bad intentions, I just let them know where I was. The house was warm. I remembered she once told me she always felt cold.

One must deal with considerable stress when searching a house alone where someone might be waiting to kill you, or someone you care about might be dead. Breath control aside, my t-shirt under my turtleneck was wet. The house smelled of vanilla incense. I remembered she also liked vanilla. It was so quiet I thought I heard my heart beat.

I found her in the main bedroom. She looked at me when I walked through the door, and relief washed over me. Someone killed Luca but left her alive. A light from the television illuminated the room. She was wearing headphones, which explained why she didn't hear me.

6

After another few seconds, I realized she was dead, and I went cold. The bedspread was dark red, pulled up almost to her neck. She didn't like being cold. As I moved closer, I saw the bedspread was wet from her blood. Not much blood there, but the mattress underneath had turned crimson. The heat intensified the coppery smell of her blood. She'd been shot in the chest, probably the heart, multiple times. I didn't feel it necessary to feel her pulse but did anyway. Her head faced the bedroom door, with her mouth open and eyes wide. Her skin was still warm when I felt it to take her pulse. Her cell phone lay on the bedspread.

My head dropped. "Oh, Vicks, sweetheart." I brushed her face lightly with my fingertips, knowing I shouldn't, so pushed away. My back faced the door. If I was lucky, he or they were still in the house.

I backed out of the bedroom, knowing I needed to check the rest of the house. Tears rolled down my face. In another second, I'd be in a chasm. In my mind, I slammed the steel door shut again, needing to stop everything, including my feelings, what I'd done since I was a kid. The memories, the tears, the pain, everything other than the task at hand, lay behind that steel door. For now.

I searched the other bedrooms upstairs. The attic door, like the basement door, was locked. It took ten minutes, yet felt like ten years, and I found nothing.

I reached into my pocket, shut the video off on the phone, then called 911 and reported what I found. I told them I would be outside the house, and I was armed, but would leave my weapon on the steps.

I went outside and sat on the bottom step. I removed my holster, un-chambered the round, ejected the magazine, and put the round, the magazine, the gun, the extra magazines, and the holster on the top step. The step felt cold. She didn't like the cold.

Under my jacket and the turtleneck, I was soaked with sweat. Sitting outside, painful grief taking the place of adrenaline, amplified the cold. The heat inside the house was on, and was slamming. The stress of finding someone I cared about dead, and going through an unfamiliar home with the possibility of finding the person that killed her, or him finding me, raised my internal temperatures to a boil.

Now I shivered from the cold, felt weak with grief, and powerless. She was gone, and I wanted her back, breathing and happy, with the chance to help her.

I heard sirens.

I realized I was breathing too fast, and felt the initial panic of loss. Not now. I slowed my breath to get it under control. Somebody would pay. Somebody would fucking pay. Anger removed the cold and the grief. He better hope the cops got him before I did. Mandy was home, waiting for me. Thinking of her was like a security blanket.

Two patrol cars arrived, one right after the other. I stood and raised my hands, not wanting anyone to get nervous. One of the cops, a sergeant, took my gun from the steps. I gave the sergeant my basic story about the call and me coming here. I showed him the state issued identification for the PI license and my carry permit. He said he'd hold onto the gun until he could verify the permit, and I told him he was welcome to. Neighbors emerged from their homes as detectives, forensics team, and another patrol car arrived.

I accompanied them to the precinct. Several detectives, their sergeant, a captain, and Chief Michael Mariano, an old friend of my partner, were present. Mariano stood a little over six feet, with a physique indicating a lifetime of weightlifting. His hands indicated martial arts training as well. A neatly trimmed mustache; black hair with a trace of silver. He introduced himself as Mike. My partner Jeff told me he bled blue, and didn't tolerate bullshit. He led by example and expected his orders to be followed. If you did something stupid and told him, he'd help you. He'd been shot, stabbed, and had broken bones. He had burns inside his throat from 9-11.

The murder count had risen on the island. Now, PD used Mariano as they always used him - to kick ass and get results. He didn't get those results by sitting behind a desk.

"I hadn't seen Vicky for months. Today, actually yesterday now, was the first time I met Luca. He needed help with a family court matter and a criminal matter for assaulting his wife. I referred them to an attorney who could handle both. Afterward, I went to Peter Luger with a young lady and went home with her. She's at my home now. I know you have to ask so I figured I'd save you the time."

"Could you recount your conversation with him and the woman?" the female detective asked.

"Yes," I said, and told them.

"Why did you go in the house? You're also armed. There are protocols for you to carry a weapon in New York, and this doesn't qualify." The scowl on the face of the detective asking seemed perpetual, like a kid sucking on a lemon for the first time.

"Firstly, detective, I saw a body on the floor, and blood everywhere. My friend may have still been alive. I wasn't waiting to go in. Secondly, she owns a business, and I have a standing retainer with her to provide protective services. Thirdly, my company provides armed security. We're on call 24/7. I'm contractually obligated to provide services during an emergency. All of the aforementioned makes what I did within the stringent guidelines set by the NYPD Licensing Division."

Everyone fell silent for a second. I looked at the wall and saw her face again. I inhaled, and let it out slow.

"Besides that, she was my friend, irrespective of anything else. I was going in." No one said anything. Mariano gave a barely perceptible nod.

I first met her when she came into the office and asked for an order of protection against her ex-husband. We also did escorts for her, to court. I was happy that retainer was safely filed away in my office. Many clients were repeat clients, with mostly open-ended retainers.

"How did you know he was dead?" the female detective asked. Her tone was softer, though authoritative.

"I could see from the window. The whole floor around him was red, and he had a big hole in the back of his head. Blood from his back, blood from his head, and two pools under him."

There was a pause in the interrogation. I sipped some of the coffee, which was actually fairly tasty. Mariano had offered me a bagel or a roll, but I was lucky my stomach could hold the coffee.

"I can tell you one thing," I said. "He told me he'd been in a car accident, but that was bullshit. Somebody worked him over a day or so before he came to my office."

"How do you know?" the scowl asked.

"I've done it to people, and it's been done to me," I said.

"Really? You do this often? You some kind of badass?" he asked, in an acidic tone.

"Listen, I'm very tired, and just lost someone close. If you ask me a stupid question like that again, I'll satisfy your curiosity by showing you firsthand." The detective's face flushed, and I smiled. One day my face would freeze into a smile.

"That's enough," Mariano said, as the detective opened his mouth to respond. His voice was low, but his message was clear.

"I'm sorry, Detective. I'm not in the best frame of mind."

"That was very rude," Mariano said, glaring at the detective. The detective looked at the ground.

The questioning continued for another hour. I never needed to disclose the recording. I told them about my past relationship with Vicky, and working on the case for which Luca served time. No reason not to tell.

At eight in the morning, Mariano gave me a ride back to my car. I messaged Mandy to say I'd be home shortly. Mariano turned on the radio, and the morning version of "Get the Led Out" came on. In the very short exposure I had to him, I saw he was a gentleman. I could also see he led by example, as Jeff said. Both qualities I strived for and admired.

"We appreciate your help."

I nodded.

"Hard enough to lose someone close," he said. "Harder to lose them like that."

"Yeah."

He pulled in behind my car. We sat and listened to the radio for a bit. He didn't seem to be in a rush. We listened to the end of "Stairway to Heaven."

"Great song," he said.

"Best ever."

"We know it wasn't you."

"I figured," I said. "I also realize you guys have to ask those questions, so I figured I should get that out of the way, although the idea of kicking 'The Scowl' hard enough he could wear his ass for a hat is appealing."

Mariano chuckled. "Might do him some good. Anyone with a half a brain knew you didn't do it. The questions need to be asked, but there's no reason to behave like that. I'll set him straight."

I nodded.

"It's not your fault," Mariano said.

"You're a mind reader in your spare time?"

He smiled. "You did right by going in. Your friend was there, but I don't need to tell you that. If there's anything you need, if I can help, please let me know."

He handed me a card with his personal cell number on the back. I did likewise.

"If there's any way I can help, you do the same," I said.

"Okay if I call you Jonathan?"

"It's a long story, Chief, but most of my friends call me Jim."

We shook hands then I got in my car and drove home. What struck me most about Mariano was, had I not known Jeff, I believe he would have treated me the same way. When I left, I told him I would send his regards to my partner.

I drove Mandy home so she could change and get ready for work. She looked sad and held my hand most of the way to her place. She asked again if I was okay. I lied and assured her I was. She kissed me gently before she got out of the car.

I got home and threw on sweats. I had a specially made four hundred pound heavy bag downstairs along with other equipment. I went to the gym sometimes, but most of the time I stayed home.

I didn't favor hand wraps. I just used sports or medical tape around the hands and wrists. I wrapped my hands in tape and put the bag gloves on. It has the added bonus of a waxing on my hands if I didn't break a good enough sweat. I was tired, and it took a few minutes to find my rhythm. I pounded the bag for a half hour and got rid of frustration, at least temporarily.

I took a hot shower, followed by a quick nap. I woke up, but not as refreshed as I would have been a few years ago. Hell, a few years ago I wouldn't have needed the nap. I threw vegetables, fruit, and protein powder into a super blender someone bought me for Christmas, then dressed and went to the office.

Once I got to the office, my partner was waiting, anxious to know I was okay. Once I told him I was fine, he asked if I happened to go online yet.

"No, why?"

"You're on the front page of the Advance, at least their online edition. We got calls from the News and the Post as well."

"Nuts." I shook my head.

I went into my office. Mandy brought coffee for both Jeff and me. I nodded to a chair for her to stay, then pulled up the Advance on my laptop.

"They called," Jeff said. "I answered honestly and said you weren't in yet."

The Advance had my name. It said they tried to reach me for comment but couldn't. They also said they had no idea why I was there and what my connection was. The headline read: "Private Investigator Contacts Police, Finds Two Murder Victims."

It also didn't name the victims, since their families hadn't yet been notified.

"I'll add to your ulcer a little, Jeff," I said.

"Uh-oh," Jeff said.

"Mandy and I are together. We agreed it won't impact work. We're not going to advertise it, but we won't go out of our way to hide it." I looked at Mandy. She smiled and nodded her approval.

"Oh shit," he said. "I thought you cleaned out the bank account or something."

"Wouldn't get far on that little."

"Stop going to Peter Luger," Jeff said.

"So you can spend all the money on prunes and bran?" I asked.

Jeff laughed, and Mandy shook her head.

"By the way," Jeff said, "it's about time you two realized it. Everyone in the office has been talking about what a great couple you'd be."

"Oh?" I asked. "How long has this been going on?"

"About three months," Mandy said. "I made a comment that you were very kind, and a girl would be lucky to ..."

I grinned.

"Don't get cocky," she said.

"That ship has already sailed," Jeff said dryly.

"I have some work to do so I can hopefully get paid later, knowing the company coffers are so low," Mandy said, getting up. Her smile lit up the room. "Should I close the door, bosses?"

"Yes, thanks," I said.

I kept thinking the cops would get whoever killed Vicky. I was angry last night. Let them handle it. I'd trade a year of my life if I could lay my hands on whoever killed her. I should stay out of it. I should do a lot of things. This wasn't my fault; it *was* my fault. I should have ... I should have done something.

"Where'd you go, kid?"

"I'm sorry, Jeff."

"You can go home. Take some time."

I took a deep breath and shook my head. I shouldn't get involved. If I was close to it, the cops wouldn't like it. Stay away from it. I should stay away from it.

Not going to happen.

7

I told Jeff about Luca and Vicky coming in. I reiterated everything I told the cops. There didn't seem to be anything about Vicky and Luca that would impact us any further. P.D. was in control. Mariano was involved personally, and Jeff said he was put here to make sure things like that were handled. We talked about other work going on. I dictated a few reports, and Jeff left for an appointment. Mandy came back about an hour later and ordered lunch.

When lunch arrived, she brought in my turkey club with a side salad. I did miss fries, but as the war against aging continued, sacrifices were necessary. She was having a grilled chicken salad. We ate and talked lightly. I saw concern in her eyes.

"It's okay for you to miss her," she said, then reached out and put her hand on mine.

"Thank you. I feel sad, like if I stayed in touch, maybe ..."

"This wasn't your fault. She could have asked for help. You offered it."

"I know."

"You could have been killed."

I smiled. "I'm not easy to kill, girl."

"Uh-huh."

"Don't believe me?"

"Actually, I do, but I worried about you. I was scared."

"Me, too, but I can't do what we do if I let things scare me off. If it makes you feel better, I was very aware of my surroundings when I went into the house."

"It does, but I don't imagine you running in there thoughtlessly."

"Brings to mind something else worth mentioning, I think. As soon as I was safely able to think about something else, all I wanted to do was come back to you."

Her eyes opened wider, and her black hair cascaded around her face. Her eyes, although blue, had a quality of warmth in them.

"You're staring," she said, smiling.

"It hits me now and again just how beautiful you are."

She blushed and looked away.

"I want to always be honest with you," I said. "I care for you enormously. This hit me like a truck, as if I stepped off the curb looking the wrong way."

"Me, too," she said. "The night I called you I felt lonely. There were other people I could have called, but I kept thinking about you."

"I'm very glad you called me," I said, and our eyes met. "When I was in the house after I saw Vicky dead, I was overcome with sorrow, but I also couldn't stop thinking about you."

"Well, I was so worried about you I thought I was going to have a breakdown."

"I have for the longest time avoided commitment," I said. "There's something here; you fit. And again, even though we just talked about how we're going to take this lightly, it feels like more than that."

"I feel the same, not what I was planning," she said.

"Sometimes people are drawn closer together because of tragedy. It might be something to be careful of."

"I thought about that," she said. "Does it feel that way to you?"

Her eyes were wide open, and it felt as though she was looking into me. Sometimes you're fortunate enough to get what you didn't realize you wanted.

"No," I said. "It feels like you belong with me. What happened last night, maybe that makes it easier to recognize."

"Yes," she said, with a nod.

"I don't want to rush things, but I was hoping you might want us to be exclusive."

"I would love to be the one who finally talked Jonathan Creed into a monogamous relationship."

I laughed. "Good Lord, woman, what kind of reputation do I have?"

"I've heard you're quite the ladies' man," she said, smiling, "but also that you're a gentleman, and quite the catch."

"Also, if you read the ladies' room walls in half the bars on the island, a demon on the mattress."

She laughed. "Jerk."

"I never saw a woman as a trophy in any way," I said. "I've loved every woman I've ever been with, and some I haven't. I tried my best not to lie or mislead."

"That's part of your charm," she said.

"What about you?" I asked. "Are you ready for something like this?"

"I didn't think so. My ex, the first one after the divorce, got too serious too fast. He had trust issues, and was overwhelming. I don't feel that from you." She paused. "Yes, I think I'm ready."

"I'm not the jealous type, Mandy. It doesn't mean I don't care, but I know I can trust you." I laughed. "I'm also not looking for a reason to get the hell out after we're intimate."

"Baby, I could stay in those arms of yours for days." She flashed me a wicked smile.

"Knock it off, lady. My desk just rose."

She laughed. Her cell phone rang. I have no problem with employees with kids keeping their cell phone on. She rarely used it, but the expression on that beautiful face changed to worry. She hit the button for the phone to go to voicemail.

"Everything okay?"

"Yes, speak of the devil," she said. "That ex I mentioned."

I was concerned. "Do we have a stalking situation?"

"No, I don't think so."

"Okay." I smiled.

We finished eating then talked a little. She told me about growing up, how great her mom and dad were. She and her ex-husband initially had a hard divorce, but toward the end, the situation improved, and they're friends now. He found someone else. When she talked about her son, her eyes lit up. I smiled at that.

"Have you often dated women with children?" she asked.

"Substantial talk, hmmm," I said. "I have. It was never a disqualifier for me, but knowing what I do, I never involved myself in the kid's life unless the relationship got serious. Not fair to the child."

"How do you like kids?"

"Love them. I'm a huge hit with the nieces and nephews."

"Would you ever want kids?" she asked. "I know, it's a serious question."

"Maybe," I said, surprised at my answer.

She smiled. We ate lunch late, and then returned to work after we talked more. She went to her desk, and I watched her walk away. She turned and grinned, because she knew I had.

She stayed late an hour last week, and asked if she could take that hour today to spend time with her son. I told her it was okay.

When she left, I walked her to her car. She turned and kissed me then got in. Her touch, even in an innocent kiss, made me feel warm. I watched her drive away, and as I turned, I saw a black Cadillac with tinted windows parked down the block by the doctor's office, pull away. I went back in and finished my paperwork.

My cell phone rang. The number looked familiar, but I couldn't place it. I rarely answered the phone if I didn't know who I would be talking to first, but did this time. Unusual things were happening. Mariano was on the line.

"Chief, how are you?"

"I'm okay. I wanted to off-the-record clue you in. We're running phone numbers on both of their phones. We're having a hard time running down their activities before last night, other than your office. The weapon was a nine millimeter. She took three in the chest, two went through the heart. Tight grouping, if she felt anything it was only for a few seconds. No clue why she called you."

"Thank you, Chief. If there's anything further I can do, please tell me. I imagine it's not often a Chief calls and follows up like this."

"I spoke with Jeff. Both he and the D.A. speak very highly of you."

"Managed to fool a few more."

"Attaboy, keep at it," he said with a short laugh.

It was late in the day. We owned the small building we worked in. Half a dozen lawyers and a few other professionals rented space. Mary, the receptionist, left at five. I called upstairs and told her if it wasn't urgent, take messages for me before she left. I went to the little bar in the office and poured myself a bourbon. I reflected on Mandy, and thought about Vicky. Her voice resonated in my head.

"How come you didn't love me?"

I got a heart text message from Mandy. I looked at it for a while. I missed her, but still felt guilty over Vicky. I sipped the bourbon. It tasted good, but the want had passed, so I put the glass down. The cops would handle this. Mariano had a history of results. Most of the detectives working homicide were proficient. Absolutely no use in my getting involved. I'd end up pissing Mariano off, and we'd lose a valuable contact. I wouldn't do anyone any good. I hadn't done anything wrong. I never lied to Vicky.

"How come you didn't love me?"

I'd never know why she called me. It could have been a misdial. She was wearing earphones, so probably didn't hear them. It didn't matter why.

8

Bill Sanders looked worn. His mother was with the children in the basement of the home, converted into a large family room. They were eight and nine. He won custody from Vicky a while back. She was in a bad way. Although she fought it initially, he told me she realized she had a problem. He told her they could change things back when she got her act together, and could see the kids whenever she wanted. He told me he begged her to get some help, and to get away from Luca. He even offered to help with that.

"I knew this bastard was bad," he told me. "I knew something like this would happen. I begged her to let me help her." He shook his head. "What do I tell the kids? She was supposed to have dinner with us tonight."

"I'm sorry, Mr. Sanders."

"I know she hadn't worked in weeks. She merged her company with another one. I know Luca was a partner in a restaurant. To tell you the truth, I know very little."

"Which restaurant?"

"La Sala da Pranzo, in Bay Ridge." He was quiet for a bit. "Mr. Creed, may I ask, who's your client?"

"I don't have one, Mr. Sanders."

I told him I went to the house and found the bodies, and that Vicky and Luca came to my office. We were quiet again.

"You feel guilty."

I didn't answer. I wondered again what I was doing here. The cops would handle this. My phone vibrated in my coat pocket. I took it out. It was a message from Mandy.

"Are you okay?" it read. I sent back a heart.

"Would you like a client?" Sanders asked.

I looked at him. "You feel guilty," I said.

He smiled grimly.

I thought about it. Apparently, I was going to look into this, so it would look better if I had a client. The cops frown on people looking into an active investigation. The frown becomes a snarl if vigilantism looked like a possibility.

"I would," I said.

I explained a few things to him, and he said he would make sure his attorney knew. He asked me a few questions.

"I'm a qualifier for Precision Investigations and Security Services, LLC. The company itself is licensed to do the work, and I'm one of two qualifiers, meaning I passed a test, background search, and my required experience was properly vetted. As investigators, we don't have a privilege with you the way an attorney does. If a law enforcement agent discovers I'm working for you, and they can demonstrate my information may impact their investigation, I'm obligated to share my information with them."

"We shouldn't mind that here?"

"No, if I begin to feel differently, I would work for your attorney, and the attorney client privilege would offer more protection, but they'd get past that eventually."

"What is your normal fee?"

"On this case? Five dollars."

He nodded.

I got my briefcase from my car, then opened it and took out blank retainer forms. I made the appropriate entries and filled in the dates, the amount, etc. He made a copy on his printer.

He wrote a check out to my company for five dollars. We shook hands. I promised I would keep him updated, then left to tell his children their mother was dead.

I called Jeff and left a message. I needed to tell him what I was going to do. I hoped he wouldn't be too upset. Carol Miller purred into my radio speakers as I drove, and Jeff called back. "The Immigrant Song" wouldn't get second billing to most calls, but it was Jeff.

I told him everything, how I felt, and how I needed to do this. I apologized for not telling him first, but didn't even know for sure I was going to do what I did.

"Jim, I know there's no way to fully rid you of that compunction you used to have for charity cases."

I laughed, "I've done fairly well, boss."

"That you have. I think you can be allowed a slip up or two. I'm on board for any help I can give you." He paused. "That being said, Jimmy, it's not your fault."

"I know I shouldn't feel that way, but I do. I need to do this."

"Clearly you do, my boy. I wouldn't even try to stop you. The quicker you get this over with, the quicker your head is back in business, so my help benefits us both. First suggestion," he said.

"Do tell," I replied, smiling.

"Let's meet with Mariano and let him know. Better to do that. I have an idea where you may actually be of use to them. I'll arrange a lunch meeting for us tomorrow and we'll discuss it in the morning before we go."

"Good. See you in the a.m."

"Goodnight," Jeff said.

"Night pal."

I talked with Mandy on the phone for a while when I got home. It struck me how much I enjoyed talking to her. I realized I missed her.

The next day, I sat down to lunch with my partner and Chief Mariano at the Portabello Café on Hylan Blvd. The menu was pleasing to the eye, and the food tasted exceptional. Adam, the owner and head chef, stopped at the table, and Mariano introduced us. He shook our hands in a very honest way, and thanked us for coming.

A little while later, a bottle of very good merlot arrived at our table, compliments of Adam.

"This is quite good," I said.

"He knows his wine," Mariano agreed.

The Veal Capricciosa I ate tasted good. Jeff ordered a cheddar and apple stuffed pork chop, and Mariano ordered Veal Sorrentino.

The merlot disappeared quickly, and we all declined dessert, but ordered coffee. The front room was crowded, so we were the only patrons sitting in the back room. We came to the reason for asking him to lunch, during coffee.

"Vicky Sanders' husband asked me to work on the case, Chief. I wanted you to know upfront, and I wanted you to know I won't be a bull in a China shop, and walk over anyone's toes."

"We can't stop you," Mariano said. "It's not generally looked on with favor by most in the department."

"I realize that," Jeff said. "However, we may be useful in areas that might be difficult for you."

"Such as?" Mariano asked.

"The restaurant where he was a partner in Brooklyn. They may not talk to me, but they sure as hell aren't talking to you guys," I said.

"Would you agree to keep us apprised?" Mariano asked.

"Yes," I said.

Jeff smiled. "Anything you can share with us?"

Mariano laughed. “You know we can’t do that, Jeff.”

Jeff smiled, and Mariano was quiet as the waiter brought three shots of Sambuca, also courtesy of Adam. He put his lemon rind in his espresso and stirred it. I ordered brown coffee; Jeff ordered cappuccino.

“We have nothing so far,” Mariano said quietly. “No one saw or heard anything. Only one surveillance system on the block, not working. Any others in the vicinity, not sharp enough even with video enhancement, but we’re trying.”

We sipped our coffee and Sambuca. Jeff appeared thoughtful. Mariano, I didn’t know well enough to read, but he also appeared pensive. The coffee, like the food and the wine, tasted exceptional. I thought of Vicky again.

“Chief, if you guys have a chat with his partners, how far are you going to get?” I said.

“Not far, unless we find someone with a big mouth.”

“Why don’t I work that angle?”

“Those aren’t Cub Scouts,” Jeff said pointedly.

“I’m aware,” I said. “It was your idea. Oh, I keep forgetting the life insurance policies,” Jeff snickered.

“I’m of the opinion you can handle yourself,” Mariano said to me. “But Jeff is right. They’re not to be taken lightly.”

“I understand. If you look at it, and I can get through to them, if it wasn’t them that did it ...”

“Maybe, but that’s a reach,” Mariano said. “If that’s the case and you can get them to talk.”

“I’m an ambassador of goodwill,” I said.

“You’re also full of shit,” Jeff said, smiling.

“That too.”

I returned to the office. As I pulled into the parking lot, I noticed the same black Caddy that was sitting by the doctor’s office yesterday. This time it faced the parking lot eight car lengths away. I felt tired, but was sure it was the same car. I went in the office without mentioning it.

No appointments in the afternoon. I looked at my schedule for the upcoming week, and changed what was necessary to free up time. I asked Mandy to come in for a bit when she was done with the file she was working on. After a while, she came in and smiled at me.

"Door open or closed?"

"Closed, please. Confidential case."

As she turned to close the door, I leapt out of my chair, spun her around, and kissed her. When I stopped, I held her as hard as I could without hurting her.

"Well, hello," she whispered.

"Hello back." I kissed her neck and moved my lips up close to her ear. She shivered.

"Unfair to do that to me here. We can't do anything about it."

"We could if you were quiet."

She laughed and lightly slapped me on the arm. "Behave, sir."

I sighed. "Yes, ma'am."

She looked at me. Maybe better to say she looked *through* me, or *into* me. I saw concern on her face. I felt many things the past few days: sadness, anger, loss, but also felt love. I actually allowed the L word into my thoughts. Seeing she was concerned for me made me feel good for some reason. I didn't want her to worry.

"Are you all right?" she asked.

I smiled back. "I'm okay."

Her eyes scanned me, top to bottom. She reached out and her fingers caressed my cheek, then leaned in and softly kissed me.

"I promise I'm okay."

The truth was, I wasn't, but the idea of her being worried and upset didn't sit well. She stayed for a few seconds. Her eyes looked into mine; looking for a sign as to the truth of my words. Eventually, she seemed convinced.

I went over things with her. Jeff would handle things for me, and other things could be delayed. I also had her put a few of the people I used on notice in case I might need them. She was going to stop by my place later in the evening. I left first.

I got in my car, and the black Caddy sat in the same spot. I pulled my cell phone out, and had a pretend conversation with my voicemail. I saw no other cars on the block. I got in my car, pulled out, and left. The Caddy didn't move.

I went around the block and parked on the street facing the block the office was located. Mandy would pull out and drive that way. The black Caddy, if it was there for her, would need to pull a broken U-turn to follow her.

It felt cold, so I put on the heater and stayed out of sight. The clock on the dash read five to five. I turned the radio on. "Do You Feel Like We Feel," by Peter Frampton came on. I liked Ken Dashow, Q104's afternoon DJ. He announced that live at five, would be Heart from a *Dreamboat Annie* concert. I could deal with that. Good surveillance music. "Magic Man" started. In a bit, Mandy's car drove by. With the broken U, I estimated it would be twenty seconds or so before the black Caddy went by, if it was there for the reason I thought. I was hoping I didn't see it. I got to nineteen, and it passed. I pulled out, turned the lights on, got to the stop sign, and did what is commonly referred to as a Staten Island stop. I slowed, saw no cars, and blew the stop sign.

Normally, I drove well and obeyed traffic laws, but conducting surveillance wasn't conducive to obeying the rules of the road. I figured if I drove normally when I wasn't tailing, it made up for the craziness during the tails. Overall, I bet it increased my odds of not kicking off in a car crash. I'm sure there's logic to disprove that, but no one wants to be logical all the time.

Mandy went home. She entered her house, and the Caddy stopped up the street. I stopped further back. The Caddy left after only five minutes. I pulled out, gave them a while, and then pulled behind when they got to a red light. I noted the plate number. Two people, both men by their outlines, sat in the car. The one in the passenger seat was a big guy.

I let them go. I was certain they didn't know I was there, but didn't want to take the chance and reveal myself. I had the plate, so odds are I had them. Of course, I had the strong urge to stop them for a chat. Having learned the hard way and acquiring scars from mistakes, it's a good thing to know what's going on before the bull is released into the china shop.

When it came to my surroundings, I picked things up quickly. I'd been followed a few times before, and it looked as if the black Caddy was there for Mandy, not me. I would've noticed if they followed me. No reason for anyone to be following me, not at the moment anyway. Mandy was on good terms with her ex-husband. She hadn't spoken much about it, but said her first relationship after the divorce didn't end well. It didn't mean it was true, but the odds were in favor of that. I was far from happy about this. The cold anger I felt about Vicky coalesced with the anger over the black Caddy following Mandy. "Take a deep breath," I told myself.

I needed to talk with Mandy before I did anything. I had no idea how she would react. Someone following her isn't acceptable. Maybe she wouldn't want me involved. I'm not a brute, but I'm also not a misogynist. She had a say in what happened; so did I. The loss of one person close to me this week was enough.

We always kept someone on call. We used subcontractors, and people working directly for us. That week it was Mikhail. Mickey was young, in his early thirties. He had his own license, was trustworthy, and knew what he was doing. He had a Russian accent, having emigrated when he was young. We would pay them a small fee to be on standby, and for overtime rates.

He picked up his phone on the first ring. "Good evening, boss."

"Nephew, I have a job for you."

"I'm lucky to have such a good Dutch Uncle looking out for me. What do you need?"

I told him about the black Caddy, and gave him Mandy's address. I told him to be armed; he was doubling as security. I asked him if he wanted relief, but as his wife recently gave birth to twin girls, he was happy to work and make money.

He was smart, with a great work ethic, but most of all was trustworthy, and I knew I could trust him with Mandy. Any sign of trouble, he'd call me.

I didn't sleep well that night. I dreamt about Vicky. I dreamt I found Mandy in Vicky's place at Luca's. I woke up mad, and worked out lightly, but neither that nor a shower released the tension.

Tom sent me a text, no activity, so he headed home after Mandy left. I returned him a text to thank him. He offered to do it as a favor. I messaged him back, he'd do no such thing, texting I resisted, like the people at the Alamo resisted Santa Anna. A good try, but eventually it overwhelmed me.

First step was the background search, followed by the fieldwork. All PI's have their sources. I had reliable ones, and the best one rented an office from me. I had Mandy tell him I needed him the day before, and he was waiting in his office for me at a quarter to nine. I wore good jeans that I could move around in, a blue turtleneck, heavy brown leather shoes, and a light brown leather jacket. I took the .45 I carried, and put it in the desk drawer and locked it. I had four extra clips in the draw. I walked down the hall to Eddie's office.

Eddie Martin wouldn't stand out in a crowd if he waved a flag. He looked like a nice guy. He was a few inches shorter than I was, and a little overweight. He was starting to do a comb over. He wore a decent grey suit and a blue tie, and white oxford dress shirt. We talked often; he was a friend, and the best information broker I ever met. He operated a marketing business as well, but I believed that was a front. He could build a computer from the ground up, and design programs. He worked for years for various government agencies before he retired young and went off the radar, now he worked only for P.I.'s. He was particular about who he worked for and what he charged, but needed only a few clients. Eddie and I spent hours playing chess. I was good, but he was better, at least so far. He led by four games.

He had coffee in a carafe and poured me some as I sat across from him.

"Who's your client on this one?" he asked.

That's a standard question. If he was going to retrieve something he wasn't supposed to, he wanted to make sure it wasn't a crazy person. Some of the stuff he came up with, you wouldn't want to go walking into court with it as evidence.

"The client is me, Eddie. My friend was murdered."

"The girl in the paper?"

"Yeah."

He was quiet for a while, then nodded. "Well, at least I know your client is trustworthy."

I smiled. "Thanks Eddie." I provided the background.

"What do you need?"

"All the information you can get me on Luca, both of their cell phone records for the last month, and anything else you can think of. I also have a license plate I need checked on a different matter." I gave him the plate for the black Caddy.

"You can run plates," he said, as his eyebrows rose.

"I need to know, or at least have a very strong indication, not just who owns it, but who was in it last night. There was a driver and a passenger. Driver was small to average. Passenger was big and tall, if that helps."

"I'll do what I can," he said, "but I can't guarantee I can develop enough information to know exactly who was in the car."

I nodded and reached into my pocket to give him cash. He waved me off.

"Expenses only on this, Jimmy. I'll let you know after."

"Eddie, please let me know the moment you have the info back on the Caddy, would you?"

"Done," he said.

Running the plate I could do, he was right. He would use all kinds of hard to get supplemental information, and it was possible he could find out, or at least make a very good guess. If his track record was an indicator, he'd find out.

I thanked him, we shook hands, and I left his office, taking my coffee. I went to my office and called Mariano. I got his voicemail and left a message. Anger grew underneath the sadness and the loss, and unsettled me. I felt like I needed to do something, but didn't know what.

9

Mandy came in a little while later, wearing a tastefully short skirt, but not as short as I'd like. She wore a black and blue top, and looked a few cents more than a million bucks.

"How's my personal, living work of art doing this morning?"

She blushed. "Mr. Creed, you're so good for my ego."

"I speak only the truth, madam."

She came around and kissed me. It hit me like a shot every damned time I saw her, how beautiful she was. It occurred to me, I knew many beautiful women in my time, and so far was fortunate. Everything here with her lined up. In such a short time, I had trouble imagining life without her.

"I need your ear," I said.

She sat down. "You have it."

"Being you're giving parts away, there are a few others I'd like, too."

"Jerk." She laughed that genuine musical laugh that would have me following her out of a town off a cliff. I smiled, and enjoyed her for a minute.

"I do need to talk with you, babe."

"Okay, is everything all right?"

"I'm sure it will be," I said. "Someone is tailing you."

A look of confusion crossed her face for the first time. "What?"

"A black Cadillac followed you home last night. The other day, it left right after you did. I didn't think anything of it at the time."

"I don't . . . my son," she said, understanding now. "Is he in danger?"

"Honey, that depends on who it is and what they're looking for, but there's no information to indicate any danger at this point. I had Mickey stay outside your house last night. After they left, they didn't come back."

"It has to be my ex."

"I never pried. It has nothing to do with us, but knowing what I know of you, nothing else makes any sense."

She bit her lower lip and shook her head. "Why didn't you tell me?"

"I wasn't sure until last night. I got the plate, and I'll know for sure who they are in a bit. They left after you went in. I'm sorry, Mickey was probably an overreaction. I just wanted to make sure you were safe."

"Honey," she said. "I love you, but please, next time clue me in, okay?"

I swallowed hard. She looked at me from across my desk. Her eyes were bright, and the words hung between us like a tether. She looked down; afraid she said it too soon. I spoke before I realized.

"I love you, too." Always trust your reflexes.

Her eyes rose and met mine. She smiled, and it lit up the room. I never saw warm blue eyes before, and felt sure someone outside could hear my heart pounding. We were silent for a bit, but it wasn't uncomfortable.

"Well, now that we've established that, we need to keep you healthy and safe, as that body of yours has become my exclusive plaything."

She threw her pen at me. "Jerk." She tried to keep her face serious but failed, and smiled again anyway.

"Okay," I said. "I need to know about him."

She got serious. "Okay."

I leaned forward, picked up the pen she threw at me, and prepared to take notes. "Name?"

"Mark Stanton. He's a builder and a realtor, owns a lot on ..."

"On Van Buren Street," I finished, then exhaled. "In addition to being a builder, he sells drugs and does some loan sharking."

She nodded and looked down. "I didn't know about those other things."

"He's very good at portraying himself as a normal citizen."

"You know him?"

"Not directly. He's popped up from time to time in relation to work."

"I don't think this would bother you, but I was seeing a psychologist for a while, after my divorce, after I broke up with Mark."

"Sweetheart, if you have a fever, you take medicine. A foolish person is someone that needs help, but doesn't get it."

She smiled. "I knew you'd say that, or something like it."

"She told me," Mandy continued, "Mark wanted me to add legitimacy to him. He wanted me for breeding. Within a few weeks of dating, he was talking about having kids, moving in. We didn't know each other."

I nodded and sipped coffee.

"It's not like us. There was an attraction in the beginning, but he was ..." She struggled for the word.

"Needy?"

"Yes. Right away, he was jealous, I caught him looking at my phone. He took it on himself to meet my mom and dad. It got weird and creepy pretty fast."

"You're educated, refined, and beautiful," I said. "He makes donations to charities; he tries to come off as one of the good guys. He also doesn't like being rejected."

"I don't think he's a real problem," she said.

"Mandy," I spoke softly. "He likely has two people following you around, or he's following you and has someone with him."

She was quiet.

"How often is he texting you or calling you?" I asked.

"A lot. It's been getting worse, not better."

"Disregard the fact I'm an Alpha and I care for you. It's my job to protect you. He's someone that if you came in here as a client and ask my advice, I tell you to be careful, file police reports, etc. And I'd be concerned."

She was quiet. "I know it was putting my head in the sand, but I was hoping this would just go away. I didn't have much time to breathe after the divorce."

"How long has this been going on?"

"About six months."

"You also have a child to worry about," I said.

That unsettled her. "Is it that bad?"

"Probably not, but I can't say," I said, then paused. "You have to approach this bearing in mind the threat is real, and prepare for the worst case scenario."

"What would you tell a client to do?"

"I have to ask you more questions so I can get a better picture."

She nodded.

"Look, what I can tell you is we'll handle this, and you don't have to worry."

She smiled. "Okay, ask away."

"Any threats?"

"Kind of, but not at first. When they are threats, it's like, 'Hey! Are you ignoring me? That's mean! Don't let me find out you have a new bff!' And he'll put 'lol' and a wink at the end of it."

"Okay. How often? And is it just text?"

"Mostly texts, but it's from a number other than his. I get hang up calls. Sometimes texts from other numbers, too." She paused as if getting ready to add something, but didn't.

"Something else?" I asked gently.

"He may have taken pictures of me in bed. I wasn't aware at the time, and he made a reference to it. He ..."

"He what, honey?"

"He seemed to be obsessed with my son, too."

"How?"

"He always asked these odd questions about the relationship Sean had with his dad. He would tell me he was going to take Sean under his wing and make sure he turned out right, like his dad did for him."

"What did you say?"

"I told him, although I wasn't with Sean's dad anymore, he was a good man and a good father. I wasn't going to try to replace him."

"Go on."

"He got even weirder then," she said.

"Weirder, how?"

"I tried to pull away, he tried to hold on." She paused and thought for a few moments. "He would stare at me, at Sean. He had this faraway look in his eyes I can't explain. He just scared me."

Anger built in me since I found Vicky, and this surely didn't help. She clearly looked ashamed. She looked at the floor.

"Hey," I said, we'll take care of this. Just tell me it's okay to handle this."

"I feel badly about that, too. I'm a big girl. You have a lot on your plate."

"Always room on the plate for more, especially if I'm in love with what's being served."

She looked up and smiled. Her eyes were bright. The words hung between us like a tether. She took a deep breath, and we said nothing for a few seconds.

"I need for you to let me do this," I said, when I regained the ability to speak.

"Okay," she said.

We talked about it a while longer. I made notes and asked questions as though it was an interview with a new client. I was more distracted and struggled to control it, but managed. I knew she was worried by the way she looked down, or there was more to it than she wanted to say. It was hard on her, and I had enough to go on, so I stopped pushing. When we finished, she asked me if I wanted more coffee. I replied in the affirmative and she took my cup. She turned around at the door and looked at me. For a second, that tether tugged.

"I love you," she said, and her eyes shone.

My voice failed me again for a few seconds, then I managed to say, "I love you."

I didn't mind saying it, but saying it to her made me wonder. She hit me with that smile that only recently became part of my life. Then, she spun around and left the room. Yeah, I know I said the word love a few seconds earlier, but that was a jab. This was a left hook.

Just a few weeks ago, I'd have given anyone ten to one odds this wouldn't be. Maybe I should buy a lotto ticket. I'm sure there was work I needed to do, but just stared at the wall until Eddie walked in about an hour later.

10

Eddie's envelope had the name and owner of the car, along with the car owner's cell phone number, and a long list of the numbers that phone called from last night, going back a month. There were ten numbers, with the name of each person that owned the phone.

Joseph Bertone owned the Caddy. He served time on both the state and federal level. He was 5'5," although I had no idea how the hell Eddie knew that. Mark Stanton's number was called a lot. The other numbers were women, a popular pizza place, and someone named Thomas Sullivan. He was 6'2." I gave Eddie twenty five hundred. If this was a paying job, it would have been five thousand. I would have charged a client at least ten thousand.

Under normal circumstances, it wouldn't take me long to find out more, but I was pressed for time. I had work to do, but I needed to know Mandy was safe. I called Mariano.

"Hey, Jim. How are things?"

"Complicated, Chief. I was hoping you could simplify them."

"If I can. Shoot."

"There's a guy, a lowlife who pretends not to be. His name is Mark Stanton. I want to know if someone there might know his connection to two people. Joseph Bertone, who I think goes by Joey Burt, and a guy I don't know, named Thomas Sullivan."

"Pertaining to the case?"

"No, Chief. In truth, they're following my ... better half around. Stanton was an ex, and still has a thing for her. Bertone's car's been following her."

"Stanton I heard about around here," Mariano said. "I'll call you back. Give me fifteen." We hung up. He called back in ten.

"Both of those mutts work for Stanton. They handle collections, supplying dealers, whatever. Bertone did time. He's a mean little shit, not much to him physically, but he caught a body or two. Sullivan is muscle who can use his hands. He was a promising heavyweight boxer. With a detached retina after surgery, he was never as good. He ended up working for Stanton. If they aren't at Stanton's yard, there's a Tex-Mex bar, Adobe Blues, they hang out at."

"Thanks, Chief."

"Your plans?"

"In the mood for some Tex-Mex."

"I'm hungry myself."

"Chief, I appreciate it, but I don't want you to end up in hot water."

"Not a problem. I'll see you there, or maybe not."

I laughed, "Okay. Thanks, Chief."

Adobe wasn't crowded. I saw Sullivan and Bertone. They were at the bar talking, with drafts in front of them. Stanton was sitting at a table with a few people, about twenty-five feet away from the goons at the bar. A man and a woman sat at a table about fifteen feet from Stanton.

I walked up to the bar and stood about five feet away from Bertone and Sullivan. A good bit of anger and the static charge brewed inside me. I would see how this played out. You plan only up to a point.

"Afternoon," I said to them.

They didn't respond.

"I'm actually here for a reason," I said. Still no reaction. I said it in an even, moderate voice, but it carried a little, because there were so few people there. The bartender, a pretty blonde, asked me what I wanted.

"Seltzer, a glass of ice, and napkins." She smiled and got it for me.

"Gentlemen," I said to them a few minutes later. They still ignored me.

"I'm here to give you this year's award for the single worst tail job to date."

That got their attention. Bertone, who was wearing his sunglasses, turned and looked at me. Sullivan looked at me briefly, his face blank, and then turned his head again. Bertone kept staring.

"What the fuck are you talking about?" Bertone asked me.

"Joey, Joey, Joey," I said, shaking my head sadly. "No need for that kind of language. The failing of many people is not admitting they're no good at something. I could give you a few pointers. But as a wheelman for surveillance, you leave a lot to be desired. By the way, do you find it sunny in here?"

"What?"

"You suck, Joey. You've been following a friend of mine named Mandy. You started about three days ago, and you're going to stop. You should also stop wearing sunglasses inside. You're crying out to prove you're cool, and you're not."

"What?"

Irritation and confusion crept into his voice. Stanton, involved in conversation, looked over at me for a few seconds and continued speaking. I smiled.

"I ain't followin' nobody. And watch your mouth when you talk to me, shithead."

"I've tried that before," I said. "It never really works."

"Tried what?" Bertone asked.

Sullivan quietly and calmly stared at his drink. He was big through the chest, and his neck was thick. He also had large hands and wrists. Bertone had small shoulders and a gut. There was plenty of room. Bertone was about four inches shorter than me; Sullivan about four inches taller.

"Watching my mouth. Bad strain on the eyes. And I look like Daffy Duck when I do that. I care about my appearance." I smiled, and my heart rate accelerated a tad. "Perhaps, people like yourself, born with less than average looks and intelligence, find that a foreign concept."

The barmaid, who also apparently doubled as the waitress, brought the couple a bill and a bag of food. She seemed relieved to be away from the bar.

"Okay, fucko, take a walk." Bertone turned his head toward me and stared. He spoke in what he hoped was a menacing voice.

"I jog, Joey. Did that already, today. Not just for the cardio, but again, you want to have a nice appearance. You could take steps to improve yourself. Within reason."

He turned his whole body to face me. "You makin' fun of me, fucko?"

"Sharp as a marble, Joey. I'm betting a lot of people make fun of you."

Sullivan also turned toward me. "You should go," he said, in a deeper voice. There were civilians in the bar, and Stanton didn't own it. If there were civilians, there wouldn't be gunplay.

I laughed. "It's like you're a ventriloquist act. Size difference is about right. Joey, what do you wear? A child size - medium?"

Bertone's face turned red. Stanton paid attention now. "Get the fuck outta here before you get hurt." His voice was on the high side, but mean and sharp. He raised his right hand to push me. Sullivan rolled his shoulders and shook his head.

I was leaning on the bar a little, and had moved my right leg back and set my weight. I move quickly. People see I have weight to me, and often judge me as slow, but I'm not.

I slapped Bertone's right hand down hard with my left hand, which I was just resting on the bar. The motion, because Bertone threw weight behind the push, moved him forward and down. I landed a nice overhand right on his jaw. The sunglasses achieved escape velocity, and landed on the floor behind the bar. His knees buckled immediately, and the elevator went down to the basement. I shuffled quickly, and caught Sullivan a good left hook on his chin. The way Bertone fell, his piece was off the board. It wasn't the best or hardest left hook I ever threw but it was solid, and I had weight behind it. I caught him by surprise, knocking him back a couple of steps. He got his bearings, shook his head, and set his weight. That hook would have put most people down.

Stanton stood up at his table but stayed put. Sullivan snapped a decent left jab at me. I deflected it with my right hand, shuffled to my left, then threw a much heavier left hook. He brought his right hand up, elbow in, fist by his ear, and caught it on his arm. It knocked him back a step and off balance. He was in shape, and obviously had training. I dropped a little and caught him in the gut with a hard right hook. I'm a fan of the hooks. He doubled up involuntarily, and I hooked him high off the body and landed solid. He went back a few steps and tried to shake it off again, less successfully than before. He was strong. Few people would still be standing. I moved in fast, threw a good stiff jab. One of the guys that trained me years ago was an old timer. He taught me this heavy jab, where you drop your weight when you throw it. Sullivan's head snapped back, and I hooked off the jab. I landed the best of the three left hooks I threw. The old timer also taught me to get more force with that combination of hooking off the jab, and to step right just before throwing the hook.

He went to sleep curled up, not far from his buddy Joey on the floor. I rolled my shoulders and neck, and through effort, kept my breathing under control. I walked back to the bar where the seltzer, ice, and the napkins sat. I took a few cubes of the ice and wrapped it in the napkin. The place was dead quiet. I took out my wallet and put a hundred bucks on the bar. I opened the can of seltzer and poured a little on the napkin, and the rest into the glass. The couple sitting at the table got up and left with the bag. Stanton and the people at his table looked up at me.

I drank some of the seltzer, and then held the ice on the knuckles of my left hand, which hurt a little bit. I'm sure I'd feel it more, later. Stanton got up and left the people at his table, and walked over. He stepped over Bertone.

"If you say good help is hard to find, that'd be really cool," I said to Stanton.

"I know you," Stanton said.

"To know me is to love me. You might know who I am, but you don't know me. I can't say I know you, but I know who you are."

"You don't really want to know me."

"Mark," I said, as I turned and held his gaze. "If your pet monkeys there keep following Mandy around, you and I will get to know each other very well. And you don't really want to know me."

"I heard she had some trouble. I just wanted to know she was okay."

"I'll let her know that. If I see Ren or Stimpy again, they may not get up next time."

"So," he said, "you're not just her boss." It wasn't a question.

I put the ice on the bar and drank seltzer. "I don't want to see anyone following her again."

Stanton looked at me coldly. He was no match for me, but that didn't matter. I knew when people were afraid, and he wasn't. I was a little, but that was for Mandy. I drank more of the seltzer, then picked up the napkin with the ice in it, and headed toward the door.

I turned halfway there and looked back. Bertone was groaning, trying to sit up, and Sullivan was starting to move. Stanton still looked at me with the same cold, dead eyes. I looked at Ren and Stimpy, both stirring on the floor.

"Just curious, Mark. Do you provide them with health coverage?"

I turned and walked out. I got in my car and saw Mariano sitting and eating in the passenger seat a few cars down in an unmarked car. His car was backed in the wrong way, so he was closest to the street. He saw me and smiled. I nodded slightly. He jerked his head slightly toward Richmond Terrace. I pulled out, drove down the block to the Terrace, and turned left. A little way down on the left was Gerardi's, a farmer's market. I parked there and Mariano's car pulled in behind me. He parked and got out, eating a taco. He had the white take out bag the couple sitting in Adobe left with. He passed me the bag. I had taken the ice with me, but dropped it in favor of the food. I took the bag, removed a soft taco, and took a bite.

We walked toward the vegetables. Signs said "Jersey Corn," but that was weeks away. They sold Christmas Trees during the holidays, pumpkins and fall vegetables around Halloween, vegetables, saplings, and groceries in the spring and summer. We walked a bit. The market wasn't crowded. We passed the bag back and forth and killed off five tacos each. There was one left. I offered it to him.

"I had one when you were still inside."

He didn't have to ask me twice. Working over Ren and Stimpy gave me an appetite, and truth be told, I felt a lot better. I still carried Vicky around, and was still worried about Mandy, but *did* feel a lot better.

"Thirsty?" I asked

"Yes."

"Rolling Rock? Stella?"

"I'm on duty," he said. "Rolling Rock."

I walked over to the refrigerator and bought a six-pack of Rolling Rock, then walked over and handed the bag to Mariano. He walked back to the car, and handed one to the driver. He came back, and we each took one. We both drank about half the bottle to quench our thirst, and then continued to walk while sipping. Mariano waved to one of the workers. The worker waved back and smiled. Mariano took the lead. We went through the market to the back, out the door, and outside again.

The market was located in what used to be an enormous warehouse or factory, well over a hundred years old. The building was constructed of solid red bricks. A huge silo with other buildings sat behind it. Piles of red bricks lay all over; one of them almost two stories high, and looking post-apocalyptic. We looked out over the water and saw the large storage tanks in New Jersey.

"There was speculation a tooth or two might have been left on the floor."

I snorted. "Not that either of them has a smile anyone would miss, but I just wanted to put them down. They'll both be fine."

We drank more Rolling Rock.

"You've had a bit of training," Mariano said. "The knuckles on your hand say 'martial arts,' but my detective told me it looked like you were a boxer. You're built like a powerlifter."

"You have some of those same symptoms, Chief," I said. "I started Karate when I was thirteen. My teacher was a Golden Gloves champ, learned how to box before he could write. He grew up in Hell's Kitchen. Boxing was incorporated into the training. The emphasis was a little different, but it worked. Got to work with a bunch of different people here and there, learned grappling, and spent a lot of time in boxing gyms."

He nodded.

"Smitty used to say I was a concussionist," I said.

"Interesting term."

I laughed softly at the memory. "'A knockout artist' he said, is like watching ballet. He taps you on the chin just right, you go to sleep. A concussionist hits you, and you go to the plastic surgeon, if or when you wake up. He said it was one of my advantages."

"Any disadvantages you'd like to share? Just in case you end up on the other side of me?"

I smiled. "Chief, based on what I know of you, I wouldn't want you to be on the other side." I swallowed more Rolling Rock. "My main disadvantage was, I don't like to hurt people."

"That's a good disadvantage to have, Jimmy."

"He told me that, too."

"Smart man. Sounds like a good man."

"The best."

"Stanton is bad news," Mariano said. "He's been on the rise, an up and comer. He's also smart, very cruel, and has discouraged people from ratting on him."

"That's my impression," I said. "He had his goons following my woman. I believed my demonstrating disdain for said activity was necessary."

"He's very ruthless," Mariano said, looking at me to be sure I understood. "Let me know if he keeps it up."

"Thanks, Chief. There's always that possibility. I should be able to concentrate on my work now. I'm hoping this is over."

"It goes without saying, but I will anyway," he said. "Keep your eyes open."

"I will. I owe you."

He shook his head. "Jeff is a good man. I take for granted, if he speaks highly of you, you are, too."

The beer was done, and there were three bottles left. I took one and handed him the bag with the other two. We both tossed out empty bottles in an old oil drum with garbage inside.

"Any new developments?"

"Nothing," he said. "The video enhancement is worthless so far."

I nodded. A huge ship came into view, a freighter heading back from Howland Hook, now called the New York Container Station. Trucking and warehousing was in my family's blood, and I spent a lot of time there when I was a kid. The ship, as big as a skyscraper, glided along smoothly. A tug floated beside it, but the ship was moving on its own power.

There was an unexpected beauty in the man-made panorama. The sky was a light mid-afternoon blue with a scraping of thin, white clouds. I thought of Mandy, and wished I were with her. There used to be a restaurant nearby, R.H. Tugs. Great food, great view, and a well-stocked bar. Luke, the head waiter, was a fixture on Staten Island. The restaurant closed shortly after he died unexpectedly, and way too soon. Blue was now the new establishment there, and offered the same views and people I knew. They said the food was good. I'd bet ahead of time I'd like it, but it wouldn't be Tugs. I hate change.

Mariano and I were quiet on the way back. He reached into the car and handed the bag with two Rolling Rocks to the cop driving. He reached into his pocket and handed me a folded up paper.

"This is the info we have on the restaurant, and some of the people he ran with. Fresh from OCCB."

"Thanks," I put it in my pocket. Organized Crime Control Bureau was an elite NYPD unit. Their information was solid.

"By the way," Mariano said softly, "guess who's on the list of known associates?"

"Al Capone? John Gotti? Tony Soprano?"

"You just used two of his slugs as heavy bags."

I shook my head. "It's a small world after all."

"Or a small island," Mariano said.

11

I felt like taking a nap, but reminded myself I was too young for such things. I drove the Terrace west toward the Goethals Bridge. Apparently judging by feel, I would have to stop drinking beer and eating so much in the middle of the day. I pulled to the side of the road. It would be best to have a different experience at the restaurant; the place in Bay Ridge Luca had a piece of, than I did at Adobe.

I called Bobby Bianchi. He was a couple of years older than me, and one of the guys I looked up to as a kid. He fought in the Gloves and did well, then went into the family business, but we stayed friends. Once in a while we helped each other out. Bobby had his hand in many different businesses, legit and otherwise, but his greatest trait is keeping his word. No one could ever say he hurt someone who didn't have it coming. People respected him and his father wasn't someone you wanted angry with you.

"Nuovo, Voi Salone. This is Rachel. How can I help you?"

"Hi, may I speak with Mr. Bianchi, please?"

"Who may I say is calling?"

"Tell him Jimmy Creed, his moral compass."

I was now at the end of the Terrace, where Proctor and Gamble used to have an industrial complex. I made the left turn. A lot of people used to work there, but now it was almost abandoned. Part of the New York Container Station began to spill into it.

"Jimmy, how goes it?"

"Hey Bobby, all is well. I was hoping you might have a few minutes to talk in person."

"I'm free for a while. Can you make it by the Salon?"

"There in ten," I said.

The Salon was back a few miles from the direction I came. I took the Terrace back as far as Bement Ave., and then from Bement to Forest. I arrived at the Salon in nine minutes. When I walked in, I asked for Mr. Bianchi. The Salon was something you might ordinarily see in Manhattan or Rome. Three floors worth, everything from hair to massage, and you could eat off the floor. The girl behind the reception desk called the manager. She shook my hand, told me Mr. Bianchi was expecting me, and there was already espresso in his office. She led me to his office, opened the door, announced me, then turned and left.

Bobby was a little taller than I was, and leanly muscled. He moved fluidly, and although he was a few years older, he looked younger. Bobby was dressed well, and if you didn't know him, you wouldn't expect his grip to be so strong.

I sat in one of his client chairs. A double espresso with a shot of Sambuca sat in front of each of us. We talked for a few minutes. I wouldn't describe it as pleasantries, which usually connotes meaningless drivel. When I asked about his family, they were people I knew, people I liked, and vice versa when he asked me. I ate dinner over at his house more than once when I was a kid.

The espresso and Sambuca tasted good. We talked about old friends, Jimmy Hannan, Pat Merillo, and their brothers, Joey Lavelle, Tito Alvarez, all guys a little older than me, and I looked up to as a kid. Jimmy and Bobby had legendary sparring rounds where they would beat each other senseless, but were the best of friends after.

Joey Lavelle got me into working out when I was a kid. He also had an uppercut to the body that he, fortunately, never used on me. It would almost send the bag high enough to go over the beam. His older brother was a politician, a breed of human I didn't care much for, but he was the exception. The Lavelle family had good blood, considering they endured more than their fair share of tragedy. They lost their parents too young. Joey's brothers, John and Tom, and their sister Rita, bore up under the pain with dignity and grace. Jimmy became a nurse and eventually moved away. Joey worked as a supervisor for the City Parks Department. Pat moved to Florida, and Tito ran his own business.

Pat was still an honorary member of the Grateful Dead, and looked like he played for ZZ Top, or starred on *Duck Dynasty*. I could still see him riding on his skateboard while doing a handstand, with his German shepherd, Captain, following him. His brother, Anthony, passed away when he was young, one of my first lessons in the unfairness of life. His sister, Felice, started out as a gangly kid, but cute enough to warrant a pull of the pigtails. She grew up to be hotter than the surface of the sun. My first girlfriend, Dawn, was her best friend, and I still remember her moving away. You never love another woman the same way you love the first. It might be better, it might be worse, but it isn't new. I looked at the house they used to live in when I happened to drive by, and still remembered it like it was yesterday. When I was a kid, you could still get lost in the woods on the island. My best friend Sal and I frequently did just that.

They were all great guys when I was a kid, and still were. They had almost all moved away, except Bobby. Bobby was an honorable man who kept his word. He wasn't someone you wanted to cross, but if you were fair with him, he was fair with you. A lot of the "good guys" couldn't say that when it came down to it.

"So, Jonathan? Tell me what you need, little brother."

I told him about Luca and Vicky. I also mentioned Stanton, as it may figure in the mix. He nodded his head respectfully when I mentioned Mariano.

"I'm sorry," he said. "Vicky wasn't a bad girl. Luca was no good. He used too much of what he sold. Woman beater." He said that last phrase with sour disdain.

"Thank you."

"Mandy, I have to meet the girl that made you monogamous."

"She's amazing."

We each had a little Sambuca left. "Tutto il meglio per voi e la vostra donna fratellino." It meant, all the best to you and your woman, little brother.

"Grazie, grande fratello," I replied.

He paused and then chuckled. "We have something in common. I once knocked Bertone on his ass too."

I laughed. "Sometimes, I do enjoy my work."

"Sullivan was supposed to be tough."

"I hit him when he wasn't ready."

"Modest still."

"Have to call them like I see them, Bobby," I said.

He nodded thoughtfully. "The first shot I hit him with would have put most people down."

When I was a kid, a lot of people on the island spoke Italian. We were alternately referred to as Staten Italy or Staten Ireland.

"La Sala Da Pranzo. What's the story?"

"One of the best in the city. Chefs come from Italy. Legit business owned by colorful people."

"I need to talk with them about Luca."

"Go on."

"The cops are working the other angles. I'm interested in finding who killed Luca, but more importantly my friend."

"Say they had nothing to do with it ... would you share that information?"

"I can't, Bobby, not if I'm working with the cops. They're sharing info with me. I'm sure they could get to him if they want, when we find out who did it though."

"True enough." He paused. "There are several big people that own a piece of that restaurant. Luca was someone's half-brother. I know Luca did some unsanctioned business with Stanton. Stanton is paying a percentage to operate, but he's growing."

"Problems with Luca?"

Bobby shook his head, but said, "Yes, but not serious enough to warrant Fredo status. His brother isn't happy."

"His brother is?"

"Eddie Siciliano."

"Oh shit. Crazy Eddie?" I asked. "Who the hell would kill Crazy Eddie's brother? Is it common knowledge Luca was his half-brother?"

"Yes, to the people that should have that knowledge."

"Who would chance that?"

"No idea yet, Jonathan."

"Crazy Eddie," I said, and shook my head.

"Yeah," he said, with a nod. "You know who works for him, right?"

"A lot of people," I said. "Anthony Tempesta stands out though."

Bobby nodded. "He ain't Sullivan."

"He surely ain't."

Anthony the "Widow Maker" Tempesta. He was a top ten-ranked heavyweight who killed one man in the ring, and put several out of the fight game. The one guy who beat him ran the whole fight. A few weeks before a fight, they bumped into each other in Manhattan. The other fighter started taunting him, and when they went outside, Anthony was the only one who walked back in. He served five years for manslaughter.

The cops figured he was good for over twenty bodies. If he went to see you, and if you were lucky enough he was there only to talk, you did what he said. He was cold yet quiet, and absolutely loyal to the Sicilianos. At the beginning of a war some years back, the other side made the tactical decision to take out Tempesta, which is like taking out Luca Brazzi in *The Godfather*. Take the wind out of the sails. Great idea … tactically brilliant … except it didn't work. With two bullets in him, and another passed through, he strangled the shooter then drove himself to the hospital. He was never charged because the bodies of the two accomplices were never found.

"Be careful there, Jonathan."

"I will, Bobby."

"Let me make a few calls, see a few people. Maybe we can go there together."

"Don't put yourself out, pal, and please don't do anything that will generate heat for you."

"Let's keep you alive. I want to be the one to say I was at Jonathan Creed's wedding."

"One never knows," I said.

"Uh-oh," Bobby said. "The first time I didn't deny it, I actually did end up married."

"I have no idea how this happened, Bobby, but I'm not at all upset it did. She's the most amazing person I've ever met."

"She must be, to quell such a legendary libido."

"It's funny when the wise guys go to college and learn big words," I said.

We both smiled. The floor manager knocked on the door, came in with a small pot, and refilled our espresso cups. She also had new lemon rinds.

I left, and despite the events of the day, I felt better. Seeing Bobby reminded me of a time past. You could still get lost in the woods on the island. Warm summers, good friends, grandfathers, and grandmothers. The amusement park formerly in South Beach. My grandfather's house in Travis.

I think a lot, probably too much. I wondered how things might have been if I stayed with the family business like the rest of my family. My brothers owned a medium-sized Trucking and Warehousing business. I loved my work but it drained me mentally and emotionally. I made money from people during the worst times of their lives. I spent many years detaching myself, and it became necessary. I worked too many cases for not enough money. On those occasions, where a client was raped by the system, and there were far too many of those, their loss became mine.

My brothers all did well financially. They went home to their families, and while they had worries, they weren't my worries. If I hadn't detached I'd be in a psych ward, or afflicted with multiple sicknesses, including poverty.

It might have been an easier life. Maybe the magic wouldn't have rubbed off so fast, and there would be some remaining. I was raised to respect authority, and sometimes that respect was deserved; other times not so much.

One case I often thought about happened a few years ago. I didn't just think about it often, it was like a semi consistent headache ... heartache would be more accurate. A divorce case where the judge wanted joint custody. Made the job much easier, a trial meant work. The layman's version of the story is we were hired because the father thought there was abuse and maybe neglect. Drug tests provided overwhelming evidence the mother endangered the child, but the judge never considered anything but joint custody. He appointed a Law Guardian and held a hearing. Visitation was supervised for a while, then unsupervised on the application of the mother's attorney and the Law Guardian concurred. That was followed by splitting the time the child spent with the mother and father again. The mother hired an expert and sought help. The Law Guardian agreed with her attorney, every time but my client's attorney fought like hell. Judge told them settle it, because if it goes, he'll rule shared custody. The case lingered for a while, and the judge punished the father for making him work. Sometimes they forced settlements that way. Schedule a trial over the course of a long period of time, then threaten and intimidate the parties off the record, and the money flows and then usually dries up.

The father shared with me that his son told his Law Guardian, "Mommy yells at me. She hits me. Mommy sleeps all day. Mommy talks funny sometimes and cries." Law Guardians in New York were supposed to be independent counsel for the children. They were appointed in cases of allegations of abuse or neglect. A great idea, but then the law changed, forcing them to specifically advocate for the wishes of the child. Maybe not a great idea - what ten-year-old kid wants to watch TV instead of doing homework? There were supposed to be guidelines about what to do if the kid wanted what wasn't good for the kid, or was being unduly influenced. No one seemed to have a handle on that.

There was training required to be a law guardian but no tests, no performance reviews. They were supposed to be selected on a rotating basis, or specific ones could be appointed if the judge felt they were suited for the case. Not going along with what the judge decreed meant you wouldn't get a case for a while. If the Law Guardian just thought that, same effect.

The judge ruled shared custody, and my client's lawyer started the appeal. The child resided with his mother.

A few days after the ruling, the mother was driving with the child. She was drunk and on Xanax. She bumped the curb and hit a pole. There was enough sufficient evidence presented during the trial to prove the mother was a danger to the child, but the judge didn't care. When her hired guns testified, he agreed. The Law Guardian agreed. The Italian sports car the woman bought for herself as a present after the divorce, after it hit the curb, was two feet off the ground when it hit the pole and disintegrated. They scraped what was left of the kid up with a putty knife. Throughout the proceedings, the Law Guardian was too busy flirting with the mother and pontificating how he was raised by his mother. Parenting was in the genes. Neither the judge nor the child's attorney seriously considered the forensics that said the mother was a risk. She slipped up due to the stress of the divorce and then got better, they reasoned. The judge didn't like squeezing a trial into his schedule.

When the father came to see me, I saw his punch coming from a mile away, but didn't move out of the way. He was big and strong but didn't know how to throw a good punch. When it hit me, it rocked me back, like being hit with a club, and opened up an old cut over my left eye. I heard that dull thud you hear when you get hit, and felt the heat and disorientation normally accompanying that kind of impact. I felt the warmth of my blood as it flowed down my face. My hands balled up instinctively, but I kept them at my sides. He cried and kept yelling at me that I didn't save his son. The guys in the office all moved on him, but I waved them off. After he hit me he stopped yelling, and the rage was replaced by a deep, soul crushing grief. He fell into me, weeping. I put my arms around his shoulders. His tears and my blood mingled on the front of my shirt. For a long time, his body jerked with uncontrollable sobs.

A few days later, he returned to pay me the money he owed but I told him I didn't want it. He asked me to give it to a charity for abused children. He apologized then fell quiet. No tears, no anger, just an abyssal chasm of sadness. He told me he knew I did everything I could, but I wasn't so sure. I couldn't think of anything else I could have done, but felt I missed something. He left an envelope thick with cash on my desk.

Later that week, he killed both the Judge and the Law Guardian. He killed the Law Guardian at his home in the morning. He knew he couldn't get the gun past the metal detectors at court, so he waited in the area where the judges parked their cars. He shot the judge twice then turned the gun on himself. The judge recovered, sort of, then retired from the bench. I heard they gave him a standing ovation at his retirement dinner. He died three months later. People still talk about him as though he was a hero.

I once read a physics paper about something called the theory of many worlds. Quantum mechanics claimed there was a good possibility that, for every possible reality there existed a reality. It had something to do, I think, with an electron existing in multiple places at the same time. Somewhere, I was in the family business. Somewhere, that kid was still alive.

That also meant somewhere I never met Mandy. I felt sorry for those versions of me. The difference now was, when I had conversations with myself they would usually end with a question – what if? Now, the conversation ended with, "I wouldn't have met her." What's next, a Volkswagen van with flower decals? A few times before, I was with someone, and thought that was meant to be. Those relationships didn't work out and I figured maybe it just wasn't for me. I was younger then. Now I feel as though my whole world is cloudy and gray, and she's a break in the clouds. Maybe sandals and a tie-dyed t-shirt.

I usually hated change but sometimes it's not so bad. I always used to think I'd never retire. Grief and pain aside, I love the challenge of my work. Thoughts, no, the *beginning* of thoughts, were creeping into my mind. Maybe someplace warm, or any place she wanted to go with me.

The task at hand. Plenty of time to think about the future. It's easier to focus when you don't have so many balls in the air. I could still hear Vicky's voice, could still see the blank stare on her face when I walked into that bedroom. My stomach still drops when I remember realizing she was dead.

The task at hand.

Part 2: Coalescence

12

Mandy picked her cell up on the first ring. "Hey!"

"Hey back, baby girl. Where are you?"

"Getting ready to leave. Can we hang?"

"Yes, I need to see you."

"What's wrong?" she asked.

"Not a damn thing. I need to see you."

She laughed. "My house or yours?"

"Mine, you're going to be crying out, loudly. We don't want to disturb your neighbors."

"Hmm, I think that can be arranged. If I get my way, you might be making some noise yourself, handsome."

"We ain't waitin on me."

I told her where I kept the spare key in case she got there first. She asked if I wanted her to get anything. I said, "No." She told me she'd be there as quickly as she could. We hung up. I called her back.

"You had better not be canceling. I'm almost there, and I'm undressing in the car."

I laughed. I did that a lot with her. "No, I forgot to tell you something."

"Oh, okay, what's up, sweetie?"

"I love you."

When she didn't respond right away, I asked, "Hey, are you there?"

"Yeah, I'm just enjoying the moment," she said. "You called me back to tell me you loved me."

"Well, I do."

"I'm going to cry," she said.

"Hey, no tears. Get to my place and strip or something."

"I love you," she said.

I smiled. "I'm not going to keep saying it. I don't want you to get spoiled."

She laughed. "Me? Spoiled?"

"No, not even close."

When I arrived home, she was waiting for me. I swept her up in my arms and carried her upstairs. We went to bed and were there for a long while. Afterward, when we lay together, I realized what an amazing experience it was to feel her next to me.

"It's good that I go to the gym often."

"Speaking for any male that can see, we appreciate it."

"I may have to increase the cardio thing if you keep doing that to me."

"It was only one more than last time."

She slapped my shoulder lightly. "You keep count?!"

"A man needs goals."

She laughed. "I almost fainted."

"I'd stop if you did."

She hit me again and squeezed my left hand. "Jerk."

I winced involuntarily when she squeezed my left hand.

"You hurt your hand?"

"Sort of."

"How?"

"Connecting on Tommy Sullivan's jaw with a decent left hook."

She wrinkled her brow. "Jimmy," she started.

"It's okay. Had to be done."

She was quiet for a while. "Is it bad?"

"The situation or my hand?"

"Your hand."

"No, just a bruise. My guess is we haven't seen the last of Stanton."

"I'm sorry," she said with her eyes down.

"Don't dare be sorry. It's not your fault."

"I shouldn't have."

"Hey, stop. Do you think people like him prey on other people like him? He realized you have a good heart, but didn't count on you being smart. We all make mistakes. We love each other. We're here for each other. We deal with our problems. End of story."

"Can I ask something? Is part of the reason you did that because you're angry he's following me? Because I'm with you?"

"That's deep. Yes, but only a small part."

"It's okay. You're my man. I'd feel the same way if it was reversed."

"There's something up with this guy, Mandy. He's crazy, yes, but it's something more."

She was quiet again. "Something very weird happened once."

"Tell me."

"You may not want to hear parts of it."

"It's okay."

"Right after sex he got up and went to the kitchen. Shane was sound asleep. I never asked him over. He pleaded with me on the phone. I said it was okay, and I made him promise to leave after. I was very tired. He said he was going to get some water and was going to leave. The sex was mechanical."

I waited. The ceiling fan was on low, and cooled the room soundlessly. It felt a little chilly, so she moved under the covers to lie against me.

"I fell asleep. Shane sleeps soundly, like a log the whole night through. I wish I could sleep like he does. His bedroom door was open. I woke up and saw twenty minutes had passed. He was in Shane's room. I whispered his name. He was startled and turned around. He was wearing baggy pants and it was dark, but for a second, it looked as if he was ..."

"Aroused?" I bit my lip. That motherfucker.

"Yes."

"He said he heard a weird noise but I couldn't tell for sure, because the radiator in Shane's room makes noises."

"Well, that's hardly proof, but going by my gut, it's not good," I said. "What happened then?"

"He wanted to go back to bed. I thought it was mechanical."

"Mechanical?"

"Maybe that's not the best word." She bit her lower lip. "Manufactured."

"As if he thought you might've realized he was aroused?"

"Maybe."

"What happened then?"

"I was really freaked, so told him I was tired and didn't feel well. Then, he left."

"How soon after was the break up?"

"Not long after."

We were quiet for a while. There was absolutely something wrong with Stanton. I'm the first person to say facts are important when coming to a decision. If I thought Stanton was out of it, I wouldn't bother with him anymore.

"Can I ask you something?"

"I'll be ready in another five minutes."

She laughed. "Oh my God! Are you trying to kill me?"

"No, but if you have to go, that's the way to go."

"Jerk."

I laughed. "Ask."

"What happened today?"

"I went to a bar Stanton hangs out at."

"Adobe Blues?"

"Yeah."

"Great place. I miss it. I haven't gone there since I broke up with him."

"I loved the food."

"Me, too."

"What happened?"

I took a breath. "The two men following you were there. I attempted to dissuade them from such actions in the future. I told them I knew and it had to stop. They took exception to my direction."

She sat up and looked at me. Worry washed over her face. "So there really was a fight."

"They chose to escalate the matter. I took care of it."

"Oh, Jesus."

"It's okay. I can't have two thugs following you around."

"Jimmy, I'm afraid for you."

"I'm okay."

"And Mark?"

"Well, considering I knocked both of his hitters on their asses, he was rather calm. He claimed he was worried about you, and he realized we were more than employer and employee. It's a fairly safe bet he and I won't ever be friends."

She lay back and wrapped her arms around me, burying her head in my neck. She held on to me fiercely. I felt tears. I stroked her hair.

"Hey, it's okay, baby. Nothing is going to happen to me or you."

"I'm sorry. I'm so sorry."

"Nothing to be sorry about."

"This is my fault."

"Hey, look. Look at me."

She did. Her eyes had tears in them. Her face looked sad, and I hated that.

"We're together now. It's us. *You* don't have problems; *we* have problems. No blame. I love you. You're worth any problem."

She lay back down and I held her a while. She still cried. She fell asleep for a little while, and we lay still until she awoke.

"Hey," she said, a little sleepy.

"Hey back. Are you hungry or thirsty?"

"Both."

"What would you like to drink? And would you like to go out or stay here?"

"Water, here." She reached under the covers and held me.

"That's not the way to encourage my departure from this bed."

"You're not leaving yet."

Turns out, I stayed a while.

13

Just before seven a.m., after she fell back asleep, I put on a pair of black sweat pants and a t-shirt and went downstairs. I turned on the television to hear Jeopardy while I cooked.

I got out a wooden cutting board and cut several kinds of cheeses, added the slices, crackers, and black olives. I got a bottle of water and ran back upstairs to leave it next to the bed for her, then returned downstairs and took out a bottle of Italian red wine from a small wine fridge on the back porch. I opened it and put two wine glasses out, then took out a spreadable cheese from the fridge and a knife from the drawer.

I opened the fridge. I hadn't shopped for a while but it was fairly well stocked. I took out Marinara sauce I made a few days ago, and took out tortellini from the freezer and set the oven to 400. I took one of several loaves of frozen Italian bread and put it in the oven. I took out a baking dish and put the tortellini and sauce in it. After the bread defrosted, I took it out and left it on the counter.

As I sliced the bread, I called out an answer. I mashed up garlic and spread butter and olive oil on the bread, then called out another answer. She walked downstairs, wearing one of my flannel shirts.

"Wow."

"'Wow' in regard to my ability to bring you to a state of ecstasy? How good it smells in the kitchen? Or my being right with the jeopardy answer?"

"Smart ass."

"True."

"All three."

I smiled.

"That's twice, which isn't bad for a man my age, Miss."

I put the garlic bread on the side. The Tortellini took forty-five minutes to cook; the garlic bread would take twenty. I took out greens, olives, cherry tomatoes, and goat cheese, cut everything up, crumbled the cheese, and tossed it all in the bowl. I prepared a quick Italian dressing out of oil and balsamic vinegar with spices, then tossed the salad a second time with the dressing added.

I put the garlic bread in the oven. I still called out the answers, and she listened to see if I was right.

"You got all those right."

"Show is a repeat."

She narrowed her eyes, walked into the living room, and hit the info button. I whistled as she walked by. She came back.

"Not a repeat."

"Luck."

"No." She smiled. "I have a problem."

"I shall solve this problem, milady. Pray tell."

She laughed. "I don't know what to call you. I wanted to say your name before when we were in bed. When I called you 'Jimmy,' it didn't fit."

"When you're that loud, I don't think it matters what you scream out, honey."

She threw a dishtowel at me. "Jerk." We both said it at the same time. I did love her laugh.

"You did call me Jimmy after," I said. "You could refer to me as 'Stud Muffin' or 'Love God.'"

"Jerk," we both said again.

"I know," she said, then laughed.

"Don't say it," I said, laughing too.

"Jim and Jimmy aren't your real names. I think I called you Mr. Creed once, and then Jonathan."

I called out another answer. She smiled. I considered her conundrum as I put the bread in the oven. We drank wine and ate cheese. I called out another answer.

"My first girlfriend and people from my early childhood still call me John, or Jonathan, or Johnny."

"You should try out for the show."

"I've done the computer try out several times."

"Nothing?"

"Nothing yet."

I removed the pasta and bread from the oven then plated the food, put the bread in the middle, and cut it into smaller pieces. She watched me with genuine interest. I put her food in front of her, and then mine. I leaned down, and she leaned up to kiss me. She ran her fingers from my face to my chest. I felt a pleasant sensation from the tips of her short nails.

"You know, you're like steel or stone. It's as if you're wearing armor, yet you're so kind and gentle. I never would've thought that. That first night, when I felt alone, you were there."

I just listened. I didn't eat or drink the wine. Only a few things diverted attention from food.

"You were there when I needed you. I just didn't realize I needed you."

She tried the food. Her eyes shone. “This is so good.”

“Key is to make it in the sauce.”

“You made the sauce?”

I nodded. “And the tortellini.”

She laughed. “You did not.”

“I did not.”

“Just a question for later.”

“Shoot, babe.”

“Any chance you might want to continue where we left off?”

“Three times! My god, woman, I’m not a machine!”

“Oh well, if you’re not up to the task.”

“I didn’t say that.”

“Good, then I won’t have seconds.”

We talked while we ate. She told me more about her son and her marriage. They married young, and she had a baby fast. They remained friends, and he loved Shane. He hadn’t been greedy. They still talked all the time. I went in at some point and turned on the stereo. Carol Miller came on with, “Get The Led Out.” She was playing some of Plant’s solo stuff.

“He fired his first lawyer because the lawyer kept trying to sell him on revenge. He had to fight for his assets. His second lawyer listened to him, and we worked out a deal right away. He gave me more than I wanted, and his business became very successful. He told me to stop working so I could be there for our son. He was able to build the business because I took care of the home.”

“Wow. If more guys were like that, there’d be a lot less business for attorneys.”

She smiled. “He’s a good man.”

Ship of Fools came on.

I asked her if she knew it. She said, “No,” and listened. “It’s beautiful.”

I smiled. “The lyrics are very moving.”

I heard my cell phone ring and went to answer, but didn’t get to it in time. It was Bobby Bianchi. I called him back.

“How goes it, little brother?”

“It goes well. And on your end?”

“Any day above ground ...”

“Is a good one,” we finished together.

“I have a meeting set at La Sala for an early dinner tomorrow night. Five fifteen.”

“Okay,” I said.

“I’m going with you. Siciliano will be there.”

“Thanks, Bobby.”

“You’re buying.”

“I can already see you skipping a couple of meals tomorrow.”

He laughed and said, “Goodnight.”

I went back inside and sat down at the table. I saw she waited for me to get back before she finished eating. I smiled, and we sat and talked of other things. She spoke of friends and her parents. I told her more about what it was like growing up. She was pleasant to talk with and I enjoyed her company. She told me about her parents then we went into the living room and watched television. When we both started to nod off, we went to bed.

I slept soundly with her next to me. At some point in the middle of the night, when she pressed hard against me, we both woke up and tended to the unfinished business of round three. All in all, it was a good night. As I drifted off to sleep, I thought, “If that was like the rest of the nights in the future, it would be fine with me.”

I dreamt of finding Vicky again. I woke up with Mandy sleeping with her arm across my chest. The alarm clock read two minutes after five. I wasn't tired. We actually went to bed early. I got up, careful not to wake her.

I watched her sleep until it made me feel creepy. I went into the kitchen and turned the Keurig on, opened the fridge, and poured myself a glass of lemon mint water. A forest of mint grew on the side of the house. Sometimes I juiced lemons, but most of the time I bought lemon juice. It was good either way. I had time to kill, so I turned off the Keurig and got out the old-style, stovetop coffee pot, then sat at the table and sipped my water. After a while, the smell of coffee floated through the room. I wasn't hungry or tired. I wanted this to move on. I wanted whoever killed my friend to pay for it.

Sometimes, I wish my memory wasn't as good as it is when I remembered things I saw, felt, smelled, and tasted. It was both the good memories and the bad. I wish I could be selective. I remembered everything about Vicky. I don't know what it was about me at the time. Now, when I thought about her I saw the image of her dead stare when I walked into that bedroom in Luca's house.

"I'm sorry, Vicks," I said softly.

14

La Sala da Pranzo was on Fourth Avenue in Bay Ridge, just a few parking spaces down from Eighty Ninth Street. The large building occupied three storefronts, with an office on the second floor of the three-story building, and a private club on the third. When you walked through the front door, a coatroom sat to the right. Straight ahead, a staircase descended to the bathrooms, a large banquet room, and two offices. A large bar and small informal dining room sat to the left; the main restaurant dining area to the right. The room was huge. A door in the back led to another more private dining area.

The paintings were all expensive and original. The walls were bright, and the whole place looked like an art museum. A hand painted border of flowers ran at the top of each wall. The food was supposed to be superb, but I'd never eaten there.

Bobby walked in first. He always looked like he could be on the cover of GQ. He wore a light blue Armani suit with a white shirt and blue tie. I wore a charcoal jacket, a lavender French cut shirt, and lavender tie; dark slacks and black loafers. My forty-five rested comfortably on my hip.

Anthony Tempesta's eye moved over us as he sat at the bar. His large frame was as imposing as ever. About half of the drink in front of him was gone. He was dressed neatly, but subdued. Bobby and I looked in his direction. He nodded slightly to us, or perhaps Bobby. We nodded back. The maitre'd approached and showed us into the third dining room to the right of the main one.

Eddie Siciliano sat alone at the table, his hands resting on his thighs, his back to the wall. There were three chairs. He stood as Bobby came close and shook his hand. They conversed in Italian. Without straining my brain, I heard Eddie ask how Bobby's father was, and Bobby asked about Eddie's family. Crazy Eddie turned to me and smiled. His lips went up but his eyes were cold steel. His grip was firm, and spoke of strength.

He got the moniker 'Crazy Eddie' because of his actions years ago when he was a soldier during a war. A gunfight broke out in a restaurant where he was eating, and despite bullets flying all over, and him without a gun, he ran at one of the shooters and buried a steak knife in the guy's neck. After aerating him in proper fashion, Eddie liberated the pincushion's firearm and took out a few more. Seven people died; a number of others wounded; Eddie walked away without a scratch.

Over the years, other syndicates moved in on the traditional Italian territory. Always the same story, the Russians would come as hard as coffin nails, but the feds would pay no attention to them unless it was forced, because they were crazy. They came from a place where prisons made our prisons look like resorts. They weren't above killing prosecutors and cops. Then they'd stay a while and their offspring would grow up easy, far easier than they did. That would break the iron. Every so often, a new ethnic group far more ruthless and crazy to deal with would arise, but nobody ratted. Much of the brutality was confined to their own ethnic group, but dissipated over time.

Crazy Eddie was still the king of his castle. He was sixty but looked forty. His territory consistently grew without ever shrinking. He didn't tolerate rats, and if you made the mistake of hurting one of his, it would be your final mistake. People with degrees in computer science worked for him. He was an efficient and ruthless combination of old and new.

He himself was measured and calm, never acted without thinking, and kept a low profile. The crazy part came out during war. The crazy was also logical, and it worked. No one ratted on Eddie and lived for very long. If you saw the crazy, it was a good bet it would be the last thing you would see. Even big talkers kept their mouth shut because Crazy Eddie hired hard people. Tempesta was the hardest.

Seafood salad and three glasses of wine already rested on the table, and music played softly in the background. Pavarotti was singing "Che Gelida Manina" from La Boheme.

"Please, gentleman, sit and enjoy the food and wine while we talk. I took the liberty of ordering some of our specialties." He smiled again, more warmly. "Bobby said you haven't been to our restaurant before.

"Grazie, signore Siciliano," I said. "Questa è la mia prima volta in questo bellissimo ristorante."

"Eddie, Jonathan, va bene. Bobby parla molto bene di te, lui dice che sei un uomo di parola, il padre dice lo stesso." Translated - "Eddie, Jonathan, is fine. Bobby speaks very highly of you. He says you are a man of your word. His father says the same."

"He told me the same about you, sir," I said in English. I understood Italian, but hadn't spoken it much since high school.

"Eddie," he said. "Please."

"Eddie," I nodded.

The frutta di mare tasted excellent, as did the wine. The bread at the table was warm, accompanied with softened butter and olive oil for seasoning. We all acted civil. I was also conscious I was sitting with a man who would send me into the afterlife without a second thought, with the slightest provocation. The wise-ass personality of mine retreated in the name of self-preservation.

We made small talk while we ate appetizers. Bobby knew the territory, and he took the lead. I actually hated small talk, but sometimes it was important, and something I needed to learn.

The plates were cleared away by a spectacular looking waitress, almost, but not quite Mandy's caliber. She brought us salad, which consisted of good greens, and an oil and vinegar dressing with a superb combination of spices. And then she further endeared herself to me by bringing more warm bread. After the salad, the main course arrived. Steak Pizzaiola made the way an Italian grandmother would; cooked all day along with homemade pasta, and a small plate of vegetables.

After dinner we were served fresh fruit, espresso, and an assortment of desserts. Italian and American Cheescake, Tortuffo, Cannoli were among the fare. I thought about animals fattened before the slaughter.

After the coffee, Sambuca with three coffee beans was brought in for each of us, with more espresso. Now the discussion would begin.

"Eddie, I want to say I'm very sorry for your loss."

"Thank you. I'm told you also lost someone close to you. Please accept my condolences as well." His eyes searched mine.

"I won't lie, Eddie. I have the feeling your brother was slapping my friend around. If I had proof or if she asked me for help, I would have knocked him on his ass."

"Fair enough," Siciliano said. "Despite what you may have been told about me, I don't believe a man should raise his hand to a woman."

I nodded respectfully. "I'm working with the police, or at least with their knowledge. I suggested I speak with you. There aren't any suspects yet. I cannot divulge details to you if I find out who it was, but when he, she, or they, are caught, I'm sure you could get to them if you wished."

"Go on," he said.

Bobby remained quiet and listened. He spoke with Siciliano as we ate dinner. He was quiet thus far about the subject at hand.

"Does anyone have any idea who may have killed them?"

"Not so far. And believe me, we're inquiring."

"Would you be able to give me a list of people he's been dealing with?"

"Allow me to consider that. I've been told you recently visited one of his associates and had a disagreement with two of the people that work for him."

"Small world," Bobby said, with a grin.

"It can be," Siciliano said.

Apparently," I agreed.

"I was aware of Stanton and he dealing with each other."

"Any reason to believe Stanton didn't have anything to do with it?" I asked.

"None whatsoever, but he remains a possibility," Siciliano said.

"Any leads?" Bobby asked.

"Not so far."

I sipped the espresso. It tasted good. Everything was excellent. I thought for a minute then sat back in the chair and looked at a painting on the wall, of what looked like Florence.

"As I said, Eddie, my hands are somewhat tied in what I can reveal, but I will say this. Thus far, no one has anything."

Siciliano nodded, "I appreciate that, and also happy you're looking into it. The police may not put so much effort into it."

"The cops are working hard, Eddie," I said truthfully. He nodded again.

Tempesta appeared at the doorway. Eddie looked at him and nodded then got up from the table, followed by Bobby and me.

"Eddie, if you need privacy we can leave," Bobby said.

"No," Siciliano said. "Enjoy the coffee. You're my guests."

"Thank you," I said, as we sat. He spoke softly to the waitress as he passed. She left, I guessed to get more espresso. He walked through the door after Tempesta.

"He's polite and a good host, likable even," I said.

"He is," Bobby said, meeting my eyes. "He will also, if you ever give him reason to, kill you in the same kindly fashion. Or will send someone to."

"Understood," I said.

I took the opportunity to look at my cell phone. Vicky's ex-husband had left a message.

> *Just wondering how things are going. Left a couple of messages at your office. Touch base when you can.*
>
> *Thanks.*

I'd call him tomorrow. Siciliano might share if they had something, or he might just have everyone involved disappear. He might even mention it but I couldn't count on it. Little accomplished but the dinner was great. There was that.

Siciliano returned after a bit and finished his coffee and Sambuca. We talked a bit more then parted ways. Siciliano told me it was a pleasure and I was welcome back anytime. I told him I appreciated his hospitality and his courtesy. He kissed Bobby on the cheek, and shook my hand firmly.

"Oh, Bobby," Eddie said, as we were leaving. "Anthony is at a table in the back of the bar. He wanted you to stop and say, "Hi" if you had a minute."

"Sure, Eddie," Bobby said.

Tempesta sat at a table furthest from the bar. The bar was crowded, but no one sat near him despite the fact there were other open tables. He was quiet, sipping on what looked like scotch and water. His large hands dwarfed the sizeable glass. His face, although vacant of emotion, wasn't unpleasant despite scar tissue around the eyes, and a nose that was obviously broken a few times. He had dark blue eyes, a full head of neatly combed gray hair, and a well-trimmed gray mustache. He stood at least six four, with a broad and lithe, but well-muscled frame. Although he was visibly comfortable and relaxed, he still gave me the impression of energy, like a soda bottle shaken to the point where its cap might pop. He gestured to the two empty chairs. I knew he was about twelve years older than me, but aside from the gray hair, there was no indication of that.

"If you like scotch, this is very good," he invited. He raised his hand, and a waitress appeared.

"Thank you," I said. He nodded. Bobby was quiet.

She quickly returned with three glasses of scotch and three glasses of water. The Widow Maker might be the grim reaper incarnate, but he knew how to drink scotch. I took a little water from the glass to cleanse my palate then poured the water into my glass. Bobby and Tempesta did the same. I swirled it around then inhaled the aroma, which was incredible. Bobby raised his glass and wished everyone good health. I sensed a glint of amusement in Tempesta's eyes. We all raised our glasses and drank.

I let the scotch linger in my mouth then slowly let it roll down my throat. My eyebrows rose, and I put down the glass. "Exceptional," I said.

Bobby said, "Wow."

"MaCallan Rare Cask, single malt," Tempesta said quietly.

"I get the feeling you need to discuss something," I said. Bobby looked like he wanted to kick me.

"I'm told you're out looking for the same individuals I am."

"Yes, you, me, and about thirty five thousand cops."

He nodded, "Eddie said he trusted you, but your goal is different."

"As I told him, Anthony (I decided on Anthony rather than Tony, or Mr. Tempesta, or Grim, or Reaper), I have no doubt once someone goes down for it, you'd get to him in jail at some point during the twenty five years to life he'd be there."

"It doesn't sit well with me you expect us to cooperate and you won't do the same," Tempesta said. "However, Eddie said to clue you in. He agrees with you about what would happen if the cops or you caught someone and they went in for it. It would also seem you'd have to violate their trust to tell us. You get a good mark for that."

"Thank you," I said.

"Respectfully, Anthony, why are we talking?" I sensed Bobby's alarm growing.

He smiled. "You can be direct and that's fine, I prefer that. You have friends and Eddie respects them, and although it's a newly formed one, he has a good opinion of you," Tempesta said. His voice was steady, quiet, and cold. I nodded and waited. "If we go for someone at the same time you do, and you don't back off, you go, too." I had no need to search for a hidden meaning there.

"I'm sure it won't come to that, Tony," Bobby said.

Tempesta nodded, but kept his eyes on mine. "Odds of that would be small," I said. Tempesta nodded.

We finished our scotch in silence. I remarked how great the scotch was. Bobby agreed again, and Tempesta nodded. We got up to leave after Bobby said he needed to get home to his family. Tempesta softly said goodnight, with no effort to shake hands. On the way to get our coats, I stopped, and Bobby turned.

"Grab my coat. I'm going to use the men's room, pal."

He nodded and kept walking. I turned and went back into the bar. Tempesta's eyes fell on me. I walked toward him, steady and slow. Our eyes stayed locked. I leaned close enough to Bobby so he could hear, and put my hands on his chair. I kept my voice low.

"Anthony," I said. "Just so you know ... if that does happen, maybe I win, maybe not. If I don't, I promise you, you won't walk away a whole man."

There was the faint smile again. "You'd be the first."

"First time for everything," I said, smiling back. "Thank you for the scotch and being clear."

"That's the way to be," he said.

"Nothing personal on this end either," I said.

He nodded, then I nodded and walked back. Bobby stood there with the coats, watching.

"Ready?" I asked.

He shook his head but said, "Yes." We walked outside. It wasn't late. A faint light in the west indicated the night sky again temporarily regaining its victory. The valet pulled Bobby's car around without the ticket. I hate to participate in a cliché, but I did have a genuine chill up my spine. Threaten the Grim Reaper, one off the bucket list.

"You're going to give me a fucking heart attack, Jimmy," Bobby said, as we entered the ramp to go back onto the Verazzano Bridge. "You're truly going to give me a fucking heart attack."

I smiled. "Maybe I'm on the short list for one myself, Bobby."

He was angry, concerned, and driving. "You had to let that ...fucking ... Angel of Death ... know. You, you had to fucking lip off to him?"

"Bobby, if someone knocks on the door, answer."

"Jesus, Jimmy," he said, with a shake of his head.

"The odds of us both closing in on the same person, come on, Bobby. Ain't happening."

"But still."

"Bobby, is there any chance he might have killed Luca and Vicky?"

"Who? Tempesta?"

"Any chance?"

"None."

"Then, it was just him letting me know he was in charge, and me protesting the thought."

He exhaled, exasperated. He was quiet, and he slowed down for the toll, drove through the EZ-pass. He turned the radio on from a button on the steering wheel. Rush hour was over, but the traffic was still heavy. He lane jockeyed, and after a few minutes made it to the far left lane.

"That was an unbelievable meal," I said.

"I hope it wasn't your last."

I laughed and put my hand on his shoulder. The traffic lightened, and we picked up a little speed.

"Bad Company," by, of course, "Bad Company," came on. Traffic lightened once we got past the part where it simultaneously sloped and curved. Even the multi-million dollar fix applied to the parking lot known as the Staten Island Expressway didn't correct.

"A fucking heart attack," he said again.

15

The next morning, Saturday, I met Jeff and Mariano at their health club. Like most dinosaurs, I did on occasion go to gyms, although for the most part, I liked the basement. It was a half-cloudy, half-sunny sky. The office was open, but only for a few hours, and I wasn't going in.

We were supposed to meet at ten, and I arrived early. I had three cups of coffee in me, and I walked in with a third; primed and ready to go. I wore an old flannel shirt with a *Breaking Bad* t-shirt underneath. The air was chilly, and I wore black sweats.

I walked up to the desk. An attractive girl with black hair and a body I bet was a combination of good genetics and a lot of hard work, hit me a smile. She had jet-black hair, dark eyes, a perfectly portioned Roman nose, and darker skin that suggested either Mediterranean, or hours spent tanning. I struggled not to stare.

"Hi," I said.

"Hi back. Any chance you're Creed?"

I smiled. "I am. Are you prescient?"

"I was told by Chief Mariano a friend of his would be by. He paid for your day."

"Very kind of him."

"He's a nice man."

"That he is." I smiled.

She smiled back. "You look like you know your way around."

"I do." I winked at her.

"If you need anything, my name is TJ."

"Thanks, TJ."

The gym was not overly crowded. Two juice jockeys off to the right in the back screamed at each other. A number of people worked the treadmills, and an aerobics class was in progress. A few other people were lifting weights, including an old timer who passionately attacked his workout.

A big room where they probably held aerobics class offered heavy bags, speed bags, a couple of double end balls, and mats, with plenty of room to stretch. I stretched first and did the usual hundred knuckle push-ups, leg raises, and crunches. I took my own bag gloves out of the bag. I had a timer, but there was also one on the wall. I set it for four three-minute rounds. I punched the speed bag first to warm up then used the double end ball for the second round. I made it move pretty good. On that rest, I stripped off the flannel shirt and sparred lightly for one round on a two-hundred pound heavy leather Everlast bag. Jeff and Mariano walked in together as I finished the first round.

We all said 'Good Morning,' and they both started stretching. The second round, I rocked the bag and felt good. I always warmed up on the bag. On time-challenged weeks, I kept the punches sharp. I usually got a few other martial arts or bag workouts in addition to the weights. While I waited for my companions, I walked over to a standing bag in the corner used primarily for kicking. I played with that until they warmed up.

They walked over and we spoke. Jeff was going to work the machines and run on the treadmill. I did strength training, and it was a bench day. I did two or three days a week. This was a three-day week.

We went over to where Mariano was benching. I put my bag down and took out a towel. I used a medium grip. His was wide, and he warmed up with 135 for eight; he did it for eight. I lifted 185 for five; he lifted for eight. I lifted 225 for five; he lifted for twenty-five. I thought at first he was miscounting. I did 275 for five; he did it for twenty. I did 315 for five; he did it for fifteen. I paused after each first rep for two seconds. By the time he finished the last set he was breathing heavy. So was I, but didn't expend near the effort he did. I was forty. Although he didn't look like it, he had to have fifteen years on me. That was why.

"I'm done," he said. "You?"

"Couple of heavy sets."

I loaded three sixty-five, and he moved to the Incline Bench closest to the flat bench I worked on. I walked over and helped him lift off the 135. It's bad for your shoulder to take that off, even light by yourself. He did eight reps and then came over to the flat bench.

"Lift?"

"I'm okay. If I can't get it, you'll know," he said, with a nod.

I paused it on the first, and did five reps, shaking a little on the last. He nodded his approval. We alternated. I managed three more sets, and shook on the last two, but managed. No help that he finished on the incline. I did three sets of incline with dumbells - just three sets, eight, six, and four with eighty, ninety, and one hundred pound dumbbells, then returned to the bench and did three sets of close grip benches, the same eight, six, and four, increasing weights on each. He finished his support work, and I did grip work.

Jeff finished too, and we all ended up on the treadmill. When we were done, we went to the café, sat, and ordered three coffees and water.

I recounted for them the events of the evening. I looked at the menu and ordered a protein shake with greens and nuts. Mariano and Jeff ordered similar fare.

"Not bad," Mariano said.

"The key to eternal youth," Jeff began, "is slow and steady wins the race."

"You do look great for eighty," I said.

"How old are you, now?" Mariano asked.

"Seventy two," Jeff said.

"He actually looks the same as he did when I first met him twenty-five years ago," I said.

Jeff smiled. "That's the advantage to losing your hair when you're young."

"Less expenses for barbers and shampoo," I said.

"More money for retirement."

"Don't waste my inheritance, by the way," I said.

"Never," Jeff said.

We drank the shakes; it really wasn't bad. I didn't go for all that "healthy" food industry garbage. I did try to eat well most of the time, a little extra protein to help keep the muscle I developed for thirty odd years. It didn't taste bad though, and it was loaded with raw greens, nuts, bananas, and vanilla protein. It tasted like a banana milkshake.

"That was some good weight," Mariano said.

"You didn't do bad yourself, Chief."

"Not as easy as it once was."

"Few things are," I said.

"Speak for yourselves, kids," Jeff said.

TJ, the hot girl at the front desk, came over and asked if we needed anything, and specifically asked if she could get us coffee, which of course, put her on my favorite person list.

Over coffee, I told them about the meeting last night and the meal, and Tempesta. Jeff shook his head at that part.

"Must you always poke the bear?" my old friend asked.

"If someone knocks ..." I started.

"Answer," Mariano finished for me.

"Or let them think you're not home, go outside, and shoot them from behind," Jeff said.

I took advantage of a pause in the conversation to check my cell phone. Some messages from the office, but not many, since Jeff was covering for me. We had a service for the office phones for nights and weekends, but if something heavy was going on, the girls at the service would call. Mandy often checked the service messages on the weekend. Mandy texted. Vicky's ex-husband called several times. I hadn't wanted to call him too early, and planned on it after the workout. My phone notified me of another text. It was from him.

"Hey, please give me a call today. Been trying to reach you."

I'd been lax and hadn't stayed in touch with him, but I was only on it a few days. Nevertheless, he volunteered to be my client, so I could do this legit. "*Very little to talk about yet, I'll be in touch soon*," I texted him back.

"We have nothing as of yet. Five blocks away, there was a silver or gray middle 00's Hyundai driving at a time. It could have something to do with the murders, or nothing to do with them. Plate is indiscernible, despite the best we can do." Mariano sipped his coffee after he spoke.

"I wonder," Jeff said.

We waited.

"We're proceeding on the premise it had to do with Luca. What about Vicky? What if it had something to do with her?"

"We're checking that," Mariano said, "but the emphasis is on Luca."

"Being as all I got last night was in close contact with the Angel of Death, and a very good meal, I can start talking to her friends, too. And my client for that matter."

We kicked around everything we know, which is a good idea to do with any case. And we knew nothing more than when we started. Maybe I should read a few Holmes or Wolfe novels to brush up.

"I thought you hotshot private guys usually had one up on us," Mariano said.

"Only in books and movies," Jeff said.

"Besides, if a key law enforcement official like yourself is stumped, Chief, what could we know?"

Mariano smiled. "Not much."

We left. I got into my car and looked through the sunroof while I thought for a while. The sky was blue, with the occasional dreamy wisp of high white. It was normally Mandy's weekend with her son, but her ex was attending a function. Her son wanted to go, and she had no problem with it. She was meeting me at the house about noon, and we were going to spend the rest of the weekend together.

I got home, and she was already there. The day was warm, but not overly so. The sky was a gorgeous light blue. The buds were coming out on the trees, and the flowers starting to bloom. She was talking to Hank, my neighbor. He was a decent man and retired cop. She kept reaching down to pet his dog, a big barrel chested Rotty named Harley.

I looked at her for a moment. She was wearing a floral print spring dress, and sunglasses. With inflation in mind, she looked a like a billion dollars. I got my bag out of the trunk, and Hank moved off to continue his walk with Harley, waving to me as he did. I waved back and walked toward Mandy.

"You must have had a lookalike in England in the nineteenth century, my love."

"And what makes you say that, my handsome man?" she asked, and kissed me hello. Since I was drenched in sweat, I resisted the urge to pull her closer.

"Tennyson must have known a woman like you," I said. "In the spring, a young man's fancy lightly turns to thoughts of love."

She blushed and smiled brilliantly, then looked down at the ground first, and then up at me. I felt like a sailor hearing the call of the siren through the mist, and realized I would do almost anything she asked.

"Remember to use this power only for good," I said.

She leaned in close and whispered in my ear. "I have no idea what you're talking about, my love."

"Are you sure you want to go out today?"

"Yes," she said, slightly puzzled. "Why? Are you feeling okay?"

"I feel great. Something just came up."

Her eyebrows went up, and I cast my eyes down at my lower half. She punched me in the arm, laughing.

"Jerk," she said.

"I could ravage you, cook for you, ravage you again. We could take a nap. Then, more ravaging ..."

She laughed. "That's tomorrow's schedule."

"Then let me shower and change, and I'll take you wherever your heart desires to make up for the strain. I'm going to make you go through tomorrow."

"Maybe I'll outlast you tomorrow."

"Well, considering the gift of your anatomy is multiple orgasms, you have a considerable advantage. However, I'm always up for a challenge." I looked down again, and she punched me.

I went in, showered, and shaved. She sat on the edge of the bed, chatting on her cellphone. I dried off and dressed. I smiled when she tried to catcall me, but she had a whistling deficiency. I put on jeans and a short-sleeved shirt, then went into the safe in the closet, and took out the small .38 included on my carry license. This was almost unheard of these days. The police department technically allowed it, but almost no one but retired cops had it. I got away with it because I hit it off well with the investigator at the licensing division, when I first got it over twenty years ago.

Under normal circumstances, I wouldn't have been carrying on a Saturday during a date. With the current circumstances, however, there's no way I wouldn't. The .38 was smaller, and had a much lighter round. As I was a civilian, I had hollow points and a speed loader with trauma shock rounds. I had several light jackets that would cover it fine. I also had a surgically sharp, but legal, pocketknife.

I sat on the bed next to her when I was dressed, leaving the gun, bullets, and knife on the dresser. I lightly started kissing her neck. After a few seconds, she lost concentration on the call. She giggled a little then told whomever she needed to go. She put the phone down on the bed, placed her hand softly on my face, and looked into my eyes.

"I feel as if I'm melting when you touch me."

"It's very difficult not to touch you when I'm this close to you," I said. "Come, milady, we must go."

She laughed. "I thought you wanted to stay."

"I want to take you out and make the world jealous," I said.

"We can stay and then go out later," she said, lying back on the bed.

I'm not quite sure what the world's record is for removing one's clothes, but if I didn't break it, I came damned close. She laughed, again. I loved her laugh. It was soft and sweet. I reached out and she took my hand. I gently pulled her up and drew her close.

"If you want that lovely dress to remain intact, Miss, you better remove it." I swept the covers back. She slipped out of the dress and neatly laid it on the chair. I scooped her up in my arms and put her back in the bed.

A few hours later, we were holding hands and walking around Snug Harbor. Years ago, Sailor's Snug Harbor was a retirement home for sailors; now it housed a botanical garden and museum. The buildings were stunning, and there were always events going on. We went to the Noble Maritime Collection and walked around, looking at the paintings. I'd been there many times, and the paintings were beautiful; deep and rich, and made part of you yearn to be on a ship somewhere. Despite the magnificence of the art, my thoughts kept returning to the living, breathing artwork holding my hand.

We took our time and eventually made our way to Ruddy and Dean's. The air had cooled a bit, and she was wearing my jacket. Ruddy's was a good steakhouse, and I was partial to the lobster mac and cheese. In point of fact, few things on most menus I wasn't partial to.

We ordered drinks. I had my usual cold weather Manhattan, made with Southern Comfort on the rocks. It made me feel like Cary Grant. She ordered a vodka with seltzer and lime.

"I believe I made a discovery," I said.

"Please share," she said. Her eyes shone and she smiled.

"We, and more so you, are a miracle."

"Oh?" She smiled wider.

"Yes."

"And your proof?"

"Well, baby girl, it might be a long explanation, but I'll impart it if you so desire."

She laughed. Jesus, I loved it when she laughed. She regarded me for a second then sipped her drink. Mine was gone.

"I'm all ears."

"Okay. First, does the subject of space, stars, creation, et cetera bore you?"

"Not at all. My son watches the Discovery Channel all the time. I started watching it with him, and it's interesting."

"Very good, luv," I said. "This will be easy, then." She smiled, and again I shivered.

"Well, first, creation for all intents and purposes explodes into being. Then, there are unimaginably hot temperatures in the trillions of degrees, thousands of times hotter than any star. Forgetting about time spans and such, eventually matter and anti-matter are formed. Eventually, by an incredibly narrow margin, as they cancel each other out, matter wins. Then, incredibly, particles of energy sort of collate and make matter, specifically Hydrogen."

I finished my drink, and the waiter came and took the glass. Mandy declined another but wasn't too far behind me. We were in a corner. It was just after five, so we were alone.

"As the universe began to cool to billions and then millions of degrees, atoms formed. Hydrogen was everywhere. Space itself was expanding." I took another sip. Jesus, I felt corny. But she listened, her eyes fixed on me.

"Eventually, gravity caused massive clouds of hydrogen to collapse on themselves, igniting the first stars. Gigantic stars, they were first called "generation stars." They burned hot, fast, and at the end of their lives, they collapsed in on themselves, and exploded in titanic supernovas. When that happened, due to the tremendous heat and compression, the heavier elements were formed and scattered through the new universe."

"Okay," she said. "I follow." She smiled.

I got caught up looking in her eyes for a few seconds. The waiter brought our appetizers, she ordered shrimp cocktail, I ordered clams on the half shell. While I talked, I was careful to load each clam with the right amount of horseradish, tabasco, lemon, and cocktail sauce. That's important.

"Eventually, a massive cloud, made mostly of hydrogen and some of those new, heavier elements like iron, was floating around in space, and became heavy enough to collapse again into a star and the planets in our solar system. Eventually, the earth formed. Likely after it formed once, it was hit by another planet, maybe as big as Mars, and rather than be destroyed, we get the Earth and the Moon."

"Wow," she said. "My son is going to love you." She cut one of the shrimp into smaller pieces, and ate them slowly. "Keep going," she smiled.

"We would likely not exist if it wasn't for the moon, or if we weren't in just the right position with the Sun." I ate a few more clams. "We wouldn't exist without our magnetic core, Jupiter, the right atmosphere, too many factors to cover with the time we have."

"I didn't know that. Incredible."

"Indeed, very much so, baby girl." Another swallow, and half the drink was gone. "So then, life forms, lots of theories about that. Maybe from comets, maybe from here, who knows?"

"We evolve into humans. We create civilizations and colonize the world. From living in trees, outlasting the dinosaurs, not killing ourselves off yet, all of these things are incredible, miraculous. Let's jump ahead so I don't monopolize the night," I said.

"I love to listen to you."

"Oh goodness, you shouldn't say things like that," I said.

She giggled. "Jeff actually warned me about that when I was hired."

"Of course," I said, laughing. "Off topic for a second, I almost didn't hire you."

"Oh?" She sounded surprised.

"I was afraid I'd be too distracted. You were so beautiful. I was attracted to you immediately."

Her hand reached across the table and found mine. "I'm so glad you did."

"Well, despite the fact I wanted to rip your clothes off that second, I was afraid, and by the way, if you didn't happen to be interested, I figured I'd be crushed. So damned if I did, damned if I didn't. You were so bright and efficient when we gave you the typing test. You were the most qualified, by far."

"I want ..." she started.

"To ask me for a raise is cruel and opportunistic," I said, and we both laughed.

"I want to say," she finished, grinning, "I felt the same way."

A knot formed in my throat. "Wow."

"You were so handsome, with a gentleness about you, and so strong. You wore this amazing aftershave. When I sat at the desk, you reached over to take a file. You came close and I actually wanted to kiss you."

"Double wow!"

"You were so easy to talk to. You cared about me. You care about everyone at the office. You're smart and funny."

"Okay. I'm going to get misty, so stop. Let me get the rest of this out."

"Oh, please do," she said, her face beaming. Her eyes grew big. Jesus, she was living artwork.

"There are millions of other things that had to happen for us to meet. Jeff was supposed to do interviews that day. For you to be so perfect."

"Oh sweetheart, I'm not," she said. Her eyes lowered a little.

"Hey," I whispered. "To me, you are. I love everything about you. I wouldn't change a thing. Your eyes, your hair, your fragrance. You taste like candy. Your lips are perfect. I can go on, but to me, you're perfect."

Her eyes glistened.

"When I'm with you, it fits so well," I said. "For all of those things to happen, in that order, and the result to be you, that's the first miracle. You sitting there looking at me, through all these random actions going back almost fourteen billion years. You becoming the person sitting across from me, that's a miracle."

Tears fell from her eyes, but she smiled brilliantly. My voice was getting hoarse, and my eyes were misting.

"And us finding each other is the second miracle. I love you, Mandy. You're it for me. It feels like I've been missing a part of me my whole life, and you filled that gap."

I had no idea I was going to say all of that. Well, I was going to say some of it, but not that much. It was what I felt. Both of us sat crying at the table, but I couldn't think of any place I'd rather be.

We managed to eat dinner without more trips to the emotional bank. She ate a Chicken Madeira, and I ate the house pork chop. The rest of the meal featured a much lighter conversation. We split cheesecake for desert. I drank a nice blended port; she drank Frangelica.

As we walked back to the car, she whispered a suggestion into my ear. I laughed, and she squeezed my arm. I made a comment about my advancing years and the strain I felt. She said I'd survive. It was cooler, but not too cold. If the effect was her pressing against me like she did, I didn't mind one bit.

I drove home leisurely, and she fell asleep for part of the ride. I drove carefully to prevent waking her. We got in and settled on the couch for a bit. I asked what she'd like to watch, and she didn't have a preference. There was a channel called METV, airing old sci-fi shows on Saturday Nights like *Lost in Space*, *Voyage to the Bottom of the Sea*, and *Star Trek*. She fell asleep as I explained the finer points of William Shatner as Captain Kirk.

She woke up about nine and kissed me. I asked if she needed anything. She said, "No." We sat and watched a while, with her head resting on my shoulder. She got up and stretched as I watched.

"Tired?" I asked.

"No, but I'd like to go to bed after a hot shower."

"Would you like me to soap you up?" I said, with a grin.

"That's kind of what I had in mind, sir."

I jumped up and she giggled again. I locked up the downstairs then went upstairs with her and set the alarm. We showered and went to bed. I didn't have a better day within my memory. I really felt like I was twenty when I was with her. She fell asleep, and I watched the bedroom TV with the closed captions on. I fell asleep about midnight, woke about two, and turned off the TV. We both slept long.

I woke up and smelled coffee and bacon. I went downstairs, and Mandy was making breakfast. Eggs, bacon, French toast, coffee, and juice. She grabbed the papers and brought them in. It was warmer out, apparently, and she had opened some of the windows. I went up behind her and kissed her. She leaned back into me, and I ran my hands over her legs and abdomen. She kissed me and woke me in another way.

"Easy, big boy. I'm making you the perfect breakfast here. I don't want it to burn. We have all day to satisfy your carnal desires."

"As you are providing fuel for said desires, I shall contain myself – for now."

She told me breakfast would be ready in fifteen minutes. I went into the living room, moved the coffee table, and stretched. Even on off days, I moved better if I stretched. I did a few push-ups and crunches, washed up in the downstairs bathroom, and joined her in the kitchen. She set the table. The house smelled as a home should.

She poured me coffee. I tried to get up to help her, but she insisted I sit. I read an astronomy magazine and glanced surreptitiously at her. She glanced back. The coffee was very good. She had added cinnamon to it.

"Hey, I got a call earlier from my ex. He wanted to drop Shane off a little earlier."

"Do you think it would bother him if he spent the afternoon with us?" I asked.

"I don't think so," she said, smiling again.

"If things are smooth with you and the ex, please ask him in for coffee."

"I will," she said.

She served us breakfast and we chatted. The food tasted delicious. She went upstairs to shower and get ready. I took my magazine, poured another coffee, and went into the living room.

Although we had the rest of the day, I was already feeling the regret accompanying the ending of the week. I had concentrated so fully on her, so hadn't thought about the case, nor thought too much about Vicky.

"I'm sorry, Vicks," I thought. "I'm not forgetting. I'll take this all the way. I'm still grieving you. I needed a little time."

I thought a bit about the week coming up and then went back to the magazine.

Being I'm a child at heart, Shane and I got along well. He was interested in astronomy. I promised him that one night we'd take my telescope out and I'd show him Saturn's rings. I had spent a bit of money on a Celestron CPC 1100 last year. I loved astronomy since I was a child. I picked out a spot not too far upstate where we could go and not worry about the light pollution.

He had many questions, and I had some answers. We used books and the internet to find the ones I didn't have an answer for. Mandy took it upon herself to clean and make dinner. I kept a fairly clean house for a man, but she seemed to enjoy doing it.

She went out to the supermarket while Shane and I talked, bought food, and set about making dinner and desert. When Shane left to make a phone call to one of his friends, we talked.

"Sorry I didn't get a chance to meet the ex," I said.

"He said the same, but needed to get back. His mom is going into the hospital in the morning. He said he'd get together with us soon."

"I really think it's amazing you guys get along so well."

"We were married young. We both love Shane. He's a good dad."

Shane came back from the phone call and asked if he could bring his friend when I showed him Saturn's Rings. Mandy admonished him gently, as I said it was okay. I winced and looked at her, but she realized I didn't intend to usurp her authority.

As we ate perfect Chicken Cutlet Parmigiana, salad, mixed vegetables, and linguini, the three of us talked. He asked me questions about martial arts and fighting. I told him if he wanted, I'd take him to a martial arts school one day, run by a person close to me. He could watch or try it out. Mandy smiled and nodded yes, as I looked to her for the okay. She made a chocolate cake and bought vanilla ice cream. She knew that was my favorite. It tasted good.

They left a little after seven. Shane wished they could have stayed, and truthfully, so did I. He was a great kid; bright, respectful, and inquisitive. My phone rang three times that night, because he thought of other questions for me. It was a warm evening. I poured a small glass of good port wine and found a decent cigar. I opened the windows and smoked the cigar inside as I watched television. I kept thinking how good it would feel if they hadn't left.

I remembered walking into the room and seeing Vicky. I remembered the relief washing over me when I thought she was alive. Then I saw the blood, and knew I had no reason to feel guilty. That sure as hell didn't stop me though. I would find out, or the cops would.

"They won't get away with it, Vicks," I said softly, but aloud.

I put the cigar out, closed the windows, brushed my teeth, washed up, and went to bed. I fell asleep thinking of Vicky and Mandy. I smiled when I thought of how many questions Shane asked. It took me a while to drift off, but I eventually did, and slept long and well.

That was the best weekend I ever remembered.

16

My mind drifted back to the weekend as I made the short drive into the office Monday morning. I would put together a list of people who knew Vicky and lay out my other steps. Still no word about the wake. It was three to five days at the coroner's with the current backlog. Yesterday would have been the fifth day.

When I got back to my office, Bill Sanders was waiting for me. I had called him before leaving the house, got his voice mail, and said I would call him when I arrived at my office.

He was sitting in the waiting room, looking gaunt and pale. I shook his hand then told him to give me a minute, and someone would come up to get him. I asked if he wanted anything. He said, "No."

I went downstairs. Mandy followed me into the office and kissed me hello. I pulled her close and ran my hands over her body. She smiled at me and whispered in my ear what she'd like to do to me.

"Okay, but you should close the door."

"Maybe later."

"I'm just going to meet with Bill Sanders."

"He left at least six messages in two days," she said.

"Any other messages?"

"Nothing that Jeff isn't handling. We have everything scheduled for him."

"Okay."

"What do you need?"

"Bring Sanders in. For anything else, I'm not here."

"Okay." She smiled again. "Coffee?"

"Only if ..."

"Yes, I'm getting myself some."

A few minutes later, Sanders sat in one of the comfortable client chairs in my office. He looked around the room at a few of the paintings. My client looked rumpled, as though he hadn't slept in days. His eyes were bloodshot, and he looked tired.

"I apologize for taking so long, I was working on the case, and in the field, I haven't been in much."

"It's okay. I don't know what to tell my kids," he said, then paused.

My head cocked. I thought the kids were four and five. "Nothing yet," I said. "I'm working angles the police aren't. No point in me running down their leads."

"Nothing yet? What angles are you working?"

"I spoke with Luca's brother."

"Who's he?"

"Eddie Siciliano."

"I never heard of him."

My head cocked again. It might get stiff like this.

"Crazy Eddie Siciliano? The mobster?"

"Yes."

"Jesus," he said. "They have different last names."

"Half-brother, but Siciliano isn't pleased."

His brow furrowed. "Do they have any idea?"

"None yet."

"Should I worry about my family?"

"I wouldn't think so, why?"

He shook his head. "This is strange to me that she was mixed up with these people." He kept shaking his head.

I've been playing poker ever since I was a kid. I loved cards. Hearts, Gin, Tunk, but could never be a serious gambler. I liked to take risks when I played. Eventually, the odds caught up with you either way, but more so when you took risks. I did pretty well though, because the idea behind a poker face hit me early on. I once bluffed a good friend in a hearts game. I was so sincere. Even though he kept track of the cards, he thought he miscounted.

I also became adept at playing roles and lying. It was part of my work. We needed to get to the truth. You can't flash a badge and get cooperation with what we do. You have to be creative, and you have to lie. I kept that part out of my personal life, but I was good at it.

Something hit me. Something was wrong. My face didn't show it but my mind was racing. I made a decision a lot of people would disagree with, but my gut was right more often than not. If the murders happened because of something having to do with Vicky, then everyone she knew at this point, Sanders included, was a suspect. I might tip him off, or might learn something. We were all going with the idea they were killed because of Luca. God damn it, it never even occurred to me they might be dead because of Vicky, not Luca.

"Off the record, they did mention they had a suspect in mind."

"The cops?" he asked.

"No, the wise guys," I said. "Trust me. You wouldn't want to be responsible for this and have them catch you. Not Siciliano's people."

"Did they say who?" he asked quickly.

"No, but they did say," I said, then paused to hit the intercom. Mandy came in.

"Mandy, would you do me a favor, please?" I asked. "Coffee if you could?" I looked at Sanders. "Care for some?"

"No."

"Could you bring a menu in when you come back, please? I haven't eaten since yesterday. Bill, I know it's early, but can I buy you a late breakfast or early lunch?"

Mandy's eyebrows went up, and Sanders looked back and forth between us, his mouth open. Maybe he was worried. She smiled, said sure, and left, closing the door behind her. His face paled.

"No, no, I'm okay," he stammered.

Okay, all in. "There's speculation they weren't killed because of Luca, but because of Vicky."

His eyes widened for a second. "No," he said. "Can't be."

"Are you sure?"

"No, I mean yes. I'm positive. She had problems, but nothing that would make someone kill her."

"Are you sure?"

"Trust me. I'd know," he said.

"Well, the wiseguys are going in that direction," I lied. "I am too, I think. PD has Luca covered."

"I think it's a waste of time."

"That would help. PD will swing that way too, if nothing comes in soon with regard to Luca's activity being the reason. Can you think of anyone that had a problem with her, enough to make someone want to kill her?"

He paled a little. Could be just the idea of it. "No," he said, after a pause.

"If nothing comes of it we can eliminate it then," I said.

"I guess you're the detective." He got up. "I need to get back and see how the kids are doing."

"There's another guy that may have been involved with Luca. A guy named Mark Stanton."

"The construction guy?" Sanders asked.

"Yeah, among other things. You know him?"

"He might have done work for me a while ago. His trucks and signs are all over the place."

His attitude and demeanor changed. Maybe he thought this was a bad idea. Maybe it was something else. My head was spinning. Mandy came back in with my coffee and one for herself and sat down. For the first time since I can remember, she wasn't the universe. Maybe it was the shock of the suggestion. Maybe he did it.

We shook hands. "It would be very helpful if you could put together a list of anyone that she was involved with," I said.

"Sure, um ... I guess I can do that," he said.

"Thank you," I said.

He smiled weakly then left.

"What's up with that?" Mandy asked, as she sat in one of the client chairs and crossed an exceptional leg.

"Don't move. Stay there unless you want to take something off,"

"Jerk," we both said, as I dashed out.

I ran upstairs to the reception area and looked out the window. Sanders seemed worn, grief stricken, and tired. He was walking quickly to his car, cell phone on, and talking loud. I couldn't hear what he was saying, but he was considerably more animated than he was moments ago.

"Excuse me, ladies," I said. "Did anyone notice if the man that just left got a call, or if he called someone?"

"He took his phone out and made the call," Mary, our receptionist, said.

"Can you describe his demeanor?" I asked.

"Umm, agitated," she said. She was originally from Ireland. In addition to be being pretty, she had a brogue I enjoyed listening to. She was smart, but the brogue was the reason I hired her. Good legs, too.

This was proof of nothing. It could very well be a coincidence. It might have tipped him off if he had something to do with it, but I had enough to go on.

"Everything okay?" she asked.

"Yeah. Thanks, hun. I just wanted to make sure he called someone I told him to."

Mandy looked worried as she stood at the door of my office when I returned downstairs. She followed me into the office, and I closed the door and filled her in.

"What are you going to do? You said yourself, babe, there could be nothing to this."

"The cops and wise guys have everything else covered," I said. "They have a lot more manpower. I'll look under different rocks."

"I hope it's not true, my God," she said. "Imagine how the kids would grow up?"

"We're a million miles away from proof of anything," I said, "but you're right, the thought is very disconcerting."

"Do you really want something to eat?" she asked.

"No, I just wanted to see his reaction."

"Okay, do you need anything? If not, I have some billing to do."

"I'm okay, hun, but need to think a bit. Close the door when you leave."

She smiled. "Okay, let me know if you want more coffee or something."

17

Two hours later, she knocked on the door. They were ordering lunch, and I declined. I felt disconcerted, as if I received bad news. I needed a break. I asked her if she had a lot to do, if she might want to take the rest of the day off. She refused and said there was a lot of work and didn't want it to look like she was favored. I smiled then left, got in my car and drove off, not knowing exactly where I was going.

After a bit, I drove home and picked up *Two Trains Running*, by Andrew Vachss, a book I started reading. I tried to find a book written by his wife, Alice, about her career as the lead prosecutor of a sex crimes unit, but it was available only in e-book. I swore I would only ever read a book if I could feel the papyrus, but I ordered the Kindle anyway. It sat home with Alice's book loaded on it. I'd figure out how it worked next weekend. Right after I got the Kindle, she announced it was coming out in paperback.

I threw on jeans and a t-shirt, then stopped at a Salumeria on Forest Avenue. I bought an Italian hero, a half a pound of roast beef, roasted red peppers, and because the owner was a friend, Pieroni.

I stopped at my brother Chris's house. My nephew was home playing video games. His parents were at work and his sister was at school. I asked him if he'd like to go to the Conference House, but he declined. I anticipated that, so settled for taking Archie, the black lab mix my brother adopted. I let him out first, grabbed his leash, and drove to the Conference House.

I worked for so many years that I burned out, so it was important to take time now and again. My work was certainly not physically grueling, but did take its toll. I had something I needed to think about. The weekend was great, but what crept into my brain about Sanders felt like someone pulled the plug on a bathtub full of water.

I was waiting at a light on Hylan Blvd. A kid in a Mustang roared through the light just after it turned and almost struck another kid on a bike. The Mustang driver skidded to a stop. The kid riding the bike got off and walked toward the Mustang.

The kid on the bike was bigger, but a couple of years younger than the driver of the car. The kid in the car got out and started yelling and cursing. I waited and watched while the cars in the other lane continued driving. No one was behind me. The kid on the bike paused a second, doubled down, and walked toward the kid in the car. As he got close, the kid on the bike told him it was his fault, and he had no business driving like that, which was correct. The kid in the car backed down, mumbled something, got in the car and drove away. I grinned.

I slowed as I drove. "Good for you, kid."

The kid, back at his bike, looked up and smiled. "Thanks," he said.

I drove a little further and arrived at the Conference House. I alternated running and walking toward the building. The park was beautiful, with beach and greenery, but little used. I took the tour a few times. John Adams, Edward Rutledge, and Ben Franklin met Lord Howe there in a half-hearted attempt to stop The Revolutionary War. It was ideal for a picnic. It was located at the southernmost point of the island, which also made it the southernmost point of New York.

I found a tree between the house and water then retrieved a bowl from the trunk of the car I kept, in case of dogs. I sat with my back to the familiar tree. Archie sat and watched the few people, birds, and squirrels. There were actually deer on the island again, although none visible at the moment. My side arm was uncomfortable so I removed it and the light jacket I wore, wrapped the .45 in the jacket and put it between Archie and me.

I took my phone out and turned on the radio to a low volume. I read the book and ate my sandwich. I gave Archie the roast beef and poured him some water. He attended to his business. I declined to offer him my Italian Hero. I had no idea what the various Italian spices might do to the canine digestive system, but he watched closely.

"You shouldn't have eaten yours so fast."

He tilted his head as dogs do and watched me eat. When I finished, he laid his head in my lap. I read *Two Trains Running*. The book was excellent. I always liked Vachss' writing. This book was a period piece set in 1959 and made me feel as though I was there. I normally breezed through books, usually reading several at a time, but I had a lot of fun with this one, so wasn't rushing it. A light breeze blew and the temperature hovered at about 70. If Mandy was there, it would have been better, but it was pretty damn good.

A ship cruising by attracted Archie's attention. He sat up and watched. When it was out of sight he laid his head back on my leg again. I didn't think about Vicky, Sanders, or anyone but Mandy. I read my book and sat with my friend. I thought about getting a dog. I loved them and donated to a couple of local rescues. I thought about adopting. I had a cinnamon chow named AJ for many years and worried about having a dog at home when I got busy. There would likely be a co-habitational thing going on soon anyway. I didn't do much field work these days, present case aside, so maybe it was time.

I dropped Archie off, headed home, and took a shower. I finished three of the beers and put the other three in the fridge. Mandy called. She was helping her son with his homework.

The sandwich I ate for lunch was large enough to feed a small city, so I ate a light dinner - scrambled eggs, and rye toast. I spoke with Mandy, wished I was with her, but in general felt reinvigorated. I made a list of people Vicky knew. I looked up her divorce case on the New York State Unified Court System website. I didn't have access to Family Court cases but the divorce would give me a place to go.

Her divorce, although the judgement was signed four years ago, was still active, with a date a few months ago, which meant the dispute was likely being heard in Supreme Court versus Family Court. Chris Costigan had the case for Vicky. I knew Costigan well, and was surprised he hadn't reached out to me when it hit the papers. He was a good attorney who actually cared about his clients. Sander's attorney, Mark Gains, was someone from New York, I never heard of. It didn't say whether a law guardian was assigned to the case.

Turning on the laptop I kept at home, I researched basic background on Sanders, something I do at the start of every investigation. It gave me whatever was available from voter registration, property records, liens judgments, and hard assets like cars and property.

It was enough for me to study, and I had Eddie Martin if I needed more. It was only nine but I was tired. I made a list of people to contact or see tomorrow.

I took a long, hot shower, left the shaving until the morning, and fell asleep watching *Snatch*. I must have seen it several dozen times. The movie disturbed me at first because it forced me to like Brad Pitt.

I woke up early but went to bed early and slept well. I woke up thinking about Sanders and Vicky. I get a feeling every so often. I spent years trying to put a name to it, an empty feeling combined with a good measure of despair. One day it occurred to me, it felt like my soul was bleeding, but this was part of my work, and I recharged enough to view it as a spiritual shaving nick.

I was a long way off from knowing whether Sanders was involved with Vicks' death, but that feeling in my gut was strong. Maybe I just dreaded the possibility.

I went downstairs and made stovetop coffee. It wasn't five yet. I opened the back door and looked up. The cool morning air rolled over me slowly. I was awake, and felt like smoking a cigar. I didn't smoke often but when I did, I enjoyed it. I watched the morning stars for ten minutes then went in and turned the coffee down as it started to perk. I opened the humidor and found it empty except for one Jeff gave me the last time we had a big retainer. I cut the end off, brought it into the kitchen, and turned the coffee off. It was just after five.

When the coffee cooled enough to remove the filter and grounds and pour, I prepared a large cup then took it outside with the cigar. I sat on the steps and fired up the cigar with the lighter Jeff gave me on my last birthday. It produced a flame from four jets hotter than the core of the planet, apparently. I lit it properly as Jeff showed me years ago; without drawing on it as I did, puffed out on the first puff, and sat with my coffee, gazing at the sky. Not a bad breakfast.

There were woods in the back behind the house, and birds sang. It was too early for crickets. I watched the clear sky and remembered something Carl Sagan said along the lines of, "If there was a God, there was no greater tribute to him than the night sky." It made all earthly churches and monuments pale in comparison. Sagan was, in my mind, right about many things. He was right about that, too.

After a while, the sky brightened. I made a list last night of people to call and see about Vicky and Sanders. I went inside and got my phone. I knew Costigan would be up early so I sent him a text. He responded shortly that he had an appearance in matrimonial court, but it wouldn't take long, and he'd meet me for breakfast afterwards.

I sent Mandy a good morning text. A little while later I got at least forty thousand hearts back in a text. I smiled. After a shower and a shave, I grabbed my notes and headed out.

18

There was a coffee shop around the corner from the St. George Supreme Court called The Gavel Grill. I was seated in the back when Costigan walked in. He was another one of those guys that aged gracefully. I got up and we shook hands. He had salt and pepper hair, was athletic, and genuinely pleasant. We often did business. I interacted with many people out of necessity, but never minded seeing Chris.

The waitress came with coffee and necessary accoutrements. We ordered, and she took our menus.

"I just got back from vacation. I just found out about Vicky," he said.

"I figured something like that," I said.

He shook his head. "Horrible." We were both quiet for a bit. "It must have been hard finding her like that."

"Not a pleasant memory," I said. "Or one that's likely to fade."

He nodded. "Do you have any reservations about talking to me about her case?" I asked.

"None. She was my client. She had her problems, but I liked her. It would be in her best interest for me to talk with you."

"What can you tell me in general?" I asked. "If you could give me an overview I'd appreciate it. I met her after the divorce."

"Well, she did have problems, but she tested clean on the last follicle test. She was foggy but clearing up. On the surface, the husband seemed like the better parent for sure. She wouldn't give up on the kids though, and the kids loved being with her."

"How did she lose custody in the first place?"

"She tested positive for marijuana," he said, with a tinge of bitterness.

My eyebrows rose. "That's it?"

"It gets better."

"Pray tell."

"She used the weed during a week she didn't have the kids. Sanders made the allegation about drugs."

"How was that confirmed?"

"The first follicle test."

I shook my head. "Then how ..."

"I don't know," Costigan said. "There's no uniformity in the unified court system. The court's always a good five years behind what's becoming common knowledge as far as what's best for the kids. The thing is, most judges wouldn't have done that. We actually appealed it."

"And?"

"Still waiting." He paused, and we both drank coffee.

"I don't smoke," he continued, "and have strongly cautioned my kids against it. Who knows what else might be in there. They're easily distracted. Brain matter isn't fully formed, but honestly, I can't see it's any worse than alcohol. You and I both know a few judges known to smoke weed on occasion."

"Yes, we do," I said. "And for sure the test gave the time frame? She didn't have the kids when she smoked it?"

"Yes. They were on vacation with the father for two weeks."

"Chris, when I saw her at my office, she looked strung out, like on coke or something worse."

"Maybe she fell into it after. Maybe it was just the grief she was suffering by losing custody, I don't know, but the second follicle test was just a few weeks before she died, and they found nothing but an anti-anxiety prescription medication."

I thought about that for a while. "What's your opinion on the husband?"

"It's just a feeling," Costigan said. "There's no evidence to support it, but there's something about him. My gut says bad. If we had gotten to the forensics ..."

He was lost, I thought for a second, considering the question.

"Are you concerned about your client?" he asked.

"I'm just trying to get a feel."

"If you were concerned about him, you wouldn't say at this point."

I smiled. "I promise, Chris, if I find out something you ought to know about, you'll know about it."

He nodded. My word was good with him, as his word was with me. The waitress brought our breakfast. I ordered two buckwheat pancakes, since I was intending to have lunch with Mandy. Costigan ordered a mozzarella omelet, bacon, and rye toast.

"What about the law guardian?"

"Freida Link-Johnson."

"Not familiar with her."

"Consider yourself lucky," he said.

The Gavel offered real maple syrup, one of the reasons I liked it so much. I took a few bites of the pancake. Costigan also reduced his food surplus and we both drank coffee.

"Like a lot of other people, when the mission of the law guardian was changed to advocate for their client's wishes, as opposed to what they felt was best for their clients, I had significant misgivings. In this case, the kids wanted to go back with their mother."

"Most kids that age would."

"Yeah," he said, "but according to Vicky, they desperately wanted to go back with her. The father scared them."

"Scared them, how?"

"I don't know. She taped them, which is useless in court, but I listened. I don't like that either, but since she did, I listened, and it sounded genuine. They said they kept asking their lawyer to go back to living with their mother, and she never mentioned that in court. They wouldn't be specific, just that they were afraid of their father."

"You asked her?"

"Yes, she said they weren't firm about it, and they wavered back and forth."

"You don't agree with that?" I asked.

"No."

"Will she talk to me?"

"Not a chance."

"Can she talk to me?"

"Technically, if the kids gave their permission, or if it's restricted to her conversations with Vicky."

"How about the husband's lawyer? Anything interesting there?"

Not really. He's mainly a criminal attorney, doing I guess what a lot of lawyers do, branching off because of the economy."

"Adequate?"

"Not particularly, but the judge was on his side."

"So, let me ask you something, Chris. Being objective and removing bias, would you say that maybe half of the divorce cases present a custody problem, insofar as parental fitness is concerned?"

"I wouldn't disagree with that."

"Would you say, given how many things can go wrong, starting with selecting inexperienced or inept counsel, getting dealt a bad law guardian, a bad judge, or incompetent forensics, there's at least a fifty percent chance those cases won't get resolved as they should?"

"Hard to disagree with also."

"So let's be generous, and instead of the fifty percent we're left with, I'm off, let's say twenty five percent. We have twenty five percent of these cases decided in a way, for various reasons, not in the best interest of the child."

"Okay. I'm with you so far," he said.

"Let's say half of those are abusive, but something the kids can recover from."

"Well," Costigan said, "there are different kinds of abuse: sexual, physical, emotional, and neglect."

"Right," I said, "and every one serious. The only real difference is the scars they leave."

"I read that somewhere," he said.

"Not to diminish it, but say it's not quite as bad, the level, the danger on half of those cases, for the purpose of this point."

"Go on."

"We're now left with twelve and a half percent of all custody cases, where there are serious problems. To the detriment of the kid, the wrong decision is made."

He nodded. "Not a pleasant thought."

"No."

"Probably not accurate," I said.

"It's probably considerably worse, but even if it was half of that, it's still thousands of cases."

"So, pertaining to this case, we agree the kids shouldn't have been taken away from the mother on testing for weed while the kids were on vacation with the father."

"Yes."

"That could be attributed to any of the factors," I said.

"Minus bad forensics, they were just about to start."

"Could it be a fix?"

He exhaled. "I'm sure that happens, but I'm equally sure it's rare."

"But could be?"

"Yes."

"So, near impossible to say what went wrong with this case?"

"Yes."

"Incompetence, design, or a degree of both?" I asked. "Give me your best guess."

"Why is that important?" he asked.

"It gives me a direction to go. You have good instincts. I trust you."

He did, in fact. Not only had we worked together, we also worked on opposite sides of cases. He looked out for his clients, and was a man of principle. He also wouldn't do anything to hurt a child. Not many left. He looked left; he looked right, and then down at his almost empty plate. We were quiet for a bit.

"What I can say is, I don't like the husband. On the surface, he's okay. The Judge made antiquated rulings like this before. Freida troubled me. Just the way she seemed to look at the husband's lawyer, the way she verbally supported him in court."

"And the forensic examiners had been chosen?"

"Yeah. Forensics was just about to start."

"Who was chosen for mental health?"

"Jackson Bishop."

"He's actually very good."

"Yes, he is. He's unorthodox but tends to get to the bottom of things. And he cares about kids."

"Freida and Sanders' lawyer would have known this," I said.

"Jonathan," he said. He was one of the few that called me by my given name. "Anything is possible, but murder? Over this?"

"It increasingly looks like they aren't dead because of her boyfriend. The cops are running that angle in every possible way. I spoke with Luca's family."

"And his family is?" Costigan asked.

"Eddie Siciliano."

His eyebrows went up. "Oh shit."

"Yeah," I said. "Not many people making their living on the wrong side of the law would take that kind of risk. They tell me they've been looking but haven't found out. I doubt they will. There has to be something to this."

"Which is why you're asking about the husband," he said, mostly to himself. "An anonymous complaint was filed early, alleging the husband abused the kids."

"That's new," I said. "Abused in what way?"

"Not specified. It didn't go anywhere. Vicki eventually told me she reported it. She never admitted it, but everyone thought it was her."

"Did she tell you how she thought they were being abused?"

"No, just that the kids would start to get stomach pains the day before they had to go with their father. They tried to say they were sick, but never actively resisted going with him."

"That's unsettling."

"It is," he agreed.

"Was her boyfriend an issue in the court case?"

"The husband said he was afraid for his kids to be around a 'mobster,' and they bitched about it."

"And?"

"And," Costigan said, "she agreed to sign off on something that said when she had them, he wouldn't be around."

"The Law Guardian's position?"

"Agreed with Vicky's ex."

"And Vicky was willing to forego the pleasure of Luca's company when the kids were with her?"

"Frieda asked how they could trust her."

"The kids have a position about Luca?"

"As far as I know, they never met him."

"Similar with Sanders?"

"In what way?" Costigan asked.

"Kids weren't allowed around his girlfriend," I said, then paused, "or boyfriend," I added as an afterthought.

"To our knowledge, there wasn't a significant other."

"Then, going by the current interpretation of what a law guardian does, which I don't really agree with, she's not exactly advocating for her client's wishes.

The waitress came over with our bill. He grabbed it as I reached for it.

"Hey, let me."

"I got it," he said. "I have an afternoon full of meetings and new consults, but if you need anything else, I'm around.

"Any chance I can take a look at your file? Something might light up."

"I have no objections to it. Call Jennifer if you want to look at it, and I'll have it available in the conference room."

"What about her family? Her parents? Siblings? She didn't talk about them much when I knew her."

"She was still tight with her mother. Her mother, as of yesterday, was off sedation and called to schedule an appointment." He paused. "She and her father didn't get along. He never forgave her for getting divorced."

"Can you say why her mother wants an appointment with you?"

"She didn't say."

"I know this goes without saying ..."

"I won't tell a soul," he said.

"Thank you. It's a long shot, but the cops are covering the other things."

He nodded. "Be careful, Jimmy."

"Count on it, pal."

We walked outside. The morning sun was shining on us and the new court building. It was a beautiful building, but complaints already started. Not enough bathrooms, courtrooms too small. The Empire State Building was built in a little over thirteen months. It took five years to build the new five-story courthouse. I liked the old courthouse better, with its marble, tiles, and artwork. It upheld the illusion we had of a justice system versus a legal system.

"By the way," Costigan said, "I know Becky Jordan. She was Vicky's therapist. I'll call her if you like. I think she may be helpful."

I told him I'd appreciate that but decided it couldn't hurt to try the Law Guardian anyway. Costigan thought something was up. It was worth checking.

"Chris," I said. "How did she come to you?" If a friend referred her, maybe they talked.

"You."

"What?" I asked.

"You were on surveillance or in court or something. She couldn't reach you. She called your office and got Jeff. He gave her my number."

We went our separate ways. I called the office. Mandy's voice greeted me. Her voice had a husky, maple syrup sweet quality. I felt it wrap around me. I was beginning to wonder whether she really was as flawless as I believed. The answer came before the thought was completed.

"Hello, handsome."

"Well, hello bauble, are you overbilling my clients in a way that would make me proud?"

"No," she said and I could tell she was smiling. "I'm too busy looting petty cash."

"That's my girl."

"Are you coming by?"

"I am. Want to grab lunch?"

"Love to. Listen, Sanders called."

I was stopped at a light so I looked at my cell. No missed calls. "He leave a message?"

"Yeah, I just hung up with him, and was reaching for the phone when you called."

"Do tell."

"He said to stop working on this case for him, immediately."

"Son of a bitch," I said.

"Sweetie, what the hell is going on?"

"I'm not sure, Mandy."

"Are you going to stop?"

"Soon as politicians stop lying."

"I thought so. This is very strange, isn't it?"

"Yeah, in a bad way I think. He could just be nervous."

"What are you going to do?"

"I find a new client, or I am my own client."

After a pause she said, "Jonathan Michael, please be careful."

"Jonathan Michael?" I said. "I don't know if I would be a fan of anyone saying that ordinarily, but given the way you say it, I think I could get used to it."

"Well, everyone else calls you Jimmy or Jim. I'm special."

"Damn right you are."

"Jonathan Michael is how I'll address you when I'm serious and concerned about you."

"I like it."

"Okay, I'm heading back to the office to get you. We'll run over to Schaeffer's, if that's okay."

"Sounds good," she said.

"Can you do something for me? Call Frieda Link-Johnson. She's an attorney on the island. See if I can get in to see her this afternoon, about two hours from now. She was the law guardian for Vicky's kids."

"Okay. Got it."

"There's another person, Becky Jordan. Tell her Chris Costigan said I should talk with her."

"Is she a lawyer also?"

"No, luv, she's either a psychologist or psychiatrist, maybe a licensed social worker."

I heard her type computer keys at warp speed. "Psychiatrist," she said.

"If either says 'no,' offer to pay a consult fee for the time. If Johnson says no to both, call back later and schedule a consult with her about a family court case."

"You're the boss."

"Okay, strip."

"I'm disobeying." She laughed.

"Then what good is me being the boss?"

"Later, when we're home."

"Deal."

"Mandy," I said.

"Yeah, baby?"

"The law guardian. Try to avoid telling her why I want to see her, use the money if you have to."

"Will do, boss."

"That's my girl."

"Yes, I am," she said. I knew she was smiling.

"One other thing, baby girl. If Sanders calls again, no one's heard from me."

"Done, boss," she said.

I called Mariano, "Hey Chief, how goes it?"

"You must be psychic."

"I'd have hit the lotto by now."

"When you do, share with your friends," he said. "It's unofficial, but there was nothing in Vicky's system other than antidepressants. Luca had so much in him. If he wasn't shot, he might have overdosed."

"The last court ordered drug test she took said the same thing. I could have sworn she was using," I said, puzzled. "The way she acted when I last saw her."

Vicky hadn't been using. She was seeing a therapist, and made an allegation about child abuse. I handled many cases dealing with false accusations, and so far, nothing proved anything. My gut was flipping though, and I didn't like how this was moving.

19

Schaeffer's had been around for over eighty years. Exceptional draft Weiss beer, simple but tasty food. Parking was sometimes an effort but was worth it. We were sitting at one of the small, dark wooden tables. I ordered pastrami on rye. I was working my way through cashews and the hot peppers they kept on the table. Mandy had a Diet Coke, and I had a tall draft Weiss the bartender served with a wedge of orange. It was delicious. I savored it, which isn't as easy as it sounds, but I was working, and would only have one. There was the bar room and the dining room. The bar was dark brown, almost black, with pictures of former beloved staff who had moved on to the big tavern in the sky, hanging behind the bar.

I spent many a cold, winter afternoon there, sipping Goldschlager, good beer, or both. I never ate a bad meal there. I often pleaded with the staff to include hot German pretzels. Eventually they did, and I took credit.

Schaeffer's was more than just good food and drink, it reveled in its past, and its patronage revered its simplicity. Sports channels played on the televisions. The waitress took our order and brought the food fresh, not more than five minutes later.

"Becky Jordan will see you any time tomorrow if you can give her half an hour notice. Johnson wouldn't see you. I'll wait and call back later."

"I'm sorry," I said.

"For?"

"Involving you in subterfuge."

"I remember what you said when you hired me. You said we weren't the police so we had to sometimes find unorthodox ways to find out what we needed to know."

"Very good. You'll go far with this company."

"If I can avoid sexual harassment by the boss."

"I've heard he's awful."

"Not so bad," she said. She had a way of looking inside me.

Mandy ordered tuna on rye and gave me her potato salad when it came. I ate breakfast not long ago. The point of lunch was her company, but I still made it through my sandwich faster than Schwarzkopf ran through Iraq.

We talked a while. She told me she hoped to one day go back to college. She was only a few credits shy of her four-year degree in psychology.

I loved hearing her voice and learning more about her. She never talked just to talk. When she asked a question, it was because she wanted to know, not to fill a gap.

Two servicemen wearing Army uniforms were eating in the back. I motioned for the waitress, and told her to please bring me their check. I greatly respected people that did what I didn't have the balls, or if not the balls, the temperament, to do.

She smiled at me. "I love you."

I laughed. "Who wouldn't?"

"Stop, that's very sweet, what you just did."

"Maybe I'm doing it to impress the hot babe."

"No, it's you. One of the reasons why I love you."

I took a breath, smiled, and looked at her. "Kid that worked for me, I've known him since he was fourteen. He did a few tours in Iraq as a sergeant. Last day, he lent his driver to the new sergeant so he could familiarize himself with the area. The driver and everyone else in the car were blown up. Kid was never the same. Still can't find his place. He had a difficult childhood to begin with. He's family to me, and I can't help him. The VA's a joke. When I see soldiers it reminds me of their sacrifice. It's a small thing to make me feel better."

"I'm sure you feel good doing it," she said sliding her hand over mine, "but that's not why you do it."

One of the soldiers got up and went to the men's room. The waitress told the other one their bill was covered. He looked over at me, smiled, and waved. I waved back. The other one came back from the men's room.

"Sarge, we got hooked up," the soldier said, and gestured at our table.

They came over to our table, and I stood. The sergeant extended his hand. I took it. His grip was strong.

"Thank you, sir," he said. Mandy rose to stand. "Please, ma'am, don't get up." He shook her hand, as did the private.

"No, sergeant, thank you. And you as well," I said, shaking the soldiers hand. They both smiled and left.

"They're out there for us and so few remember them beyond a retweet or a Facebook like," I said.

Her eyes shone when she looked at me. I did that out of respect when I met our people in uniform. I'd do it for cops too, but that would get them fired. It was how I felt. I had to say though, if I didn't have incentive, the look in my woman's eyes would be a good reason.

It's not that all servicemen and women were good. Of course there was bad mixed in. Same with cops, firemen, and doctors, as in any profession. I remembered years ago running into a bunch of sailors, and they all apparently belonged to the same Klan cloven back home. I was at a bar with a few friends and they took exception to their black waiter. The guy that owned the bar used to be a friend, until we wrecked the place that night. I worked on cases with bad cops, but it wasn't the norm. If someone did a job for the public good, they should be respected and appreciated until they demonstrated they weren't worthy.

"So what's on for tonight?" I asked.

"Parent teacher night for me, but I can come over about ten."

"That would be exceptional," I replied.

"And what shall we do?" she asked, with unmistakable mischief in her eyes.

"Come over wearing a trench coat, a blue negligee underneath, and pour us some whiskey. Then, ask me to find the Maltese Falcon for you."

"Maybe for your birthday, if you're a good boy."

We talked a while longer, and Mandy reminded me she had things to do at the office. I left with great reluctance.

When I got in my car I called Sanders. Voicemail. I asked him to please call me back, and said I had a few developments I wanted to speak with him about, as though I hadn't talked with Mandy. At the next light, I glanced at my notes in the passenger seat and dialed Vicky's mom. She said she was free and agreed to meet with me, so I headed that way. They lived on Todt Hill, an exclusive area.

Ten minutes later, she let me into a home a little smaller than the Taj Mahal, but not by much. It would have fit at least four large houses on the land. Houses on the Hill were premium to begin with, and there was coin here. I parked my car, and an attractive young woman opened the door and informed me the lady of the house would see me in the kitchen. A short hike later, I sat in a breakfast nook at the end of a kitchen, spacious enough to cook for and feed a small city.

Jennifer Rose Hayes stood and extended her hand. She had the tired face of someone in the beginning of what would be life-long grieving. Knowing Vicky was thirty when she died, she had to be in her mid-fifties but looked younger, despite the wear and tear of recent events.

She gestured to the table and we sat. "Coffee?" she asked softly.

"Thank you. That would be lovely, Mrs. Hayes."

"Jen," she said.

"Jim."

She poured coffee from a carafe into a mug set in front of me. She offered raw sugar, regular sugar, and artificial sweetener, with half-and-half, and milk. I kept it black and sipped.

"You found her," she said, looking down.

"Yes, I'm so very sorry for your loss," I responded softly.

"The police said you were worried about her and went to check. Thank you."

"*Why didn't you love me*?" I heard Vicky say.

I took a deep breath. I didn't know what to say. 'You're welcome,' didn't feel right. Aside from the slight hum of the refrigerator, the sound of a pendulum from a clock in another room was hypnotic. The kitchen smelled good, as kitchens should. Fresh herbs grew near the window that looked out onto the backyard. I felt her pain like the vibration of a stereo when the bass was turned too high. Her hand rested on the table. I slid my hand across the table and rested it gently on hers. She still looked down but clasped her fingers around mine. We sat for a while.

"You tried," she said. "You shouldn't feel guilty."

I didn't answer. Christ, was everyone a mind reader?

"You were there for her when she needed you. I should have been."

"This isn't your fault."

We sat a while longer. The pleasant young woman that showed me into the kitchen came in.

"Mrs. Hayes, Emil Grant is on the phone."

"No calls, Eileen."

"Yes, Ma'am."

Emil Grant was the borough president. I hadn't voted for him, but I'm sure if he knew, he'd get over it.

"I can come back another time if you aren't ready for this," I said.

She withdrew her hand, covered her face with her hands, and rubbed slightly. She opened her eyes and smiled weakly. "No, I want to help."

"Jen, is there anything you can think of that Vicky was involved in? That might have had something to do with what happened to her?"

"I know so little about my daughter," she said softly. "My husband was so disappointed in her when she got divorced, even more so when she was doing drugs." She paused. "I still saw her several times a week, although not recently."

"Why was your husband so upset about the divorce?"

"Bill Sanders is what my husband would call a solid man. He's the son of one of my husband's business contacts. My husband knew him for years before he introduced him to our daughter."

"What kind of business is your husband in?"

"Too many to name. He introduced my daughter to Bill Sanders. He believes addicts are people of weak moral fiber," she said bitterly. "He's politically very active and participates in the campaigns of people he feels are worthy. A lot of people considering running for office call him."

"Well, like most people," I said, shaking my head, "he's partially right."

"I shouldn't have listened to him. I should have been there for Vicky more. We could have gotten her into a program. We could have helped her with the custody case. I talked to her by phone a lot, and saw her when I could."

"Other than anti-depressants, there were no drugs in her system when she died," I said, "but that needs to stay between us. She lost custody because she smoked a joint during a week her husband was away on vacation with the kids."

She stared at me. "That's not what we were told."

"By whom?"

The sound of someone coming in through the front door made its way into the kitchen.

"My husband, he won't approve of this, but that doesn't matter. I'll help you but it would be easier if he didn't know."

I gave her one of the cards I had with my cell phone number. "We'll finish up soon."

I stood and shook her hand, just as Michael Hayes flowed majestically into the stadium sized kitchen. I wouldn't have been surprised if I heard trumpets and heralds. He was about my height, trim, and looked much younger than his apparent years. Gray hair, blue eyes, and a four hundred dollar John Edwards haircut. He had a deep rolling voice, the sound of which he loved. This became apparent as soon as he spoke.

"Good afternoon," he said. "Michael Hayes." He extended his hand.

"Jonathan Creed." He had a politician's grip, strong from shaking hands all day long.

"Mr. Creed is investigating Vicky's death," Jen Hayes said.

"Well, anything we can do," her husband said, looking at me somberly. There wasn't any doubt he damn well knew who I was and what I was doing there before she told him. His smile was as genuine as an election promise. "Sadly, my daughter made several bad choices, but naturally we want her killer caught and punished. Anything we can do to help?"

"Thanks," I said. "Asshole," was what I thought. I choked back a few things I would normally have said to him in response to his condescending mini sermon. For the sake of his wife, I held back.

"You're a police officer?"

"Private investigator."

"Is it acceptable for a private investigator to work on a case while the police are?"

"It is," I said.

"May I ask who your client is?"

"Your ex son-in-law."

He smiled. "Bill's a good man. It's a shame Vicky didn't do the responsible thing and stay with him. She might still be alive."

His wife turned and walked out of the room. I couldn't see her face. She didn't make a sound, but I knew she was crying. Aside from choking back words, I was now resisting the urge to see to it that Hayes ate through a straw for the next six months. I had no doubt in my mind he knew Sanders wanted to drop me.

"Did you know my daughter?"

"Yes, I did," I said, meeting his gaze. He god damned well knew that too. "She was a good woman."

"You'll have to excuse my wife. Her grief is still new. I accepted Vicky wouldn't be part of our lives since the divorce."

"You'll have to excuse me," I said. "I have an appointment shortly."

He smiled. "Of course."

Man, would I like for him to smile with no teeth. He was the biggest prick I met since the start of this, and that's saying a lot. Outside, as I got into my car, I saw Jen in the upstairs window looking out at me. I raised my hand and she nodded. She made as though she was bringing a phone to her ear, indicating she would call me, or perhaps she wanted me to call her. I nodded.

Poor Vicky. Nowhere to turn. Her father had shut the door, and all she wanted was her kids back. The father, being an enormous prick, filled in a puzzle piece or two. I wondered how much help her father gave Sanders. The fact she hooked up with Luca made sense. She probably loved him. He was also a support system. Some time ago, I asked her if she needed help. I told her if she needed something, all she had to do was ask. She said she'd be okay. I never called her after that.

The sky was cloudy and the sun was well into its descent. *Lucky Man,* by Emerson, Lake, and Palmer, came on the radio. I felt a stab of remorse that Keith Emerson was gone. The sun was setting. I sat in the heavy end of workday traffic on Todt Hill for a while, and then went home. Since I ate breakfast and lunch so close together I wasn't hungry, which was uncharacteristic. I would see Mandy later in the evening.

The cell phone rang, and the radio cut off. Jack Harmon came up. I smiled without thinking. We met in court a few years ago when I was working a homicide case. He was originally from the Midwest, boxed for a while, and played basketball when he was a kid. He was a good, seasoned, investigative reporter, part of a vanishing breed. I started reading him when he covered a mob trial.

He ran a little left of center, and me a little right, but a difference of opinion was never an insult. We debated things, shared many good dinners, disagreed on a few things, and agreed on a lot more. We collaborated on things from time to time, and he was on my short list of people I trusted.

"Sherlock!" his voice boomed when I answered the phone.

"Mencken! What's going on?"

"Out of work for the day, thought you'd like a drink."

"Man, would I. Where's good for you? I'm central island."

"Duffy's?"

"There in ten," I said.

The traffic was heavy and I arrived in fifteen. Jack was seated at the bar in the front and reserved a stool for me. He stood when I came in. He was tall, six four or six five, with silver hair and blue eyes. He kept himself in good shape. He was part native and strongly identified with that part of himself. He could also play the drums and sing. I'd go see him every so often when he played in a band or two.

We talked a while about generalities. I was drinking a Manhattan, a drink making me feel like Cary Grant or William Holden. Jack drank Jack Daniels Honey Whiskey over ice, kept for him by the bar. He always said he drank the whiskey for his head and the honey for his heart. We split a few appetizers.

"At least it's not Merlot," I said, snickering.

The first time we met for drinks, two younger guys in construction clothes, feeling no pain and drinking beer, passed a few comments about him drinking red wine. They were loud enough for us to overhear. He turned his eyes on them and slowly got up from his chair; I readied myself to launch. Their faces paled when they saw how big he was. He actually went over and talked with them instead, and by the time he was done, they were laughing, and both of them tried the merlot, and bought us a round.

Although you wouldn't expect a hardboiled crime reporter to be drinking wine, it was fine by me. Hawk, the best friend of my literary forebear, Spenser, sometimes drank Cosmopolitans. Although I wouldn't admit to it, I liked the occasional or frequent Daiquiri, Margarita, or Mojito, especially during vacation, or when dining at a Chinese Restaurant. I would likely have to admit this to Mandy soon, since I was in love with her. That would be the first true test.

"How are things going on Vicky's case?" he asked after a while. He didn't need to say, and I didn't need to ask. It was off the record.

I exhaled. “The thinking is, maybe they’re dead because of her, not him.”

His eyebrows rose. “Wow,” he said, after a minute.

“Yeah.”

“What are you carrying around with you, Jimmy?” he asked.

I shook my head. I was working on my third. I knew goddamned well what I was carrying around with me, but didn’t want to deal with it. I felt guilty about Vicky. I felt guilty for feeling happy with Mandy. My phone rang. It was Sanders. I told my friend I had to take it and went out in back.

“Hi, um, Jonathan,” Sanders said when I answered. He had me on speaker. “How are you?”

“I’m well, you?” I waited.

“Um, look, I don’t know if you got the message I left for you today?”

“No,” I lied. “Everything okay?”

“Well, I’ve been thinking. I’d really rather the police handled this. I don’t want to continue. I don’t want to do anything to jeopardize my kids’ safety.”

I smiled. “That actually works out well,” I said. I rolled with the punches fairly well and then made a snap decision. I had it in the back of my head and was leaning toward it. Fuck it, why not?

“You were finished? What did you find out?”

“No, I have another client, someone interested in hiring me to look into Vicky’s death. It might lead to a conflict so I was going to tell you I can’t continue with you as my client.”

Dead silence. I could sense he was talking to someone, which meant nothing. He could be telling the truth. If you’re investigating to find the truth, it’s a different thing than working for a side. There aren’t any conclusions until one has all the facts.

"Oh, um what, what do you mean by conflict?"

"There's always the possibility of a conflict of interest. Unless you killed Vicky there's nothing to worry about." I gave a short, humorless laugh to show I was only kidding. It was painful.

"Oh, well, in that case please send me a report."

"I will. If you look at the copy of the retainer I sent you, you'll get it within thirty days or an interim report if the case goes longer."

Dead silence again.

"Still there?" I asked. I hit the mute button on the screen.

"Yes, is there any way I can get it faster?"

I took the mute off. "I have a bad signal here. I'll call you in the morning, and we can." I cut the call and turned off the phone then hit the block mode on the phone to send calls to voicemail.

When I got back inside Jack was gone, and our drinks sat on the table. Kevin told me he walked out the front door to take a call. I sipped the excellent Manhattan. He came back in a short time later.

"Everything good?" I asked.

"Yeah, work called, someone got stabbed at the ferry. I'm waiting to see if I need to head there." He finished his drink.

"What do you know about Stanton?"

He put his hand on my shoulder. "Keep a clear head, Jimmy. These aren't Boy Scouts."

I laughed. "So, as I didn't get a chance to tell you, there's info going around."

"My lady friend bartends at Adobe." He smiled.

"Small world."

"Small island," he said. "Did you actually ask Stanton if he provided health insurance?"

I smiled again. "Something like that."

"Don't let it go to your head, but sometimes you're cooler than ice."

"Can't argue with that," I said, with a smile. "Mariano says he's an up and coming thug."

Harmon nodded his head. "Charged a bunch of times, indicted twice, never convicted. He had a good lawyer."

"Who?"

"Steven Rafferty."

I nodded. I never worked for him but saw him on trial. He was actually a decent attorney, currently favored among some of the criminal culture for what was considered a few big wins, and some self-promotion. On a hunch, I took my phone out and texted Chris Costigan. I asked him if he knew Rafferty, and whether Rafferty had a connection to Mark Gains, Sander's lawyer, on the custody case. It came back thirty seconds later. "Separate firm but they share office space."

"Son of a bitch," I said.

I sent Mariano a text, briefing him as I told Jack. I let him know I'd update him in the morning. He didn't respond. That was too many coincidences to be attributed to "small island."

Jack got the call, and he needed to board the ferry. It was almost eight. I still had two hours before I met Mandy back at the house.

"Okay to drive?" I asked.

"Yeah, you?"

"I am."

I stayed and talked to Kevin for a bit. The after work and supper crowd had thinned and it was too early for the night crowd. At eight thirty, I paid the tab, shook Kevin's hand, and left. I took the phone off blocking mode. Five missed calls from Sanders.

On the way home, Vicky's mom called. "Are you sure she was clean? My husband told me different."

"Positive."

"Is there anything I can do?"

"Well, I no longer have a client," I said.

"What? Are you going to stop?"

"No. I would ask you to be my client but I don't want to cause a problem between you and your husband. If need be, I'll be my own client."

"Why would Bill do that?"

"I'm not sure."

"I know he spoke with my husband."

"When?" I asked.

"Yesterday, and again after you left."

"I can do this on my own, but for various reasons it would be helpful to have a client. Would you feel okay about not telling your husband you hired me?"

"Yes," she said, before I was done.

"Thank you. Text me your email. I'll email you a retainer."

"It would be better not to. I think my husband has access to my emails. He isn't in the house now so I can talk."

"I can leave it at my office for you to go in and sign in the morning."

"Okay, I'll do that. How much money do you need?"

"Not a dime."

"We have it to spare."

"If I run into a need for it, some heavy duty expense, I'll tell you."

"Thank you."

"Thinking about this, I may need more information from you. So, us meeting up tomorrow would be a good thing."

"I'll make sure I see you," she said, in a tone registering both strength and sadness.

I got home and took a shower then donned a pair of sweats and turned on the television. It was almost ten. Mandy texted me to say she was on her way. I watched the news and got an update on the weather. When it turned to politics, I switched to Spongebob.

The doorbell rang, and I flew out of the chair. I opened the door, and she stood there, looking as beautiful as ever.

She was wearing a kind of raincoat, similar to a trench coat but more stylish. I looked at her for a few seconds and she smiled at me. Damn.

"Are you going to let me in?"

"Depends, lady."

"On, sir?"

"What's underneath the trench?"

She opened the coat a little. I saw something light blue and very revealing. I shot my arms out and pulled her into me. I kissed her and held her for a while.

"Wow," she said.

"You're the bestest girlfriend ever," I said, grinning.

"I try for my man," she said.

"I pronounce your effort a success."

"Just wait," she said, as she took my hand and led me inside. I locked the door and she pulled me toward the stairs. We went upstairs and into the bedroom. Go with the flow, that's my motto, at least for the moment.

She pulled me around with my back to the bed and gently shoved me onto it. She removed the trench coat and tossed it in the corner. She crawled on top of me, kissed my neck and my lips, and whispered in my ear, "I was thinking that tonight, as much I love your need to bring me to the point of fainting, repeatedly, I would take charge of the activities. I'll see to it you're well taken care of." She gently took my lower lip in her teeth. " I think you'll find this, as in any other task I undertake, I'm very well versed. Any objections?"

"Absolutely none," I replied.

Time, when I was with her like that, lost its cohesion. A long while later she rested on top of me. Very well versed was an understatement. She asked me if she was too heavy and I said, "No." We lay like that for a long time, her head on my chest. I asked her if she was hungry or thirsty, and she said, "No." I drifted off for a while, and when I woke, she was in the same position.

She moved to my side and we pulled the blankets down. I kissed her and told her I'd be right back. I went downstairs and grabbed two water bottles from the fridge. I took the water and my gun then went back upstairs and set the alarm. I was always cautious, but with events taking shape as they were, now even more.

We were sitting up in bed, and I turned on the television for a bit. She rested her head on my shoulder and held my hand. Eventually we fell asleep. I dreamt about Vicky, and getting there while she was still alive. Her father shot her as I watched. I woke again later. Mandy slept silently next to me. I felt tears start but they didn't come to fruition. I fell back to sleep.

20

I made us breakfast the next morning while she got ready. I was on my third cup of coffee when she came downstairs, looking even better than she did the night before.

"I think it's not wise," I said, "that you look so lovely going to work."

"I look the same way I do every day," she said, smiling.

"You do look beautiful all the time, true, but you're so beautiful. You may distract others from working."

I had made pancakes and sausage. Knowing her habits, I put a sausage and a pancake on her plate. I had maple syrup and butter on the table. I turned on my phone and left it on the counter.

I didn't like my food overly sweet, so I drizzled syrup on my plate, cut the pancakes with a fork, and dipped it in the syrup. She told me a little about growing up, her brothers and sisters. Somewhere during the course of conversation, she asked if I might consider having a child. A few months ago, that very question might have sent me running for the border.

"I have those thoughts now and again," I said.

"And?"

"Once we're married," I said, "I think that's something we should have serious conversation about."

"Married? Have you been thinking about that?"

"Yes, a lot," I said then paused. "How would you feel about that?"

"I think," she said, grinning, "I would find that very acceptable."

We talked a little more about that, and another unusual thing happened. For almost ten minutes my food remained untouched, a personal record. When I came to my senses, I dug into the food. She asked me what I had planned for the day. First, I filled her in on the new developments.

"I'm going to see the law guardian, the therapist, and do research at the county clerk. I wonder if there's a firm connection between your ex and Sanders. While it's certainly plausible, Sanders ends up with a New York City crime attorney working on his custody case? And Stanton's lawyer shares the same office? I'm not ready to believe that's a coincidence."

She nodded thoughtfully. "I can't recall him saying he interacted with Sanders."

We both ate. She took small bites. Her intake of food overall led me to wonder how she survived. Then I had an idea.

"If you don't have any plans, what do you think about having dinner with Shane tonight?"

"He'd love that, but his dad is helping him with a science project that's due tomorrow." She smiled. "He keeps talking about you. He'd like to see you again, too. He keeps asking me about karate. I told him he could ask you about getting started, so be prepared. As you know, he asks a lot of questions."

I smiled. "Understood. I shall happily try to weather that storm."

"That's a good description. He's a hurricane. He wants to know everything."

"I got that impression. He's a good kid."

"It was hard to stop online time for books and just being outside, but his dad and I are on the same page there. They actually build things together and work on science experiments."

"Impressive," I said. "Especially today."

"They're even going camping for a week this summer."

"Good," I said, then thought a minute. "Great, that will mean you can spend a week as my personal sex toy."

"Jerk," we both said at the same time. She smiled.

She looked down, and the slightest shadow passed over her face.

"What's wrong?" I asked.

"I am so in love with you. This happened so fast. I keep thinking I don't deserve it."

I smiled. "I don't know that anyone deserves *me,*" I said. "I can be as difficult as anyone. I would say that I sure as hell may not deserve you, but I'm going to keep you as long as you let me. When I was younger, there were times I almost settled down or got married. They were all good women but something didn't feel right. I never thought I'd find someone I could be with, where "for life" appealed to me." I sipped coffee. She watched me intently.

"I'm happy I never did because had I met you when I was with someone else I would have realized you were the one. If you don't like thinking of it in soulmate terms, when I met you I would have realized you were the person I was most compatible with. Either way, I won't let you go unless you tell me to."

She got up, came over, and kissed me. I kissed her back and held her for a while. I looked at the clock. It was seven forty five.

"How is your son getting to school?" I asked.

"My dad," she said.

"You're going to have to do your hair again." I picked her up in my arms and carried her upstairs. She buried her head in my chest.

Later, I decided to drive to the office of the therapist first. Yesterday, when Mandy called both the therapist and the law guardian, the therapist agreed to see me right off the bat. The law guardian refused. Then Mandy called back later and scheduled me an appointment for a consult for that afternoon. It would cost me three hundred dollars, but at least I was in. I'm sure it wouldn't endear me to someone I wouldn't get along with anyway, and I could always put a stop payment on the check. The morning air was crisp and the day held promise. Any day that started out with a beautiful woman in bed, I reflected, would hold promise.

I went over things in my head. The therapist met with Vicky's mom, the law guardian, and I wanted to further research both Stanton and Sanders. There was a connection there. Too many coincidences.

After calling, I drove to Becky Jordan's office. It was off Page Ave on the South Shore, not far from the Conference House. The private home was well kept, with an office entrance on the side. The old house, beautiful and full of charm, was part brick and part wood, painted a sunny yellow. It was at least four bedrooms, maybe more, with three floors. There was a big, well-landscaped yard, and an old working well. The house had old-fashioned working shutters.

I walked around the side of the house to see a big yard, where apparently a lot of gatherings were held. The walkway was built out of dark slate stones set in concrete. I rang the bell at the side door. A brass plaque on the door read Dr. Jordan.

The door was opened by a very attractive woman. The doctor was medium height, with blonde hair just past her shoulders. It fell around her face in layers. She was slim but athletic, and still managed the right curves. She wore a gray skirt and a light blue blouse. She had dark brown eyes. Her smile was a very warm, very genuine smile.

"Mr. Creed?

"Yes, Doctor Jordan, thank you for seeing me," I said, accepting her hand, which was firm yet feminine.

She swept her arm in a graceful arc as an invitation for me to enter. The room was very tasteful, with decent art reproductions and original art as well. A light brown wooden desk, beech perhaps, and client chairs, as well as two small sofas, surrounded a coffee table. The aroma of fresh coffee and a faint fragrance, perhaps jasmine, hung in the air.

She gestured toward the sofas. I removed my sports jacket, and she took it from me. In response to my affirmative response, she poured a cup of black coffee for me, and placed it on a coaster, then sat opposite me and crossed her legs in a graceful way. She had good legs. I was in love with Mandy, but I'm not blind.

"I know some of what's been going on through Chris Costigan," she said. "He called me, and we discussed it."

"How do you know Chris?"

"College," she answered. That put her in her late forties, about ten years older than she looked.

"I must say, this is a spectacular place. The house is beautiful."

She smiled. "Thank you. I bought it a few years ago, except for the paint and a few rooms, just as it was."

"Wonderful," I said. The coffee was strong and quite tasty.

"The house or the coffee?" she asked smiling again.

"Both."

"A man of taste, very good."

"Did Vicky see you for long?"

"About six months," she said.

"Doc, I don't want to intrude on the issues you helped Vicky with, but I'm investigating a specific angle." She listened intently. "Although from appearances, her death was likely caused due to her relationship with Luca, the thinking is now that might not be the case. The police, who have far more resources than I do, are approaching the avenue it had something to do with Luca and the general investigation. I'm looking at it from the other end."

"I see," she said. "That does make sense. Vicky was actually a very sweet and scared woman. She was dealing with a lot. Anything I can do to help you, I will."

"No conflict?"

"No, my client is dead. You're looking to find out who killed her. That's in her, as well as the children's, best interest."

"Costigan said the same thing," I said. "Thank you. He felt this whole thing was wrong, meaning the court action. Do you share that feeling?"

"I do. I can only go on what Vicky told me but I believed her. Many people in therapy spend the entire time lying, crafting personas and situations. After a while, most of the time you can tell fairly easily who's being honest and who wants help."

"And Vicky was being honest."

"Yes."

I looked out the window. It faced west, overlooking the well-maintained yard. There was a pool and a hot tub as well. The property was huge, probably close to an acre, which was becoming unheard of on the island. It was late morning and sunlight bathed the house, but wasn't on the west side yet. The sky was mostly light blue and stretched out forever in every direction. The trees and yard presented a myriad of shades of green bathed in yellow sunlight. A spot of clouds loitered far off to the west.

I had another one of those moments where everything dropped, and I felt sad. Vicky wouldn't see a sky like that again. Her kids, when they looked at skies like that, would still be thinking of her. It would be that way for a long, long time. I'd held her, felt her, and was part of her for a little while. I still heard her voice sometimes.

"Why didn't you love me?"

"Doc, when I last saw her alive she looked like she was strung out. Now I hear from both Costigan and a well-informed source in the PD, she had no drugs in her system other than prescription anti-depressants. Why did she seem that way?"

"I believe it was the trauma of having her kids taken away and her fear of what might happen to them. She felt she was failing to protect them and was grieving over their loss. Very often, people with trauma are misdiagnosed in many ways and can have some of the same symptoms as someone under the influence of drugs."

I thought about that for a while. I'm the go to guy for most people that know me. It's just that way. People think I can help them. She didn't come to me. When I saw her, I read her wrong.

"Mr. Creed ..."

"Jonathan or Jimmy is fine, Doc."

"Don't beat yourself up. Professionals can easily misunderstand or misdiagnose themselves."

"Prescience," I said, nodding my approval.

She smiled. "Chris Costigan told me about you."

"Did he mention how, in addition to being handsome, I'm an ace investigator and cook like Bobby Flay? That I'm so clever I sometimes don't understand a single word of what I'm saying?"

She laughed. "That last line was very good."

"Oscar Wilde, if I remember correctly."

"It's not easy to see, but you're carrying a bit of grief and guilt."

I looked out the window again. The rain clouds were closer. "I should have been there for her."

"Her boyfriend was giving her the money and she had a good lawyer. You couldn't have helped if she didn't ask."

I nodded. "She may have told you we were intimate at one point, and it makes her death that much harder. She was more than a friend, although I wasn't ready for commitment at the time."

"Did you lie about that?"

"No." Branches at the top of the trees at the back of the yard swayed as the wind picked up. It occurred to me I needed to interview the doc, not there for a therapy session.

I thanked Doctor Jordan for that. She smiled again. She was a very pleasant woman. I was glad Vicky had someone to find solace. Back to the task at hand.

I asked her every question I could think of. In her opinion, Vicky was dealing with her situation better as time passed. She resolved to continue fighting for her children and secretly had them examined by a pediatrician. No physical signs of abuse were evident, but in the pediatrician's and Dr. Jordan's opinions, the children suffered from emotional trauma. That diagnosis didn't help, since the custody battle could account for emotional trauma. The children wouldn't talk about it. They loved their father's dog. They would go more readily to the house when the dog was mentioned.

Sanders was, by Vicky's account, a cold man. His comments were cruel, but in calculated and subtle ways. He used guilt and disappointment as weapons with his kids.

"Doc, let me ask you. Is there anything you can think of, a person, an incident, something that could point me toward something I could use as evidence or fact?"

She thought for a minute. "I can't think of anything. I'm sorry."

"Don't be. You were very helpful. You filled in some gaps."

"After you catch who did this, if you ever need to talk, I'm here."

"I appreciate that, Doc, the confidence as well," I said.

"It's apparent to me you're seriously committed to this, Jonathan. I have nothing other than an impression, but I imagine you're formidable to the wrong people."

"Strong as an ox and almost as smart," I said.

She laughed again then showed me to the door. The distant cluster of dark clouds had grown considerably from the speck they were before. I looked at them for a second then headed to my car. I turned to see her walking toward me.

"Jonathan, something did come to mind just now. In her first session, she told me while they were still married they took pictures of the boys taking a bath. She said he took at least a hundred pictures. She got annoyed with him and he mistook that for worry. He said something to the effect there was nothing wrong with taking pictures of your own children in the bath."

I leaned on the roof of my car and thought for a second. One thing was certain, I kept feeling worse about this case, and not just because Vicky was dead.

"Was that the only time she mentioned something like that?"

"Yes, but she did say his camera was never far from him."

I nodded. "Thanks, Doc."

"Something?" she asked.

"Maybe."

I got in the car, waited for the traffic to clear, and pulled an illegal U-turn to take Page Avenue back to the expressway.

At the light near the on-ramp, I hit the office number and was greeted by, 'She Who Had Become Part Of Me.'

"Hey, baby girl, do we have Tom on anything?"

"Not till the end of the week."

"I want a loose tail on Sanders."

"Done. When?"

"Today, if he can. Tell him not to get made. If it comes down to it, let him go. I'll have someone to help him soon."

"Anything else?"

"Well ..."

"Do not say strip!"

I laughed. "I was going to say I'll be in the office in a little while. Did you need anything?"

"Oh," she said, and giggled. "Okay, no, we're good here."

"Cool. Now strip."

Jerk," we said at the same time. The radio came back on when we hung up, and the stones were finishing "Brown Sugar." Kashmir started. Not more than a minute later, she called me back.

"You're one of the few people I would interrupt Led Zeppelin for."

"An attorney is on the phone. He'd like to come in and see you. He says he represents Sanders."

"Interesting. Sure, what time is the appointment with Johnson?"

"She's in now, and apparently hungry for business. I said it was a custody matter and asked if you could pay the consult in cash. "

"The magic words," I said.

"That's for sure," she said.

"I can get to her in twenty minutes. That would be noon. Tell him two-thirty."

"Hang on." She came back on in a few seconds. "Two-thirty it is."

"Thanks, babe."

"See you soon," she said.

Kashmir came back on and I rolled the windows down. For the moment, it was sunny and comfortable, but the storm front was a serious threat. I turned the radio up as procedure dictated when rolling the windows down.

21

"Mr. Creed," Freida Link-Johnson said, "I'm afraid I can't speak with you."

"I'm not asking you to violate your attorney-client privilege. I was hoping to speak in generalities. Give me a chance. If you can't answer the questions, just say so." She looked unsure. "I'm trying to find out who murdered the mother of your clients."

She was average height and heavy set. She had expensive nails, hair, and wore stylish glasses. The usual degrees and admissions certificates hung on the wall, along with pictures of herself and other people. From the pictures and slogans, she was feminist, vegan, and progressive. I made it a point not to care what other people believed, but I felt this was an indication this interview would not bode well. For the record, I think rather highly of Camille Paglia.

"Surely your clients would want the person that took their mother from them found."

She forced a weak smile. "Okay, proceed."

"Do you know why anyone would want to kill Vicky Sanders?"

"I would imagine it had something to do with her boyfriend."

"Actually, it's beginning to look like that's not the case."

"Hmmm. Well, she did use drugs."

"A little birdy told me the autopsy came back with nothing recently in her system other than a normal dose of a prescription anti-anxiety medication."

"That doesn't sound accurate to me," she said. "If it was, how could you know? You aren't with the police."

I smiled. "I know it's cliché, but like I said, a little birdy told me." Okay, now my face really started to hurt, and I hoped it didn't freeze that way. I was sure she was troubled, even alarmed. "Let's proceed, for the sake of argument, under the pretense I'm right. If I'm wrong, and that's happened before, we can look at it another way. But say I'm right. Where does that leave us?"

She was quiet, but beneath her calm demeanor, I'd bet my life she was rattled. I didn't have much time left. I bet on a subject change. Either way, she'd soon ask me to leave.

"Well, honestly, I don't know. Her behavior was consistent with someone on drugs."

"Okay, let me ask you some questions. Did you know Vicky's ex-husband outside of court? Did the children tell you they wanted to see their mother? Did you honestly advocate for the wishes of your client?"

"I aggressively and progressively represent all my clients, and do a good job of navigating them through a court system fraught with intersectionality."

Oh great, a sermon. If I wasn't going to get cooperation or information, the next best thing is irritation.

"I view words like progressive and intersectionality in a phrase accompanying anything other than the insurance company or weight training to be a bad thing." I paused and smiled. "It's the same thing as seeing a piece of land with a radiation hazard symbol. I know the land's poisoned, and I'm going to avoid it."

"This interview is over!"

"So soon? I was hoping to stick it out until my ears started to bleed, or my testicles shriveled."

"Typical Staten Island mentality," she hissed.

"Don't knock them. Staten Islanders appear to be enriching your coffers.."

"Get out before I call the police!"

"You would call the agents of oppression? For shame." I stood to leave, and smiled. "I wouldn't bother calling them. The way this investigation is going, you should *expect* them."

Her jaw hung a little bit, and for an instant the worry on her face was evident. I held her gaze until she looked away then walked out, humming the theme from *Conan The Barbarian*. I think it was titled, "The Anvil of Crom."

****

Mandy brought two people into my office and asked if they wanted coffee. Gains declined, and the guy with him, trying to look tough, said nothing.

"Good afternoon, Mr. Creed. My name is Mark Gains. As I told your office manager, I represent Bill Sanders. This is my associate." The goon tried as hard a look as he could manage.

"Not an adequate isagoge counselor, but it shall suffice," I said with a smile.

"Aysuh what?" the man trying to look tough asked, apparently wondering whether I insulted him.

"Isagoge means a formal introduction," Gains told him.

"Apparently, counselor, your education insofar as grammar wasn't in vain," I said with a smile. I was being smug, but the fact the goon of the moment would need a translator was undeniably pleasing.

He tried to ramp up his stare. He wore a light black leather blazer and a turtleneck. Gains wore an expensive, custom three-piece suit. The stare continued as Gains prepared to talk. Let's poke the bear a bit.

"You could look this good too, if you did more cardio," I said to the thug. He stood with arms folded behind Mark Gains, who was sitting in one of my client chairs.

"What the fuck are you talking about?"

"I'm sorry. I thought it was envy that caused you to stare at me like that," I said, smiling at him. "If you're attracted to me I appreciate the sentiment, but while I support equal rights for people of all sexual persuasions, I'm straight."

"Listen," he started, then Gains raised his hand. The thug stopped talking but continued to glare at me. He was about my height and build, but not in as good of shape. He looked like a puffer fish.

"You shouldn't hold your breath when you suck in your gut. You could break a blood vessel."

"Mr. Creed, please, can we get to the matter at hand?"

"Well, since you're into archaeology, I didn't want to ignore the missing link." My hands rested in my lap. The forty-five sat on a small ledge I installed above knee height, three inches from my hands. No one sitting across would have any idea. I noticed the ape, whose clothes weren't as well tailored as mine, had what appeared a shoulder holster. He continued to glare.

"My client would simply like his report and to ensure you have discontinued your investigation. He's also concerned about his privilege with you being violated." He took a deep measured breath then continued the undisguised admonishment. "He's also very troubled. You, just this day, harassed his children's attorney."

I laughed. "First, counselor, since you do a lot of criminal work, you should know there's no privilege with a private investigator and his client in this state. In Massachusetts and some other states there is, but not here. If you look at the copy of my retainer with your client, you will clearly see he can expect his report within thirty days. The investigation however, continues. I have a new client." I smiled again. "I do find it curious, though, that his children's Law Guardian would call him. Might that constitute an ethical breach?"

"Well, if you're saying you represent him."

"I never said who I was working for. The interview lasted forty seconds." His face showed he realized he shouldn't have mentioned that.

Trying to recover, he continued. "According to my client, he was told when he signed the retainer you would be working for him through me."

"I have the signed retainer. He has a copy. You have a copy. It's quite clear."

"That may be an issue for the courts to decide, and you could find yourself embroiled in a lawsuit."

I laughed again and his face reddened. "Are you familiar with Barren and Paris?"

"Of course."

"Steven Barren is my attorney. I encourage you to speak with him."

I did a personal job for Steve Barren a few years ago. He led one of the most prestigious law firms in the country. He was happy with the job, and not only did I gain a valuable client, we became friends.

"We're hoping to avoid that," Gains said.

"That's encouraging. Steve also personally prepared my standard retainer. I'll let him know you feel it has room for improvement."

He ignored that. "My client also feels you should be paid for your work. I have an escrow check for you." He reached into the jacket pocket of his custom suit and handed me an unsealed envelope. I opened it. Inside was a check for twenty-five thousand. You had to give a nod to that kind of money, so I bowed my head a bit.

"Not bad," I said.

"So we have an agreement?"

"No, but I'm very much in your debt."

"Excuse me?"

I smiled and slowly tore the check and envelope in half. "No excuse for you, counselor, but I have so wanted to do that for about twenty years now. I owe you one."

A flush crossed Gains's face. I tossed the two halves of the check on the desk toward the ape. He got red too, then moved so I could see the piece. My left hand rested on the desk. My right went to the top of my thigh and then down to the small shelf below the middle drawer where my gun sat. The custom grip reassured me.

"Before you move again, I need you to listen to something, Cheetah."

I began tapping the barrel of the .45 on the bottom of the desk drawer. They both looked puzzled by the sound.

"Hear that?"

"So fuckin' what?" the ape asked.

"That's the sound of your life ticking away. If you move that hand toward the shoulder holster, I let go a few rounds from the .45 I have pointed at your balls. Or where balls would be if you had any."

Gains' face color changed from red to white. Gunplay wasn't what he signed on for. The ape froze, and Gains licked his now dry lips. Deafening silence filled the room for a few seconds.

"It took me a year to find this desk. I bought it in an antique store upstate in Goshen, paid about four hundred for it. It appraised at three thousand. I'd like to avoid putting a hole in it, not to mention your femoral artery parting and you bleeding out on my floor, Cheetah."

"Wait a minute," Gains said nervously. "He didn't pull his gun."

"He was going to, or he was going to threaten me with it. If he moved the wrong way I'd have shot him. You probably would have caught a round too, since I've been so nervous and all. You actually should thank my read. I had the gun out and pointed. That gave me time to explain things to you." I smiled again. "If he caught me by surprise you'd both be dead now."

The thug was angry. Gains was afraid but still in charge. He told the thug not to move and keep his hands where I could see them.

"You ain't pulling no trigger," Cheetah said.

"Cheetah, you should consider another line of work."

"You're the one that cheated, you piece of shit. You had your gun out already."

I let out a genuine laugh. "Firstly, it was C-H-E-E-T-A-H, as in Tarzan's pet monkey, not C-H-E-A-T-E-R. Secondly, I'm compelled to ask, were your mother and father really brother and sister? You think this is a contest? You believe this is Marquis De Queensbury rules? You want a fair fight? You really need to find another line of work."

They stared blankly at me.

"Counselor, I must ask. You come here with a thug in tow, an amateur thug no less, and try to bribe me. Why is it so important to your client I'm off this case?"

Blank stares.

"Tell Sanders if he wants to talk, he should come himself."

"All things considered," Gains said, trying to recover, "I don't believe that's in my client's best interest."

"But it's in his best interest to send his lawyer, who I happen to know shares office space with the lawyer representing Mark Stanton, with an amateur thug to threaten me? Any idea how suspicious this looks? If I had to take a wild guess, I'd imagine it was Stanton who suggested this."

Gains got a little braver, since it appeared there wouldn't be any gunplay. "It isn't a crime to know people in common, Mr. Creed. My client may or may not know Mr. Stanton. That doesn't matter. I made no bribe. Perhaps I misspoke, or you misunderstood."

"So you expect me to believe a milquetoast like Sanders would find a criminal lawyer that doesn't advertise he accepts family court cases?" I took a shot there. I hadn't checked that they even knew each other yet.

"As I said, it's possible I misspoke. And how my clients came to be my clients isn't your concern."

"The cops might find it interesting. You gentleman are going to leave now, unless there's something more for you to say."

"You should take this deal," the ape said. "You got lucky."

"Do you know what a caricature is, Cheetah?"

"We'll see how smart you are the next time we see each other, jerk off."

"Google it later and you may come to know more about your limitations. Remove yourself from my sight, Cheetah. The longer you're here, the greater the odds my finger squeezes the trigger. Leave Clarence Darrow here for a minute."

"Who the fuck is that?"

My eyes rolled. "Leave Gains here. He'll join you outside."

The thug looked at Gains and Gains nodded, then shrugged and left. He glared at me and I winked at him. Good thugs are hard to come by these days.

"Counselor," I said. "I repeat, you don't expect me to think a milquetoast like Sanders would have an attorney threaten me with a half assed leg breaker. That has Stanton written over it all day long. About as subtle as a sledgehammer. If he just sent you, I might not have put it together."

"Really, Mr. Creed,"

"Let me finish, counselor. Stanton might be clever but that was dumb. It bruised his pride when I knocked two of his hitters on their asses. His dislike for me caused him to make a bad judgement call. A friend of mine has a saying, "contempt will kill you." I'm going to find out who killed my friend, and whoever that is better hope the cops get hold of them before I do. But there's another factor. Since you do criminal work, I'm sure you know who Eddie Siciliano is?"

"Yes, of course I do," he answered.

"Did you know he's Anthony Luca's brother?"

Gains didn't pale, he blanched. "What's that have to do with me?"

"I wouldn't want to be the person that killed Crazy Eddie's brother, or anyone helping him, or even in close proximity to him or her. We don't want to be sexist now."

Gains said nothing.

"If someone happened to get in my way while I was going for said person or persons, I wouldn't care what happened to them. Siciliano not only wouldn't care, he'd hunt anyone down that had anything to do with it." I let him reflect for a few seconds. "I assure you, they'd end up as chum on a fishing boat."

Still he said nothing. If he played poker, I'd like to buy into that game. He was whiter than a new sheet, and sweat was beading on his forehead. I was familiar with the feeling of, "holy shit, what did I get myself into?" because it kept me company since Vicks was murdered.

"You may want to remember that if I talk with you again, you might need a friend."

He got up without a word, turned and left. Mandy came in shortly after and closed the door behind her. I could tell she was upset. She sat across in the client chair Curtis vacated.

"You all right?" I asked.

She nodded. "I was afraid for you. That man was scary."

"The one that should have scared you was the lawyer. They're terrifying people."

I waited for her to say, "jerk," but she didn't. Her eyes were downcast, and she was quiet. The room was quiet now too. I exhaled softly and nodded.

"Sweetheart," I said softly. She looked up at me. "This is what I do. Sometimes, not too often, I run into bad people."

"I'm afraid for you."

"Don't be. I promise you I'll be okay," I said.

"Vicky wouldn't want anything to happen to you. I know this is hard and I know this is what you do. I'm ... I'm afraid."

I watched her. I knew her now. In a short time, she became part of me. She was the most beautiful woman I'd ever seen. Now that I was getting to know her, I realized it wouldn't matter what she looked like. She was *it*. If you asked me six months ago what the odds were for me to fall in love, I'd have said you have a better chance of hitting the lotto.

What I do is part of what I am. I didn't want to cause her any pain or worry, but also needed to be able to do my work.

"Listen," I said, and she looked up at me. "Sometimes there's danger in what I do, but it's my job and the work is part of me. I'm a cautious person, even more so now, babe."

"What do you mean?"

"I need to come back to you."

"Oh," she said softly, and smiled. Her eyes teared up a little.

"I can't even imagine you not being there. What matters is, for whatever time we have, and I hope it's forever, we have each other."

I got up and moved over to her then leaned down and kissed her softly. She kissed me back, and stood without breaking the kiss. We put our arms around each other. I took her lower lip gently in my teeth after we stopped, and looked in her eyes. She reached out and caressed the side of my face. I traced a line from her forehead to the tip of her nose, down the side of her neck and to her breast. I rested my hand on her heart, which I felt racing.

When I looked into her eyes, I felt the sensation of looking into an infinite horizon.

"I never knew anyone like you before. You're so strong, and you care about people. You're smart. A lot of men have wanted me because they thought I looked good. So few of them wanted to know the real me."

"Also handsome, modest, charming," I said, with a smile.

"Jerk," she said, as she punched my shoulder.

"You're possessed of great inner beauty, sweetheart, and fortunately for me, it's wrapped up in a nice package. I honestly do a lot less fieldwork these days, babe. You've seen it. I'm in the office or out schmoozing more than working on cases."

"I know. I'll be okay with it. This is just getting crazy."

"Yeah, that's undeniable," I said. "I have the feeling we're drawing to a close, though. Sanders has a connection to your ex. Small island is becoming a too frequently used phrase."

"You're stirring the pot," she said.

"Yes."

"You aren't afraid of the man that was here?"

"Well, he was a lawyer. They're pretty terrifying."

"Jerk," we both said at the same time. "No," I said. "By that I mean he's a big, mean guy, strong and used to pushing people around. I wouldn't turn my back on him, but wouldn't worry too much about him."

"This man, Tempesta?"

"He's someone I would worry about, but we're kind of on the same side. I'm not worried about him coming after me."

"And my ex?"

"Physically, as in assaulting me? No, but he's dangerous. I hate to use the term, because it's so overused. He's a sociopath, maybe a psychopath." I paused. "You don't have to be tough to pull a trigger or stick a knife in someone's back, or pay someone to do it. He has a ways to go in the human resources department though."

"My college psych professor said that 'sociopath' and 'psychopath' are basically the same thing."

"Well, to my knowledge there's a bit of a difference. I like the distinction. A sociopath is someone that utterly lacks empathy for the pain of others. A psychopath lacks empathy the same way but likes to cause pain as well. A sociopath would sell a snuff film, a psychopath would make one."

"That's an interesting way of putting it."

"I read it in an article Andrew Vachss wrote."

"He's a psychologist?"

"No, he's an attorney and an author. He writes crime fiction. He represents children exclusively. I have most of his books at home in the library. I met him once in Manhattan Family Court. He's an exceptional man."

"I can't get past thinking this is my fault. I'm afraid something might happen to you and it's my fault."

"It's not. The connection between Sanders and your ex would still have been there," I said. Besides, there's enough to deal with while I'm busy taking the blame, I thought.

"It looks as though there's a connection between them, but what is it?"

"That's the next phase of the investigation," I said.

She left to return to work. I called Mariano and filled him in. He was as interested in the new developments as I was.

22

Jen Hayes left a message to say she'd come in Thursday morning to sign the retainer. Her husband had stayed home unexpectedly yesterday. Vicky's body was released. It normally would have happened sooner, but there was a backlog at the Medical Examiner's office.

Jen came in as promised at two minutes past nine. She looked sad and tired. Her eyes were a little red, but she walked with grace and strength despite the pain she carried.

She sat in my client chair and her voice was clear. She looked pretty despite no make-up and the red eyes. She signed the paper without reading it, and we talked after.

"Jim, there's something wrong here. I think I may need to speak with the police. My ex son-in-law called my husband late last night. He thought I was sleeping. I couldn't hear what he said, but he was pacing a long time after."

"Well, there have been several interesting occurrences and the police may want to interview you. If they do, be candid with them. I say this because you want to know who killed your daughter."

"Very much so," she said. "I think my husband knows or suspects more than he's saying."

I paused and reflected. This would be a delicate question. "Is it possible he had something to do with her death?"

She was quiet for a long while. Her gaze went to the small bar in the corner of my office that had just three crystal decanters. One had Johnny Walker Blue, one had an exceptional old port, and the third had Grey Goose VX. All three were gifts from clients during the last holiday season. Although her eyes rested on the decanters, she looked through them.

"I wish I could say, 'No.' There's a cold, reptilian aspect to my husband. It rarely shows itself fully. In business he's very cold, especially to my daughter whenever she didn't measure up to his standards. We've been going through the motions of marriage for the last twenty years."

I took the cue from her and stared at the decanters. I was still a ways away from proving Sanders had anything to do with Vicky being killed. By implication there, I was further away from her father having anything to do with it.

"You'd be hard pressed to find someone as self-assured of their morals as my husband."

"History indicates he'd be in well-known company," I said.

"I wish I could say I can't imagine even he," she said, then paused, "had something to do with our daughter's death."

That hung for a bit. "But?" I asked.

"It's hard to explain. I just feel he's capable."

"Intuition isn't something to be ignored," I said, "but it's far from proof, Jen."

"Agreed," she said. "Tell me what happened."

I filled her in about the law guardian, Becky Jordan, and the visit from the milquetoast Tarzan and Cheetah. We talked for a long while. She asked questions. I answered what I could.

I told her I felt my presence would be a distraction so wasn't going to go to the wake, but would pay my respects off hours. I asked her how she felt about Sanders being there.

"He'll stand there with my husband and they'll talk about how great she could have been."

"Jesus, I'm sorry."

"I'll get through it," she said, then extended her hand. When I accepted it, she held it firmly. "I know you'll do what you can."

"Count on it," I said.

After she left, I pulled the file on the research I did on Sanders, and did the same on Stanton. I took the info I got from Eddie Martin and took out a pad to jot notes. After several hours my stack of papers sat four inches high. I like to see and feel paper. My office killed a lot of trees. I started out with the address Stanton owned near Adobe. I ran the address for both people and businesses associated with it. I ran every address Stanton was connected to for the same, and did the same for Sanders. I ran the owner of each property.

An hour and fifteen minutes later I hit a business called Promised Land Properties, LLC., where Stanton and Sanders were two of the dozen or so principles. So was Vicky's dad and surprise, surprise, Anthony Luca.

That is, of course, only proof they know each other. I spent the next few hours running the works on all the other principals, running criminal checks on all of them. By the time Mickey showed up to give me his report on following Sanders, my eyes were blurred and my company was a few thousand in the hole.

"Come," I said gratefully to the sound of a knock on my door. I had the radio playing softly in the background, and so far drank a week's worth of coffee.

"Uncle?" Mickey inquired.

"Come, nephew. What news have ye?"

The big kid plopped into one of the client chairs and his large frame settled in. Mickey had that almost perpetual grin on his face but his eyes looked tired and the wide shoulders sagged. I knew the kind of tired tail jobs cause. He had a slight accent that suggested he hailed from Eastern Europe. I knew it was Ukrainian only because he told me.

"Your buddy Sanders is playing Mister Mom. He takes his kids to school, looks like the ideal father."

"But?"

"Nothing substantial, a few things, and one I think you'll like. I did get close to him a few times. He took the kids to the food court at the Mall. I observed a bit and listened."

"What did you see?"

"Nothing unusual, boss." He opened his mouth to speak, but thought better of it.

"This ain't dragnet, kid," I said. "You have a feeling? Out with it."

Mickey nodded his head then shook it. "Sanders is fucking weird, boss. Cold. Hollow. His kids, they act as if he's the Boogie Man. The whole time I'm with them he seems detached. From the kids … I never saw kids that age do everything their parent wants them to with no trouble."

"Possibly because their mother died?"

"Not if I had to put money on it," he said. "He's a cold, creepy, son of a bitch."

"Was it hard?" I asked.

"Not too," my protégé said. "He acted like someone who suspects they're being followed. Watched a little when he would first leave his house and then stopped looking." He paused to think. "He drives slowly, cautiously."

"Anything other than normal activities?"

"Yes, once. He met a couple of guys. I think maybe the person Stanton you asked me to look out for was one of them but it's hard to say. Couldn't get close enough to see but the second guy was big. Hard looking, about my size, my age. Big bruise on the side of his face."

"Aha."

"Aha?"

"Aha."

He smiled. "What are we Aha-ing about? By the way, if Aha-ing is not a recognized word, I claim it."

I smiled back. “Is that of some import to you, since English isn’t your first language?”

“It is.”

“Then it’s yours to claim, kid. I believe the big guy was Tom Sullivan. That would make the guy Sanders met with either Mark Stanton or Joey Bertone.”

Oh,” he said. “Aha!”

“Aha,” I said.

“Next move?”

I thought about that for a while. “Okay, submit your bill for what you’ve done so far and stand ready. I have some more work for you starting tomorrow.”

“Great,” he said, and grinned again. “More surveillance?”

“No, a bunch of people to be interviewed.”

“Discretely?” he asked.

“Not in the least. Let whoever answers their door or whoever is at the reception desk know it’s about a murder.”

I called Mandy in, gave her my notes, the highlighted info on the printouts and a list of questions while Mickey listened. Mickey volunteered to help her get it ready. I left for the short ride to the funeral parlor. In the car I called Mariano and provided him with general details.

“Not bad,” he said, then hung up.

Part 3

The End Product

23

Vicky's wake took place at Matthew's Funeral Parlor. My family did business with them since my family was a family. When I was younger, I remember my grandfather passing. Jack, he never let us call him grandpa, died when I was about twelve. He was a big, sometimes, ornery Irish cop, who at six-five, stood more than a foot taller than my Italian grandmother. In those days, it was considered an interracial marriage.

The Italian side of the family sat upstairs where my grandparents lived and wailed, and the Irish side sat downstairs, where we lived and they drank to the memories. My uncles on the Italian side made their way downstairs. To this day, I remember the cop that showed up; his name was Markow. We talked about science while he stayed with us, waiting for the coroner to arrive. I remember being with my father at the funeral home, and as sad as we were, the people there made us feel better. I felt the smallest measure better that her wake took place there.

I got there about one. The viewing started at two. I knew Chris, the manager. Years ago, her brothers and I trained together. She escorted me into the viewing room, the smallest of the three in the building. She went in with me and asked if I was okay. I said, "Yes." She opened the casket for me and left.

She had the same unanimated quality of any corpse at any wake I attended. I hadn't been to church in years but recited the customary prayers. I told God, since he couldn't see fit to keep her with us, maybe he could watch over her kids. I visited this issue since I was old enough to think about it. In the end, God or none, it was a matter of belief. If there was a God, I don't think he, she, or it, would hold it against anyone if they weren't sure.

Carl Sagan once said something akin to, "If there was a God, he'd want us to use the brains we were gifted with to question everything." I don't think he would seek praise or prayer. I think if he cared, he'd be pissed at a lot of things done in his name. My mother and brothers were religious. I was a Godfather to a few of the nieces and nephews. I didn't begrudge anyone if they believed. If God was supposed to look out for good people, he should be sued for malpractice. Whenever I voiced that question in religious instruction, Father Mendori answered, "free will."

I looked at Vicky. She looked gaunt and drawn. Maybe I should have looked out for her more. I shared a bed with her, laughed with her, dined with her. I had someone now, but she died without having had that someone.

"I'm sorry, Vicks," I said, choking on the words.

I reached out and held her hand. It was cool to the touch. Chris told me no flowers had yet arrived. Daddy Warbucks apparently further showed his disapproval, even in her death. The smallest viewing room, one day only, and a quick service.

I told her I would find out what happened and see to it the kids were okay. I kept telling her I was sorry, then leaned over and kissed her forehead.

"Rest well, sweet girl. I love you. I'm sorry I never said it. You were a good woman. I never thought I'd settle down. You'd been through so much and didn't want to lie to you about that. I'm sorry I hurt you."

I wanted to cry for her but didn't. Almost. I'd let the grief have its way when I found out who did it, or the cops caught them. As I walked to my car, I caught sight of a car, a four door, blue Grand Marquis. I might have seen it when I left the office, except I was preoccupied with where I was going. Slight tint on the windows a distance away, but I thought I saw at least two guys inside.

A half hour later, as I drove and made believe I was doing things, they were still with me, hanging back. I stopped at a deli and bought gum then pretended to talk on the phone a lot, holding it to my ear so they could see. I stopped at the bank, went in, and took care of a few things.

An hour later, they were still trying to hang back, but staying with me became more important. It wasn't like it was years ago. You have to be more selective about where you do certain things. Cameras exist in many places, and I assumed many of them actually worked.

It didn't feel like a hit. It just didn't feel like it, but the .45 at my side was a source of great comfort just the same. I knew there were at least two of them. When I did listen to my gut, it was rarely wrong. I had hollow-points in the clip with two extra clips, one with steel-jacketed rounds, the other with more hollow points. Twenty-one shots – seemed comfortable when I wasn't followed by three thugs. If I lived, I'd send the governor a nasty letter. My fault though, I should have kept extra clips in the glove compartment. Fuck him, his fault too. I made a mental note that if I died, to write to the governor with my bloody fingertip, "Thanks."

My judgement in these instances is rarely wrong. I experienced enough of these instances to make sound judgments. That wasn't magic, but it was more than luck. I think when you're calm and trust your experience, your brain calculates the outcome, and the result is intuition. I could be wrong. I'm wrong at least once a month, and this month I'd already been wrong at least three times.

My shadows were being bolder, staying with me. The gut said they were going to more than just watch. I'd been warned off. It was a beating or a goodbye. It didn't feel like a hit.

An edge would be nice. There was a Dunkin Donuts on Bay St. If it was who I thought it was, the Dunkin Donuts was in their neighborhood. They would know there were cameras all over the place in that shopping plaza. I pulled in, but they didn't. Their car passed me. Had they pulled in, I would have walked through the parking lot to the side street leading to the water. If I was wrong and it was a hit, I didn't want anyone else getting hurt.

They actually pulled onto the side street. That was smart. They could pull out after me regardless which direction I went. My vet was right down the street. I walked into Dunkin. There was no line. I ordered two boxes of coffee called Box O' Joe, and two dozen donuts. A cop car sat parked in the lot.

"Please make the coffee as hot as you can. It's going to be a while before I get to drink it, and I hate cold coffee."

"Yes, sir," the girl behind the counter said. She was high school age, and I noticed a textbook sitting close by her on the counter. She had a kind face. You never knew of course, but the impression was, if she managed to stay on track she'd become something. I left five dollars in the tip cup.

I pulled out and drove west on Bay Street. In a few blocks, I stopped at the vets then pulled onto the side street. The set up was the same as the Dunkin Donuts plaza, except the street ran one way, and the side of the building facing the one way wasn't equipped with cameras. They drove past me and parked in front of a black Suburban further down the street.

I hadn't been there for months. My dog, a cinnamon chow named AJ, had been with me for fourteen years. He had bad arthritis and was getting close to contracting something called Bloat. Happens sometimes to deep chested dogs. The stomach turns over and causes terrible pain. I rushed him to the vet. Cheryl is the office manager, and all the vets were competent. I called out to her as I entered with AJ in my arms. Cheryl jumped up, sent a tech for the vet, and led me into a room. They quickly lessened his pain to a tolerable level. I brought him there regularly for injections and treatment for his arthritis.

Doctor Cavallaro, Cheryl, and I, discussed the options.

"The operation is long and difficult," Doc Cav said. "If he lives through it, it will be weeks of recovery. That would be hard even for a young, healthy dog, but torture for him, considering he already has trouble moving well. If we did the operation, it would be more for you than him, Jimmy. If he was mine, I'd let him go."

"Okay, we need to do it quickly."

Cheryl left the room, and another tech came in with the necessary drugs after Doc called on the intercom. Cheryl returned with a box of tissues.

"I'll be okay," I said.

"I know." She put the box down and slid her arm across my back. Most people using the animal hospital liked her. Hell, many people went there because she worked there. It was also her job to keep order and make sure people followed the rules.

I kept my hand on AJ's head, stroking him. He knew I was there and went to sleep. The tech left and Cheryl handed me the tissues. I was about to say, "no, I'm okay," when I realized my face was wet. I wiped the tears away. Both Cheryl and the Doc hugged me.

When I got out of the car, I took out one box of donuts and one Box O' Joe. I left the car unlocked and walked toward the animal hospital. I saw the car peripherally as I walked toward the storefront and saw Bertone and Sullivan, as well as the muscle that was with Gains, who came into the office to warn me off. They parked on the side street. This plaza had cameras too, but none on the side of the building. I parked just past camera view.

I walked in. Cheryl and a girl named Erica, sitting behind the counter, both looked up and greeted me warmly. Doc Cohen was one of the vets on duty, and up front. When he saw me, he came around the counter and shook my hand. We'd known each other for years and I considered him a friend.

I put the donuts and coffee on the counter. Doc was heading back to his office so he volunteered to take them to the break room. Construction to the practice was going on. Previously there were other stores in the shopping plaza, but as the reputation of the vets grew, they needed more room.

"You ready for a dog yet?" Cheryl asked.

I smiled. "Soon, but I need a favor."

"Shoot."

"I need to stand here and talk for a few minutes."

"That ain't no favor," Erica said.

"Speak for yourself. I have things to do and this perpetual man-child is a distraction," Cheryl said in mock frustration.

I laughed. "Perpetual man-child?"

She smiled. "Go ahead, deny it."

"Can't," I said, with a shrug.

I could see the parking lot, and saw Sullivan walk across it, talking on his cell phone. He was probably speaking to Bertone. There was only the animal hospital and a Pizzeria called Molo in the entire shopping plaza. The pizza there was good. It would take him some time to cross the parking lot if he stayed there and more time to get back.

Ritchie, a tech at the vet ever since I was a client, came in. He was a great kid who donated his kidney to his father without hesitation. Something a lot of us think we would do.

"There's a couple of guys standing on the side of the building." He paused. "They look a little scary."

"I got it," I said to Cheryl. "They might be here for me."

"Should I call the cops?" she asked.

"No, I got it."

"There's two of them," Erica said. Ritchie wrinkled his brow.

"Three, one walked over to the pizzeria. It's okay, trust me."

I grabbed a piece of paper and wrote the names Bertone, Sullivan, and Goon from yesterday, on a paper with Mariano's cell number on it.

"If things don't go as well as I anticipate, call this fellow Mike Mariano and read this to him. I left more coffee and donuts in the car. Be right back."

She looked at the paper. "Goon?"

"Hey, I've been called a goon myself," I said. "Some of my best friends are goons."

She smiled. I went outside and saw Sullivan in the pizzeria from the corner of my eye. He didn't move. The fewer guests showing up at the beginning of this party the better. I walked right to my car.

As I walked, I saw them peripherally, leaning against the wall of the building. When I opened the back door of the car and leaned in, they came off the wall and walked toward me. I used my keys to vigorously score the bottom of the box of coffee, and was rewarded with coffee precipitation. I quickly carved a smiley face on the bottom for my own amusement; it made me smile and removed the nervous tension.

Bertone's high, mean voice cut through the air. "Hey, motherfucker, remember me?"

I got out of the car and held the Box O' Joe in my right hand. I slid my keys back in my pocket.

"Of course, you're one of the Oompa Loompas from the original *Willy Wonka* movie. You're in great shape for your age."

"You shoulda listened," the Goon said. They quickly closed the distance. Sullivan was walking toward me across the parking lot but didn't rush. A second later, they were standing next to me.

"Fellas, I'm sure we can talk about this. One of you must have a pocket dictionary, perhaps an app that could enable you to comprehend me."

"Fuck," Bertone started, as he reached for me. His lips were curled into a mean sneer. I imagined "fuck," would have been followed by "you," but would likely remain a mystery.

The Goon reached for his shoulder holster. As hard as I could, I smashed the box of coffee on his forehead and the box disintegrated, causing the desired effect. Some of the coffee splashed on me, and it didn't feel good, but he took the brunt of it in his face. He screamed, grabbed his face with his hands and kept screaming, but they were muffled. The thought crossed my mind he might lose one eye or both, but I didn't care.

Bertone lunged for me, and I drove my elbow into his face with my full weight behind it. He collapsed. I was a betting man, sometimes, and wagered he was looking at cosmetic surgery. Sullivan began walking over when I opened the car door. He was about half way now and neither hurried nor slowed. I had about ten more seconds. I hit the button for the trunk. The Goon collapsed on the sidewalk, landing, poetically, in a large pile of dog excrement. He was alternately screaming, cursing, and moaning. Sometimes, I thought there must be a God, and sometimes, he, she, or it, shared my sense of humor. The tomato cans were out of the picture.

When I took out my gun, Sullivan paused. I put it in the trunk with my wallet and winked at him. Cheryl, Erica, and a bunch of people had come outside. Cheryl was holding what looked like a two by four.

"You okay?" she asked.

"Yeah, babe, thanks," I said, then tossed her my car keys. She caught them, and Sullivan resumed his march.

"Round two, Tommy?"

"Let's see how you do when I'm ready for you," he rumbled.

"Yeah," I said, smiling, "let's."

As we circled, he appeared calm, and although he probably thought he'd do better the second time, I knew he wouldn't, but at least he had the balls to try. Not easy dealing with a loss like that. Last time, I hit him before he was set. It was even up now.

He flicked a couple of decent jabs at me in a classic boxer's stance. He was strong and moved well. He was searching for a rhythm and would move in. Soon.

I threw a couple of jabs back at him, one rocking his head back, which motivated him. He landed a jab and caught my chin, which rocked my head back. There'd be a nice bruise there later. He threw another jab and a right hook, but let the hook hang there too long. We circled more. He threw a good combo at me and caught me under the eye. I was rolling away but he cut me. I shuffle stepped to his right and threw a heavy left hook. He ducked and moved away then we circled a bit more. He hooked off his jab; his left hook was crisp, hard, and short. I was moving away at the time it connected with my chin, almost right where the jab hit. If I was moving the other way, it would have put me down.

He threw an overhand right. I deflected, but it was heavy. His arm came up, and although I moved him with the hard left hook, it didn't land on anything but arm. The right would have done damage if it landed. The guy could hit, and as such, I would prefer not to be on the receiving end for any more. A left hook followed. I ducked and left myself open for the right hook, hoping he'd take it. He did.

I took a short step forward with my right leg, and blocked the hook with a left knife hand. With my right, I punched his right bicep, hard. He groaned and tried to draw back. It wasn't like getting punched in the face, which isn't a picnic either. The bicep was almost certainly torn. He involuntarily constricted his eyes, squeezed shut with pain. I gripped his wrist with my left hand to control him. As the punch bounced off and slid past him, I slammed a back fist into his kidney. It made the sound of a watermelon disintegrating on the sidewalk. He groaned again, louder, and his body involuntarily arched back. I drove the same hand down into his groin. Another grunt, and he was finished. I slid my right arm behind his elbow reflexively and almost broke his arm, but it wasn't necessary.

He was finished. I knew his bicep was torn, and he'd likely be pissing blood for a while. Although he could still probably have children, he wouldn't want to try for the next eight hours or so. He tried to stay on his feet but collapsed, clutching his right arm to his body and holding his groin with his left hand. A good kidney shot will draw you back, but a torn bicep and ball pain apparently trumped a kidney.

"You shouldn't leave the right out for so long, Tommy," I said, tilting my head. "It's different here than in the ring. Odds are you won't run into someone that would make a difference though. At least not again."

With his jaw clenched and eyes closed, he groaned and hissed a short expletive. Bertone wasn't moving. He should hire me when he has insomnia. His nose whistled.

The Goon was still screaming and moaning into his hands. I looked at Cheryl, and saw relief spread over her face.

"You can call 911 now if you like, Miss."

"Your friend, too?"

"Yeah, tell him they attempted to inhibit my forward locomotion and I was forced to resist said attempt."

"Is that what it was?" she snickered.

"If you like," I said.

"You're going to have a hell of a bruise on your face, judging by its progress so far."

My head felt light and hot; my hands were sore as hell, and post adrenaline exhaustion started to set in. The right side of my face felt very tender. I realized I tasted and smelled blood from a cut inside my mouth but it wasn't too bad. The area around the small cut under my eye was swelling.

She smiled at me, I smiled back. I looked at the two by four and nodded approvingly, then looked at all of them. Erica was definitely a Port Richmond girl so she was disappointed. She held her key ring in her hand and the keys between her fingers. I saw Doc Cohen also came out. He always had this kind look on his face, sort of like if Rockwell would have painted a young grandfather. I noticed he held a claw hammer.

You know who your friends are when the shit hits the fan. "Thanks, guys, that means a lot to me." And it did. "Doc helping out with the construction?" I asked Cheryl.

"Not a chance," she whispered. I smiled.

Doc and the girls turned and went back into the animal hospital. The adrenaline left my body, replaced by the customary exhaustion.

"Mr. Creed," Richie said.

"Stop aging me," I said.

He smiled. "I'm sorry, Jimmy. There's a man standing across the street, big guy in a suit. He's been watching for a while. He seems ..."

I turned to look and saw Anthony Tempesta. "Out of place?" I suggested. Out of place like the Grim Reaper on Sesame Street. Was he there for them or me? Disconcerting.

"Yeah," Richie said.

He stood, not leaned, near the store on the corner across the street. When our eyes met, he nodded. I nodded back. He turned, walked up the street, and disappeared.

It wasn't a coincidence; he was following me or them. Unlike the neutralized participants from amateur hour, I didn't see him following me. Very disconcerting.

Mariano had arrived not long after the squad cars arrived. Turns out he was at Pouch Terminal. Ambulances also came. The cops took statements from the Animal Hospital employees. The usual machinations.

"Three? You did two a few days ago. Are you going for a record?"

"It wasn't three at once," I said, smiling. "They made errors."

"Which you were smart enough to exploit."

"Yeah. Some luck was involved though."

"But you'll take it," Mariano said.

"As the alternative would have been off the suck scale, indeed I will, Chief." I paused while they loaded the now conscious Bertone into the back of an ambulance. "Interesting, isn't it?"

"If you mean after the turn of events with your client, I would say, "yes. Off the record, he's declining to come in without an attorney present."

"Very interesting," I said. "I'm wondering what Gains' position will be, as I'm imagining you'll bring him in for questioning?"

"Well, since he was with one of the men who assaulted you days before the assault happened, yes."

"Do we know who the Goon is?" I asked.

"No, other than asking for burn cream, he's mute. He's having trouble seeing apparently, and is in great pain. We'll print him in the burn ward."

We were quiet for a while. My left hand hurt a bit. I felt the exhaustion typical after a large adrenaline rush. My chin didn't feel good either where Sullivan landed. The small cut under my eye bled only a little, but the headache brewing promised to be memorable.

"He does have balls," I said. Mariano looked at me questioningly. "Sullivan. He took some good hits the other day and came back to even the score. He didn't bum rush me when the other two did."

"That does take balls," he conceded. "One of my guys at the precinct knows his family. He wasn't a bad kid. He showed promise as a fighter but got hurt, lost more than he should have. That's the decline of the sport. Twenty-eight, with no way to make a living."

I don't know what's wrong with me, but I felt bad. "I doubt I'd have done as well if he rushed me when they did."

"Unlikely," Mariano agreed.

"Maybe he'll be smart and talk?" I asked. "I wouldn't cry about it if he got off easy."

"Jesus," Mariano said.

"He behaved in an honorable way. He had a gripe and came to settle it. That's out of style today."

"Softy."

I smiled. "Sometimes. He'll also likely need surgery to fix his bicep. He's in for some pain." I cleared my very dry throat. "The fact he didn't puke his guts up after the shot I gave him in the family jewels indicates a strong constitution. He won't run short on pain any time soon."

We were quiet for a while. Cheryl brought out two bottles of water and a cold pack for my face. Mariano politely declined his so I took it as well. I drank the first one in three swallows then sipped from the second one. We both watched her walk away. The cold pack was big enough to cover the side of my face and under my eye.

"I'm always in favor of gym time," I said. He nodded.

"So, let's review where we are," Mariano said. "If you can tend to your grievous injuries and talk at the same time," he said, with a smirk.

"I'm game," I said.

I told him about the research and the company called Promised Land. I mentioned all of the other people involved. I told him about the surveillance on Sanders, interviewing some of the shareholders. I also mentioned the appearance of Anthony Tempesta.

"It's looking like a strong possibility Vicki was the one killed, and Luca was a casualty. The motive had something to do with her."

"Maybe, or maybe it was two birds with one stone?" I asked.

"I think I know where you're going," he said. "Elaborate a little."

"Luca was a bit of a loose cannon."

"Stanton and Sanders apparently do know each other," Mariano said.

"My ex client was doing business with Stanton," I said. "We've established that. We were told, and you confirmed, Luca and Stanton had dealings together."

"Two for the price of one. Things just lined up that way and they decided to take advantage of that. Luca just got worked over."

"If that's the case, I guarantee Sanders had no idea Crazy Eddie was Luca's brother."

"It is, to say the least, a bold move," Mariano said.

"To say the least," I agreed. "Stanton is clever but he appears to have a reckless side. He surely doesn't deal well with insult. At least two of these guys are his," I said, jerking my head to one of the ambulances arriving. "There's heat on this."

"I wonder if he might think Sanders is a weak link."

"This has been happening pretty fast. If he hasn't, he might soon," I replied.

"I wonder if Sanders or Gains knew they were weak beams in a house of cards, how they'd feel about that. Gains, I think, knows he's perilously close to acting outside the scope of an attorney. I think they're both scared," Mariano said, as he looked at the second ambulance pulling away. "Gains being in on the land company won't go well for him."

"Maybe a meeting of the minds will reveal a few things," I ventured. "Or maybe if we keep poking the bear."

"They won't come to us. Not without attorneys."

"I think," I said with a sigh, "Vickie's mom would help us out. The piece of self-important refuse masquerading as her father lied to her. I'm betting he unknowingly somehow collaborated in this."

"What brings you to that conclusion?" Mariano asked.

"Just a gut feeling. If you met him, I wager you'd come to the same conclusion."

Mariano nodded thoughtfully. "Is knowingly collaborated a possibility?"

"Jesus, Chief."

"Yeah."

"He's quite the supreme asshole, no question," I said. "Being part of killing your own kid ... I hadn't considered that."

"Maybe things are dark enough and you didn't want to."

"Maybe," I said. "Question, I know Vickie didn't have drugs in her system, but what about Luca?"

Mariano laughed grimly. "A pharmacy, an actual tribute, to modern chemistry."

"Here's a scenario," I said. "Stanton and Sanders put together a deal above or below board, a land deal. Stanton wants to play citizen but he isn't. He figures he'll gain favor with Crazy Eddie, invites Luca in, gets him some cash. Look what I did for your troubled little brother. Something has to link these people together."

"Okay," Mariano said, following my line of thought. "Then Anthony proves true to his nature and does something relatively fucked up," he postulated.

"Making his removal necessary."

"Or maybe Vicky was on the verge of discovering something. I don't like what you're telling me."

"There's something else that might tie in," I said.

I told him about the night Mandy saw Stanton staring at Shane while he slept, apparently aroused. He inhaled. We were both quiet for a while.

"They often run in packs," he said.

I looked at him and raised my eyebrows.

"Child predators."

24

I went back to the office. My hands hurt like hell. My head throbbed and my jaw was sore. The cut was small. Under the eye, it didn't look like it needed a stitch, but was swollen. I felt sore in other areas, a hazard of aging and moving quickly I guess. They hurt like that before and would likely again. I was exhausted. I would like to take a hot shower and sleep for a bit, but now since we had something, I had to run with it. I'd called ahead. Eddie Martin was just about to leave, but he stayed and waited for me.

I stopped in the office for a moment and took a shot of whiskey I kept for medicinal purposes, four aspirins, and grabbed coffee. I put a second shot of whiskey in the coffee and went to go see Eddie.

When I was sitting with Eddie Martin, his eyes lit up when I told him what I wanted. I asked if he could do it. More importantly, I asked if he could do it without leaving a trace.

He smiled. "You want me to do background checks and hack the computers of the people on this list?"

"Yes."

He smiled again. "What are we looking for?"

I exhaled. "Child pornography and any other illegalities."

He winced. "Do you know if the company owns land?"

"Not yet. I figured I'd leave that to you. I don't know if the company is a legit venture, either."

"Done," he said.

"Fee?" I asked

"Still working that case where your friend was killed?"

"Yes."

"Same," he said. "Expenses only. I'll tell you after." He was looking at the photo of his wife and kids sitting on his desk.

"Thanks, pal."

"Anytime," he replied. "So we're going after genuine bad guys?"

"Yes," I said. "Almost certainly."

"As you know, I don't leave a trail, but you should make doubly sure since the police will eventually be involved."

"Yes."

"Don't spend any time worrying about that," he said flatly, but not caustically.

I sat in my car and looked at my phone. There were some text messages from Mickey. "Rattled another cage, boss. Pissed off another one. This one is scared shitless."

I texted him back and reminded him to be careful. I debated calling Gains. That's a weak link. Sanders, for sure. A lot of time and effort would be saved, depending on what Eddie Martin found. Odds are most of them had computers, and odds are most of them would have items of interest on them. I also realized I had Siciliano.

Crazy Eddie could surely scare people, and he might do it. He might also just kill anyone involved and not care about the rest. I think I would wait a bit, let Mickey stir things up, and give Eddie Martin a chance to work his magic.

Since Tempesta saw the altercation, it might start Eddie to wondering, Tempesta too, for that matter. We were close and I knew things would come together. I called Bobby Bianchi and asked if he could get a message to them for me.

"Sure, if it keeps you from going and busting Tempesta's balls, I'd be happy too."

That brought a grin. "You didn't worry so much when we were kids."

"Don't give me that shit," he said. "I held you when you were a baby."

"I was cute then, huh?"

He laughed. "No points for that, *every* kid is cute. What's the message?"

"Tell them I believe we're close to breaking this open. I'd like them to pull back. If it doesn't work ..."

"If it doesn't work?"

"I'll give them everything I found out so far."

"Okay, done." We hung up.

I looked out the window. I asked myself if I would give them what I knew, and knew the answer. I saw Vicky's face. I goddamned well would.

It was dark when I got home. I went inside to the freezer, took out a cold pack, and headed for the couch. I kicked my shoes off and tossed my jacket across the room. It missed the chair I was aiming for. I took off the gun and belt, left them on the coffee table, and finally got my shirt off, which added new dimensions of pain. I lay down on the couch, placed the cold pace on my face, and listened to the news. Sullivan was kind enough to give me the bruise on my chin and the cut under my eye on the same side. I fell asleep then woke up about a half hour later. I heard the front door opening and Mandy's voice call out. The cold pack was warm.

"Hey, babe," I called out.

The cable box read six forty five. I felt my face as she walked in. It was sore but not bad. I stood to greet her and smiled. I was sore as hell. A cacophony of sounds emanating from various joints greeted me. I remember when snap, crackle, and pop, was the sound my cereal made, and not what I heard when I got up.

She immediately walked over to me. "Oh, honey."

"It's okay, no big deal. I don't even feel it."

"You have a black eye."

I looked in the mirror on the other wall and saw she was right, but it wasn't that bad. She dropped her bag on the living room table then reached out to gently touch my face. I smiled at her.

"I've looked, had, and felt much worse, babe."

"Can I hug you?"

"Four out of five physicians and this investigator would highly recommend it," I said.

We held each other, and I didn't mind the resulting discomfort. She let go of me and kissed me softly.

"Either we order food or I make you something."

I smiled. "Order, I'm going to take a hot shower. Maybe an Irish coffee first, and some aspirin."

"Okay, how about the Lunch Box?"

The Lunch Box was a small restaurant near me. They offered good food, and got their name from a collection of lunch boxes we used to have as kids. I took a shot of Irish whiskey I kept in the cupboard, made a cup of coffee, and washed down four aspirins with it.

A few minutes later, I finished a second Irish coffee and stood under the hot shower. There was a bruise on my chin. Aside from the little cut, it was puffy under my eye but not serious. I put on my standard I'm-not-leaving-the-house clothes, sweats, t-shirt, and Chinese slippers. I went downstairs and downed another shot of whiskey, sans the coffee this time. I grabbed Mandy when she walked by, and pulled her to me, planted a kiss on her lips, and reassured her I was fine.

The food came later. I ate a cheesesteak Panini, sweet potato fries, a salad with dried cranberries, good greens, goat cheese, and finally, for the perpetual man-child, a large chocolate malt, with real malt powder. We ate at the dining room table. She ate something called The After School Special, a grilled cheese, tomato, and salad. She declined a portion of my malt, which, if possible, endeared her to me even more. We sat at the table a while, ate and talked. I felt a renewed burst of energy from the food, her company, and a pleasant buzz from the whiskey. After a long conversation, we adjourned to the living room. I got the other cold pack out of the freezer and we sat next to each other on the couch. I offered her the remote, and she asked me to pick something.

The whiskey at the office and at home took effect, and I felt drowsy. The pain subsided a bit. I wasn't missing any teeth. I was sitting next to a beautiful woman, and spiders didn't have the ability to fly, all good.

"I already love you as much as I can," I told her. "You didn't touch my ice cream, and you're giving me the remote." She giggled and rested her head on my shoulder.

I picked out a show on the Discovery Channel hosted by Stephen Hawking. As interesting as Hawking was, I felt myself falling asleep. The tired was winning. I rested my head on her lap and she brushed my hair back. I fell asleep holding the cold pack against my face, head in her lap. I woke up an hour later, still tired. We went upstairs and I slept. I woke up about two and saw she was up, watching me.

"Hey," I said.

"Hey back."

"You okay?"

"Yeah," she said. "Just making sure you're okay."

"Define okay," I said.

"No," she said, laughing. "You tell me what's okay for you."

"Well, I think being we're both up, perhaps we should consider,"

She laughed again. "You're just fine."

"Long as you're here, I am," I said. She ran her fingers gently across my chin and under my eye. She suddenly looked very sad.

"Honey, I got tagged with a couple of punches. No big thing. There are things much more painful, like watching the news and always voting for the lesser of two evils."

"It doesn't hurt?"

"A little, it's no big thing. It's a hazard of what I do, like carpal tunnel for typists."

"Computers don't usually have the potential to kill you." I knew she said that a little harsher than intended. "I didn't ..."

"It's okay," I said. "It's my chosen profession, and there are hazards. In general there's risk, but it's not like I'm overseas in a hostile country."

"I know, but I don't want anything to happen to you."

"It would be a lot tougher if I was a cop, hun."

"I'm not so sure."

"This isn't the typical case, baby," I said, then paused. "I'm motivated by profit in my profession."

"I don't know about that." She smiled. "You do try to help people and you care about people."

I reflected about that before I responded. "There was a time, Mandy, some time back, when the economy tanked. Jeff and I were doing a case update at the time, and a lot of people owed us money. People would come to us for help, and a lot of them didn't have much money, but we'd end up working on it anyway. We have people that work for us, as well as ourselves to support. We had thirty active cases when we did that particular case update. Nine of them were pro bono. I still do it on occasion, but there has to be a limit. As Jeff pointed out, if we ended up with our homes foreclosed, or if we had to fire people because we couldn't pay them, we're not doing anyone any good."

"It must be hard for you."

"It was, not as much now."

"You're very protective, you hate bullies."

"Yes and yes."

"You also like to test yourself."

"You paid attention in your psych classes," I said, with a smile.

She smiled back. "I did."

"It goes with the territory. I want most of all to get good results, but Holmes needed Moriarty."

"And you?"

"I do like to test myself. When I was younger, I was hoping I did meet a Moriarty. Now I'd be happy if I just coasted."

"My ex doesn't fit that category?"

"No, he's dangerous and unpredictable, but so far, nothing to indicate he would rise to that level of formidability."

"He sent three men to hurt you today."

"He sent amateurs."

"Amateurs doesn't mean they can't kill you."

"No, it doesn't. There is risk."

"Honey, I want more than anything to have a life with you. I didn't even know I wanted that until recently. You're like no one I ever met, but I can't live my life running from people like that or letting them do what they want. I can't let him have his goons follow you, I can't let someone like that tell me, "do what I say or I'll hurt you." I have to respect myself, and I want to earn your respect."

She nodded and brushed my hair back. I felt myself getting sleepy again. "I'm sorry. I didn't ask about Shane. Is he okay?" I asked then fell back onto the mattress.

"Yes, he's good."

"Good," I said, and slept again until morning.

When I got up, I took a long shower, alternating hot and cold water. The cut and swelling under my eyes was still noticeable but less prominent. I didn't shave, and that helped hide the bruise on the chin. I heard Mandy downstairs, and the sounds and smells of breakfast. It hit me how much I liked hearing the sounds of her downstairs.

I put on jeans and a decent short-sleeved shirt. It was less formal and comfortable, but a-sports-jacket-can-dress-me-up-if-I-need look.

"Smells wonderful."

She was wearing a light dress, covered with an apron I think I used only once. She made bacon and French toast and sliced up a few apples, dredged them in flour with cinnamon and sugar, and fried those in bacon fat. She made scrambled eggs as well.

The table was set. There was coffee and juice. Her pocketbook hung over the chair and her phone was charging on the counter. Her eyes had a smile of their own and she looked happy.

"There's nothing in this house that belongs here as much as you do."

"That's one of the nicest things anyone has ever said to me," she said. She smiled so bright, I felt the urge to reach for my sunglasses. "Sit, please."

"Yes, ma'am."

She served our food. My plate was far more filled than hers. She put the cream out for the coffee and maple syrup from the fridge she apparently warmed.

"I have an idea," I said.

She laughed. "No, there are things we have to do."

"Oh well, I wasn't thinking of that, but we should revisit that idea," I said.

She laughed again. “Tell me the idea, sweetheart.”

“You should move in here, or we should at least think about it. I know you have to consider Shane. There’s no rush if you don’t think now is a good time.”

“What if you get tired of me?”

“That’s like asking, what if I get tired of bacon.”

She laughed again. “If you had it every day, you would.”

“Then, it’s like asking if I could get tired of breathing. I want to see you when I wake up.”

“I’d like that very much.”

“I may have to soundproof the walls to stifle your cries of ecstasy.”

She threw a potholder at me. “Jerk,” we both said.

“Can I ask you something?”

“Sure,” I said.

“What happens if Mark keeps this up?”

I considered that. “It’s coming to a head. He may try to up the game, make it more serious. He may also very soon have too many other things to worry about.”

“I hope so,” she said. “When I told him I didn’t want to see him anymore he accepted it, but the way he looked at me, it was...”

I waited.

“Once a long time ago when we were all out after work, somebody threatened you at the office. It happened that afternoon. Some guy came in and said all these things he was going to do, remember?”

“Yeah,” I said. I thought I knew, but truthfully, it happened a few times.

“You told us not to worry. People who would really do you harm wouldn't make threats like that. They just wouldn't do it.”

"I remember." Actually, that happened enough times. I thought I remembered.

"He didn't say anything. He did say it was fine with him but I knew I wasn't getting rid of him, just by how he looked at me. It didn't matter how much time went by or what he said he would do."

I was quiet while I thought about that a while. I wouldn't let him hurt her. I thought he'd end up doing time. If he didn't, and I still thought he was a threat, I'd kill him if I had to. I wouldn't let him hurt Mandy or Shane. I saw in his eyes what she was talking about the day in Adobe. If he stood between Mandy and I he was in trouble. If he was a danger to her, he was dead.

"We can't live in fear of that," I said. "When it's time we'll deal with it. The way these things usually go, and the way this looks like it will go, it may just go away."

"How?" she asked.

"When the hammer drops, he won't likely make bail. He'll probably be facing heavy time. Regardless, it'll be okay."

She nodded. Most of the time when people were afraid of someone, it wasn't with good reason. I lost count of the number of women, for example, who told me how dangerous their boyfriends were. When I started out years ago serving orders of protection, dozens of times I heard, "Be careful. He's crazy," only to have them slink away with the papers nice, as could be.

Most of the time, the abusive boyfriend was a coward, and the only person he could push around was his girlfriend. *Most* of the time. Every once in a while, there was an exception to the rule. I thought about my run in with Stanton at Adobe. She was right, there was something there. An old friend, Marc MacYoung, has a saying, "contempt will kill you," meaning, don't underestimate your opponent's skill because you despise them. Just because someone's a lowlife doesn't mean they're incapable of violence, further, they might be very good at it.

"We'll be okay," I said.

I decided last night to take the list of names, head to the county clerk's office, and get copies of the deeds of the properties Promised Land owned. I realized I could probably do that online. After breakfast, Mandy went to the office, and I fired up the laptop.

I had all the info I needed in less than an hour. I took the file, spread the contents over the dining room table and reviewed everything.

I made a carafe from the Keurig and worked halfway through. The key players were Stanton, Sanders, Gains, and Vicky's father, aka, the shit in human skin. Minor players, such as the radical and useless Freida Link-Johnson, I hoped were collateral damage. My money was on Gains as the weak link. The others had too much to lose. Gains did too, but his involvement likely didn't include the murders.

It hit me again. I didn't have to do anything but tell Crazy Eddie about all the people involved. It was pretty tempting. Before the thought fully formed, I knew I wouldn't, but it was a nice thought. I wasn't willing to be a party to murder. Not yet.

Although I dismissed the thought of giving the info to Eddie Siciliano, it occurred to me he could help. More specifically, Anthony Tempesta. I grabbed a short cigar from the humidor and went out back with coffee. It was a one-cigar problem, and didn't take much thought.

I finished the cigar and the coffee then went in and called Bobby Bianchi. Several factors bothered the hell out of me, my friend murdered heading the list. I believed she knew something bad was going on with her kids. Mariano said predators sometimes moved in packs. There were a lot of people involved in this. It could take weeks or months, and we needed to turn one of them. Mariano wouldn't likely approve of my idea to pressure one of them, namely Gains. He turned ghost white when he found out Eddie Siciliano's brother was killed. Tom told me how Vicky's kids acted around their father. Mandy told me about Stanton watching her kid and getting aroused.

This was actually all pretty thin. I didn't doubt it could be proven, but there was also a chance some of them could get away. I wanted this done. It occurred to me Vicky's kids were likely living in a place making a prisoner of war camp look like Disneyland.

I got Bobby on the phone and asked him if he could arrange a meeting today with Crazy Eddie. I assured him I knew what I was doing. When we hung up, I convinced myself the same thing.

We were at a small, quiet neighborhood bar in Bensonhurst. No great deductive power that Eddie owned it. Tempesta was at the bar with a few other guys. Tempesta acknowledged Bobby and nodded to me. I nodded back. A goddamned chill ran down my spine. Eddie sat at a table in the back. He was wearing a custom-made suit, and his nails were manicured. His hair and dress indicated he took pride in his appearance. He smiled and stood. We shook hands. He gestured to the chairs.

"Something to drink? Coffee? There's a small selection of good food here, and we have biscotti from the bakery next door."

I asked for coffee, as did Bobby. Eddie motioned for the bartender, who came, left, and then returned with three American coffees, a plate of biscotti, cream sugar, and three small glasses of lemoncello. I reminded myself of a slight variation of circumstances, and my host would be dropping me in a meat grinder.

"Anthony said you handled yourself very well yesterday. I don't see anything but a few small bruises."

I smiled. "I'm sore as hell, but I was lucky," I said.

Bobby looked at me with raised eyebrows.

"Tell you on the ride home, pal," I said.

"Three people, even not at the same time, is nothing to sneer at," Siciliano said. "At my age, I would've just killed them."

There are a lot of people walking around now that talk the way Eddie just did, but few of them actually meant it. He said it very pleasantly. He was speaking the truth, and he could do it. Normal people would likely not be able to make the distinction. I wondered if it should bother me that I could.

"Two of them were slugs," I said.

"Still, nothing to sneer at," Eddie said. "The last was not."

"No, that he wasn't, but I'm a little more experienced than him."

Eddie's eyebrows lifted. "You don't hold a grudge?"

"I hit him last week on the sly to make a point to his boss. He had the balls to come back and try again. That's not easy. He also could have rushed me when the other two did, but didn't."

"Be careful, Jonathan. You're a hard man but you have rules. When you're up against people that have none, it's a decided disadvantage."

I bowed my head in respect. He was right, and I thought he meant that for my benefit.

"Thanks, Eddie. I'll bear that in mind."

"So tell me," Siciliano said. "What's on your mind?"

"Eddie, I believe I can wrap everything up and bring this to a head but I need your help. Bobby told me I could speak plainly. I need your word, if you're willing to do it, it'll be confined to what we agree on until we know who's who. I don't care what happens after that. I've earned the trust of good people and don't wish to betray that."

He considered for a moment. "You have my word."

I laid all the cards on the table. He listened with interest and was focused. He didn't stop me to ask questions until I finished. He asked the questions, and I answered as best I could.

"You believe the lawyer, Gains, would break?"

"I do."

He nodded. "Your judgment seems good."

"It is, Eddie," Bobby said.

Siciliano nodded again.

"Anthony is very loyal and also a good advisor. I'll share something with you that I trust will never leave this table under any circumstances, but I'll tell Anthony I told you."

We both nodded.

"Anthony's younger brother was violated by an uncle and never recovered. He died of an overdose when he was just seventeen."

My eyes drifted over to Tempesta. His eyes seemed to reflect some of the lowlight in the bar.

"They found the uncle beaten to death with a hammer," Eddie said, "but no one was ever charged. Anthony was about fifteen when that happened. He never speaks of it, but still visits his brother's grave every Sunday."

We were quiet for a while. I sipped the coffee, which was excellent, and ate a few of the biscotti. My jaw hurt, courtesy of Sullivan. Eddie gazed at Tempesta.

"When he fought, he looked like Jerry Quarry, only smoother and quicker. Despite his grace, he hit like a sledgehammer. He's the most loyal of all those around me." Eddie spoke to all of us, yet no one at the same time. He won't mind helping, and he'll stay within the parameters you need.

Eddie stood, and we stood as well. "I imagine you'll hear from Mr. Gains shortly, Jonathan."

"Thank you, Eddie," I said, as I shook his hand. He kissed Bobby on the cheek and we left. Tempesta nodded to us as we left. Bobby said, "Goodbye," and I bowed my head slightly. How adept we are, as a race, at creating our own monsters.

In the car on the way back over the bridge, Mariano called me. He wanted me to meet up with him. Sullivan made bail and wanted to see me.

That's not as easy as it sounds. In New York, there's an automatic order of protection issued by the court to keep the accused away from the witnesses. I told him I'd meet with him and testify if it ever came up. I agreed, then went to meet him willingly.

"His mom bailed him out. After Stanton heard what happened, he posted bail for Bertone. The thug ended up with a few open warrants and missed some court dates, but Stanton left Sullivan hanging. Teaching him a lesson, I guess."

"How did he get to you?" I asked.

"Through one of the guys at the precinct, the Sullivans are a good family. On the whole."

I chuckled. "Pick a place that's private. Tell me when, and I'll meet you there."

25

We met off Arthur Kill Rd. near the Outerbridge. A lot of people thought it was called the Outerbridge because it was the southernmost bridge on the island, and therefore, the southernmost bridge in New York. It was actually named after Eugenius H. Outerbridge, the first chairman of the Port Authority of New York and New Jersey. I'm sometimes like Cliff Claven from *Cheers* except I'm right, better looking, and throw a great left hook.

There was an hour or so of light left in the sky. We were on a road leading to an Exxon station where they took fuel off boats and barges. An outdoor gun range I practiced at a few times wasn't far away. There was the occasional report of a pistol in the background. The air outside was cool but pleasant. I saw two cars when I pulled down the road - Mariano, in a black Chevy Suburban, and two people in a Blue Hyundai four by four.

I looked at my text messages before I got out. Mandy was suggesting supper at her parent's house. I told her I could be there in two hours, barring the case broken open. It was actually less than ten minutes away.

"You don't look too bad," Mariano said, reaching for my hand. "Good to see you."

"Chief, good to see you, and good to be seen. We have to talk later about today when we're alone."

"Done."

Tommy got out of the passenger side. He seemed to have difficulty getting out of the Santa Fe, and walked stiff-legged. I was happy he was hurt, because I sure as hell was. His right arm was in a sling and he had a few bruises. A short slim woman, whom he dwarfed, got out of the driver's side. She was too young to be his mother. She was pretty and in good shape, petite. There was a bit of a resemblance. I had my hands clasped in front of me. Tommy looked at the ground, and the woman met my eyes. She looked at Mariano first. I saw mutual respect.

"Chief, many thanks. My dumbass brother wants to talk with you guys." She turned to me, extended her arm, gave me a firm handshake, and looked me in the eye. " I'm Maureen Sullivan. I was NYPD. I'm retired now. I know you lost someone, Mr. Creed. I'm sorry."

"Jimmy," I said.

She nodded.

"Thank you."

"My brother is a good person who made some mistakes."

"Funny you should mention that, Maureen. Jimmy said the same thing."

Sullivan looked up at me. I faced him and looked at him a bit. Hard read.

"We all make mistakes," I said.

"My sister says you aren't pressing charges against me." His voice was a little hoarse.

"Tommy, you got mixed up with the wrong people but came back in an honorable way. You hit like a goddamned truck. First time, I caught you unaware. Next time, it just so happens I've been doing this dance a little longer. Plenty of people could do that to me. You're young and you can grow. That arm will heal. Anyone that trained hard enough to become as good as you are has drive. You don't have a record, and can move on from this. You came back a second time and that takes balls. Most people wouldn't." I laid it on a bit thick but it didn't hurt. He might talk easier if he felt better.

Sullivan looked me in the eye and nodded. He looked at his sister, then back at me. He opened his mouth to speak, then stopped.

"I … I was thinking I needed to talk to someone before you came into Adobe's. They told me I just was like back up. I didn't sign on for this. I just needed the money. I can't fight anymore, at least not for a while. I didn't know …"

His sister put her arm around him and whispered, "Do what's right. It'll be okay."

Tears filled his eyes. If you told me yesterday this was going to happen, I'd have said you were out of your mind.

"I drove them there," he said. "They killed Luca and that girl. I didn't know they were going to kill anyone, especially not a woman. They just wanted to scare Luca."

I looked down and breathed in deep, and then took a few more breaths. Tears almost welled up, but didn't. Almost doesn't count.

"And they got pictures of kids, little babies doing things," he stammered. I looked away to the water, but still felt every word.

"Who is *they*, Tommy?" Mariano asked in a gentle, fatherly type of voice. "Tell me who killed Luca and the girl."

"It was Stanton and Bertone. Bertone pulled the trigger."

I swallowed and took a deep breath again. The sun was now gone, and the western sky held hints of red and gold, a whisper of summer coming. A tug's horn bellowed off in the Kill. Poor Vicky. Her boys, God knows what else. I wished I wasn't there with the Chief or Maureen. I wished I was on the phone with Tempesta. I wished I was offering to go with him.

"Why did they kill them, Tommy?" Mariano asked.

"Luca was bitching about the money. Everything he made he spent like water. He was threatening to go to his brother. He cursed Stanton out, called him a baby raper in front of a lot of people."

"And Vicky?" I asked.

"She would have been a witness and Mark figured Sanders would owe him. Stanton is ice cold. He gets off on hurting kids."

We were quiet for a bit.

"I was afraid they might try to hurt my mom or my nieces or nephews," Sullivan continued.

"Did they threaten you with that, Tommy?" I asked.

"No, but they told me what they did to other people who ratted."

"And the stuff about the kids?" Mariano asked. "How many people were involved in that?"

"Sick, they all get off on it. Except that one lawyer, he never stayed for it. And me."

"My friend, Vicky, the dead girl, did her father have anything to do with it?"

"With the stuff about the kids, yes. I don't think anyone else but me and Gains know about the murders. Stanton knows the Brooklyn guys would kill him. Luca was threatening to go to his brother. He spent his money on drugs and needed more. All the people are in on the land deal. Gains knows about the murders but can't talk about them even if he wanted. Stanton gave him the same message he gave me. If you fuck him over, he'll kill you and your family."

I wished I had broken Bertone's neck. I'd have leisurely let him languish in a nursing home until I felt like going in one night with a pillow.

I sucked in a deep breath and silently counted five in hold three, five out. I needed to keep clear. I felt the anger boiling inside but needed to keep the lid on the pot. I needed to see this through for Vicky and for her kids.

Things were a bit fuzzy for a while. Mariano kept talking. I gathered, despite the fact it sounded to me as though they were underwater, Maureen was taking Tommy to the precinct at Mariano's direction. Then things cleared a little.

"I don't care if he's off. Call him and get him in now. I want him there before I get there." I was betting it was the detective with the scowl on his face, from a hundred years ago.

I recovered. "Anything else we need to know, Tommy?" I asked hoarsely.

He met my eyes. "Yeah, he fucking hates you. He speaks about you taking his woman. Those two people that were there the day you came into Adobe's?"

"What about them?" Mariano asked.

Still looking at me, Sullivan continued. "They were legit, potential real estate investors. He never saw them again. He said it was your fault. He knows about you. He's had people come in and talk about you. He also knows you've been talking with Mr. Siciliano." Sullivan paused. "He's evil, there's no other word," he continued, "he's not much to beat in a fight, but if he loses he'll come back and kill you. I saw him beat a guy senseless. We had to pull him off the guy before he killed him."

"Why?" I asked.

"The guy asked him, Mark, why do you put so much effort into trying to make people think you're a good guy?" Sullivan looked at me. "He kept hitting him with a chair, screaming, 'I *am* a fucking good guy!' It was the first time I saw him lose it. He fucking hates you, man," Sullivan said to me. "When you took us out at Adobe he didn't say a word. He kept his mouth shut but we knew he was thinking about you."

I turned to Mariano and opened my mouth. "If you say, 'To know me is to love me,' I'm hitting you myself," he said. I smiled.

His sister took Sullivan to the precinct; Mariano would follow. I briefed him on the day's activities. Sullivan also confirmed the Goon was a recent Stanton hire.

24

Dinner with Mandy's parents felt strained at first. I realized this wasn't a good time, but I couldn't disappoint her. I met and liked them instantly. Her mom was a beautiful and kind woman, her father, strong and pleasant. They were both in their sixties, but looked a good deal younger.

The aromas from the kitchen reminded me of Thanksgiving, and also made me realize I hadn't spoken to my mom since this all started. I made a mental note to fix that. I really did enjoy meeting them, but I frequently wished it was a different time. I have a good poker face, but I quickly realized my mood was dark, and they sensed it.

Her mom made Beef Wellington, and it was superb. She did something with the mashed potatoes and Port Wine cheese that was as close to sex as food got.

I noticed Mandy was concerned, and she watched me closely. Many other people would have been angry with me for withdrawing, but she was worried.

I was unexpectedly hungry and tore through dinner like knife through butter. I kept up the conversation, which was pleasant. Bill was an engineer, and Susan ran a decorating business. They also had an exceptional red wine with the dinner. I limited myself to one glass.

"I would like to thank you for asking me to your home," I said. "I apologize if I seem distant or distracted. The work I'm involved with took a bit of a turn earlier, an unexpected and serious but good turn. I'm very sorry, and please know I appreciate the opportunity to meet you. I love your daughter very much. I love her in a way I didn't think was possible for me."

They both said something akin to think nothing of it, and were both warm and genuine. Mandy sat next to me. Her hand found mine under the table.

"We know what happened, Jimmy," Bill said. "At the risk of sounding superficial, since we just met, we're both moved and very proud of what you're doing."

"We're both sorry for the loss of your friend," Susan said.

"Thank you both," I said.

Susan smiled. "I hope I'm not embarrassing my daughter, but she's been talking about you for months."

"I'm betting she told you what a lousy boss I am."

They all laughed. "No," Bill said. "I noticed several times, when she needed to be there for our grandson, you let her leave."

"It's hard these days, but I try to make it easier. I find people with less worries are more productive. She's a very conscientious worker. Most of my clients prefer her to me or my partner."

The rest of the night went well. They were happy when we told them we planned to marry. We went home a little after eleven.

I woke to my cell phone ringing at one minute to five. Mandy wasn't next to me, but her side of the bed felt warm. I answered. It was Gains, and he was babbling that he needed to see me. I asked him if he knew what time it was, but he kept babbling.

"Do yourself a favor. It sounds like you're upset so don't drive. Take a cab or an Uber to my office this morning. I'll be in at nine."

"I'm upset. I was up all night. Please, can't you make it any earlier?"

"I have an appointment first I can't break."

He agreed. I got up and dressed in my house attire - sweats and an old t-shirt. I didn't hear the normal kitchen sounds of Mandy in the house, although heard noise in the basement, music on low. The Keurig was on. I drank my customary glass of water with lemon juice and put a pod in the machine.

After I made the coffee, I took it downstairs. I heard the sounds of weight being moved. I was quiet since she was mid set. I was enormously impressed she was doing cleans, followed by a front squat.

"Wow!" I said, when she was done.

She smiled. "I figured you wouldn't mind."

"You figured right, Miss."

"I have one more set."

"Is me watching you a disturbance?" I asked.

She smiled. "No."

"It's getting late," I said. "If you wanted to kill two birds with one stone, we could try cardio whilst in the shower."

"Go make sure there's enough hot water."

I ran up the stairs.

A few hours later, I was in considerably different surroundings, in my office with Gains. He was minus the ape this time.

"You offered me your help."

"In a manner of speaking," I said. "If memory serves, you're here to threaten me."

Gains blanched again. He's one guy who would never need a mood ring.

"But don't worry counselor, I keep my word." I inhaled and let it out slowly. "The floor is yours."

"Someone came to see me, and I was told I had to come forward."

"Were you told to lie?"

"No, no, nothing like that. I was just told to come forward. I don't have a choice."

"If you're not going to lie, I wouldn't mention you were urged to come forward. I wouldn't say that to another soul if I were you. *Ever.*"

"Okay."

"As a matter of fact, I'd imagine mentioning it might bring about what you're most afraid of at this moment."

"You'll help me?"

"What do you want?"

"I need to make a deal. I need to keep my law license."

"I can't make that kind of deal for you, Gains. I'm a p.i. small p, small i. You overestimate me."

"I know you know people. And Chief Mariano carries a lot of weight."

"He does."

"I'll do what I can," I said. "I can't imagine you'll do jail time, but I don't know about the rest. You should consider a lawyer. This could get pretty involved. It's not a good idea to represent yourself. Find someone good who doesn't piss off the D.A., for marketing purposes."

"I ... I can't even think. Any suggestions?"

"Joe Mure, Pat Brackley, maybe both."

Gains waited downstairs while I sat in Mariano's office. We both had coffee. He took the donuts and pastries I brought from Renato's bakery on Forest Ave., and put them in the break room after we chose the ones we wanted. I knew a few of the guys moving about. There were a few "hellos" to me and a lot of "hey, Chiefs." Bob Doyle was on the speakerphone.

I explained to Mariano in more detail, because I owed him, and because he deserved to hear that Tempeta paid Gains a visit. He didn't care what made Gains come forward, as long as he wasn't lying. As far as I knew, only Gains, myself, Crazy Eddie, and Tempesta, knew the real reason why Gains came forward. To the best of my knowledge, no one ever spoke of it again. Mariano and I explained to Doyle everything that happened up until now.

"So we have a group of people, who on the outside appear to be good citizens, involved in a shady land deal, breaking all kinds of laws, some of them involved in a child porn ring, and some of them committed murder?"

"Yes."

"What do you need, Chief?"

"As far as Gains ... no jail time?" Mariano looked at me, and I nodded.

"Maybe in a few years, if he reapplies for his license to practice law, and sends a nice letter to the bar," I added.

"That will depend on what we find out about his full role," Doyle answered. "Model behavior and a bad decision is one thing, kiddie porn is another."

"That actually suits me fine," I said. Sullivan said Gains knew but didn't participate.

"Anything else?" Doyle asked.

"Bob, Sullivan came to us, the only person that should have a gripe with him is me, and I don't," I said. "He deserves a second chance, not a record."

"Chief?"

"After speaking with his sister and interacting with him, I agree."

I mouthed the word, "Softy." He smirked.

"You know, Jimmy boy, you're wasting your talents working for the bad guys."

I chuckled. "I'll take that as a compliment, Bob. Vicky was important to me and I should have been there for her. I need to know her kids are okay. Her mom has no idea what her husband's into, so don't hold that against her."

"I won't, Jimmy," Doyle said, "but a lot of the time ... you know how it is, the family circles the wagons."

"I give you my word, that's not the case this time. If I have any indication that'll change, you also have my word. You'll know about it."

"We have room at my house," Mariano said.

Doyle was silent when Mariano said that. I looked at Mariano and bowed my head. Doyle seemed at a loss, but then said that was very kind of him. I didn't know for sure what the procedure was, but if both Mariano and Doyle wanted the kids to be with Mariano temporarily, that's where they'd be.

"Tell their grandmother she's welcome to come whenever she wants to see them."

"I will," I said. "We need to get those kids out of there now."

"Before supper. With what we have from Sullivan and Gains about the murders, and the kids, Stanton, Sanders, and Bertone, go today. The others will come later, and a lot of them will contact us and try to cut a deal. There'll be a lot of trials here, no deals for the child porn.

"So, Bob, after the murders, the priority is the human refuse exploiting the kids?"

"Both are priorities, *major* priorities. I ran in part on kids and meant it." Doyle said.

That's why I voted for you," Mariano said. "The worst things I've seen happened to children."

"Bob, don't forget there was highly improper collusion between the law guardian and Sanders," I said. "I think Gains can shed light on that, too."

"I'm on that, Jimmy," Doyle said. "You're not to blame for what happened to your friend. She's looking down on you, and thanking you for saving her children."

"What he said," Mariano added.

"I hope, after this case, my psychological motivation is not the continual subject of water cooler talk."

"It ain't that interesting a subject, kid," Mariano said with a smirk. Doyle and I laughed.

I hoped what they said was true, but I still felt the guilt and pain of her loss. Sullivan was at the D.A.'s office, and I went downstairs to get Gains. In that time, he had taken my advice and gotten both Mure and Brackley. We exchanged short greetings.

Gains knew about the murders, but found out only recently. Both Berton and Stanton talked to him about it, so there was an attorney client issue. He swore he knew nothing about the children, and said it would be okay for the cops to take his computer. He reiterated what Tommy said about Stanton hating me. He was red in his face and sweated profusely. Tommy seemed genuine. Gains was sad because he was caught. He was desperate. His life was in danger and the Grim Reaper visited him. I felt no pity for him, but I kept my word.

I texted Mandy at some point, told her to reach out to Jen Hayes, and it was urgent I reach her as soon as I finished here. I preferred we met in person. The text came back fifteen minutes later. She would be at my office until I got there. I asked Mariano if he needed anything else from me. He said, "No." I told him I'd call him as soon as I met with my client. He nodded. Gains mumbled a thank you. Brackley clapped me on the back, and Mure winked at me. Mariano stood and shook my hand. I stopped at the door and looked at him.

"The kids?" I asked, again.

"As soon as possible," Mariano confirmed.

I spoke to Vicky on the drive back to my office. I told her, although I let her down, I would make sure her kids would be okay. I didn't hear an answer.

Jen Hayes was sitting in my office with Mandy. Before I went, I spent a couple of minutes with Eddie Martin. He had a great deal of info suggesting all kinds of illegalities. I told him to stop where he was, but to give me whatever he had to back up by legit sources. When I asked if that would be difficult, he snickered. I asked him how long. An hour was the answer.

I texted Mariano, telling him I would have an early Christmas present for him, and it would help with the investigation. I also asked him to keep me apprised of their progress, especially what was going to happen with Stanton.

Mandy asked me if I needed coffee. I shook my head. Both she and Jen had a cup. For the first time since I remembered, I didn't want coffee. I had no idea what I would tell Jen. Well, I knew what, I didn't know how. I told the ladies I needed a minute. I texted Mickey to be at the office in an hour, and take the manila envelope from Eddie to Mariano. I got the reply, "Done, boss," then sat and faced them.

"Jen, there's been significant progress, I know quite a bit. There's going to be a wave of arrests in the coming days." I inhaled. "Some of this will be hard to hear."

"I'm expecting bad news, Jim. The worst."

"Okay, I need to ask you some questions and need clear answers, so I can watch out for your interests."

"My only interest is making sure my daughter's killer is caught."

"I think you have another," I said.

She looked at me and waited.

"Your grandchildren."

That got her attention. "What's wrong?"

"Nothing at the moment," I lied. "It's being taken care of." Well, *that* was the truth. "Questions first. Does your husband have a separate computer?"

"Yes, in his office, at home."

"Do you ever use it? Is there another one you both have access to?"

"No, he has his, I have mine, but I usually use my phone."

"This is going to be very hard to hear, and harder for me to ask. I know the answer, Jen, but I need to ask."

Mandy sat holding Jen's hand, and watching me carefully. I spoke as gently as I could. Jen squeezed Mandy's hand but kept her eyes on me.

"Go ahead, ask."

"Is there a possibility there's anything inappropriate on your computer?"

"Such as?"

"Child pornography."

"What?" She asked. " Did I hear you right?"

"Yeah. I'll explain, but I need to know the answer."

"For God's sake, no." Her voice trembled slightly.

"Okay. I know this is hard. I'll answer all your questions, but you have to be absolutely sure."

"None that I know of," she said, and she knew why I asked.

"Did your husband ever use your computer, even for a minute?"

"Not that I can remember."

"There's a group of people your husband is involved with. In addition to illegal business deals for land and development, such as fake auctions, illegal loans, and a host of other things, most of them procured and circulated child pornography, some produced it. We believe your grandchildren were used to make some of it." I looked at Mandy then nodded in anticipation of the question she wanted to ask.

"Stanton and a man who works for him named Joseph Bertone killed your daughter."

She was quiet for a long time, holding Mandy's hand, and looking at the small bar in my office. Jen knew she made a mistake by not helping her daughter, and finding out for herself what was wrong. She just found out her husband, her refined, controlling, icy mate, was into kiddie porn, and he was working with the people who killed her daughter.

After a long time, she looked up and opened her mouth, started to say "what," then closed her mouth. Her face was blank. She started to say something again, but the words didn't make it out.

"You need to stay strong. When the garbage that was your son-in-law is arrested, the kids will be taken care of, but then they'll need you. Your husband living in your house may complicate things if you want to file for custody."

"It's so much to take in," Jen said.

"Take a minute."

"Where are my grandsons going to be?" she asked.

"Actually, there's already a volunteer to take them in, he and his wife have two kids of their own. They'll be removed tonight."

It was a quarter to one. Mariano and Doyle told me they were going to get the warrants for what they could, and Sanders would be the first to go.

Gains was booked and released, Sullivan was never charged. By the time night arrived, as many of the warrants as possible were issued. Sanders was taken in, his home was searched, and computers seized. Stanton's office was raided. Neither he nor Bertone were present. The news that night reported the searches and arrests, and there would be more arrests in the coming days. Mariano had Vicky's boys, as promised. Mariano told me I saved them a lot of time with the information I provided about the land company. Kiddie porn was rampant on both Sanders' and Stanton's computers, which necessitated involvement by the feds.

I didn't know what to do with myself that evening. Saying I was restless was like saying Everest was a bit of a climb. I didn't feel like working out, and had no appetite. While the former was something I disciplined myself to do even though at times I'd like to pass it by, nothing until now affected my appetite. Mandy came over with Shane. He did his homework on the dining room table as she made dinner. I tried to read and watch T.V., but it didn't work out. I thought about a drink, but had no idea what might happen that night. I called Chris Costigan ahead of time as promised.

The cops and the D.A. seized the computers at the Hayes house, but Father of the Year wasn't taken in yet. His attorney wouldn't be a slouch. Jen told me she would be alone with her husband. They didn't have live in help. She told me she would be able to appear normal.

We ate, and I was distracted, so barely tasted the food. Shane was planning to sleep at my house for the first time. *Our* home now. Before dinner, Mandy told me her ex was happy for her. I apologized to her and Shane, the same way I did to her parents. They both said it was okay. Shane almost beat me at chess after supper, and I had the feeling he would win soon enough, whether I was distracted or not. The kid was good.

He went to sleep while Mandy and I sat on the couch and talked. I apologized again. She held my hand and said it was okay. She handed me the remote, and I turned on the cable. *Animal House* was playing, and Mandy nestled into me. We watched T.V. for a while. At eleven o'clock on the button, my cell phone rang. It was Jen Hayes.

"Can you come here, please? My husband is unconscious. I dialed 911. They're on the way. He left what I think is a suicide note."

I arrived at the Hayes estate twelve minutes later. An ambulance sat in the driveway. I texted Mariano. He was on the way with the detectives. The paramedics were working on Michael Hayes. He wasn't breathing. They loaded him on a gurney while the cops spoke to Jen. I followed them inside.

Jen came over to me and asked if I wanted coffee. She acted as if she was in a state of shock. Mariano and the detectives arrived. Mariano stopped, said hello to us, and went into the house. I put my arm around her and we walked into her kitchen. I told her to sit at the table. I'd make it, but she said it would help if she stayed busy.

"I want you to know," she said quietly. "He got drunk. I made him write that note. Six months ago, his back was bad. He had most of the oxycodone left from then. They were thirty-milligram pills. I gave him some when he was drunk, crushed up the rest, and put it in the meatloaf I made for him. He liked his food spicy, so he didn't notice."

I didn't know what to say, so said nothing.

"When he got drunk, he told me what they would find on the computer, then kept talking. He told me what a disappointment Vicky was. He said he knew my son-in-law was taking pictures of my grandchildren. He said he wasn't sick, and he loved the kids. He was preparing them to be adults."

I nodded. She spoke softly enough so no one would overhear. I stared at the figurines in the kitchen's bay window. She stopped talking and got up to make me a coffee, after the machine warmed up.

"Jen," I asked her quietly, "why are you telling me this?"

"I need you to know I want my grandchildren. I can't make up for turning my back on my daughter, but I can love them and take care of them."

"Jen, as far as you knew, she was an addict. He misled you."

"I should have known. I should have found out for myself."

"Okay," I said. "Why did you tell me?"

"I don't know. I needed to. He wouldn't have left. I could never get custody of my grandchildren while he lived here. I made the biggest mistake of my life not giving my daughter the help she needed. I won't repeat that mistake with her children."

Mariano came into the kitchen, and Jen asked him if he wanted coffee as well. He said he would if it was no trouble. Less than a minute later, he sat across the table from us, cup of black coffee in hand.

"Mrs. Hayes, it looks as if your husband may have killed himself, or unintentionally overdosed."

"He kept talking about being sick, and what you would find on his computer. I told him he would have to leave our home. I'm going to seek custody of my grandchildren, and I didn't want him here."

Jen went on to tell Mariano her husband drank a lot, and she saw him swallow a handful of pills. Later on, when she picked up the bottle, it was empty. He was already unconscious.

"Chief Mariano, I won't lie. After finding out what he did, what he was doing, and what he did to our daughter, I'm not sorry. I won't spend time grieving for him."

"Mrs. Hayes," he said, in a lower voice, "that doesn't matter to me. I wouldn't care if you killed him yourself." I looked at my coffee. "You come over to our house tomorrow and see your grandchildren. We'll begin the process of you getting custody. They've been asking for you. I have no reservations after what Jimmy said about you, and after the way you helped us."

"Do you think I'm up to it, Jimmy?" she asked.

"I do, Jen."

25

During the next two days, there were headlines, radio and television news stories. Some of them mentioned me. Bertone and Stanton both skipped out, and the cops caught Bertone later that day. Mariano called me and told me he believed they'd have Stanton soon. The rats all started to jump ship. Bertone's lawyer immediately started talking about a deal. He'd be away for twenty years, but he'd avoid life. He gave them everything. Between Bertone and Sullivan, Stanton's world ceased to exist.

I ate dinner with Mandy and Shane at her parent's house the next night. We told Shane about the upcoming nuptials. Her ex stopped in, and we finally met. He was with his new girlfriend, and as awkward as that sounds, I liked them both. His girlfriend, Janice, a nurse, was lovely and sincere. I spent time talking with Mitch, her ex. I wanted him to know I thought Shane was a great kid and I wouldn't try to take his place. I assured him I did love Mandy and would treat her well. I watched him interact with his son, and thought him to be a decent man.

My family, especially my mother, was overjoyed, even more so when I told her grandchildren would likely be forthcoming. That weekend, I introduced her to the Creed Clan. I asked her if she wanted to choose the ring, but she left it up to me. She made a few requests though, nothing gaudy, nothing too big. A good friend of mine on Long Island owned several jewelry stores. I got Mandy's ring size from her mom then went early Saturday morning to pick it up. It had a teardrop cut, which he told me was less common these days. It was flawless and had one carat, with a platinum band. I was indeed fortunate to have a carry license in New York, considering how much I brought with me in cash, and the value of the ring.

Mandy's mom believed Mandy would prefer if I gave her the ring while we were alone. I returned at ten thirty that morning. She was showered and dressed, hair done, looking as beautiful as ever. With no planning and just a lump in my throat, I walked in, kissed her, and dropped to my knee, making it official. Tears filled her eyes, and mine felt a little moist as well. Neither of us needed to be anywhere besides my mom's that night. Shane was with his dad. We spent the afternoon in bed.

She met the clan that night, Mom, my four brothers, and their wives and children. She wasn't the least bit nervous and they loved her right away. None of my brothers passed a remark about the unlikelihood of me getting married, although privately there were a few snickers. There was no violence.

We left my mom's about ten, and stopped off at her apartment so she could pick up some clothes. I reminded her to call the building management company and say she was leaving. We got in, and she asked if I wanted something to drink. I took off my gun and put my wallet, keys, and phone on her small dining room table. I knew she'd be a while, so I turned on the television. She brought me a beer in a glass. I once told her only savages drank beer from the bottle.

She went into the bedroom, and there was a soft knock at the door. It was her neighbor, a pleasant, older woman. She was coming home, and had some of Mandy's mail that ended up in her box. She asked if she could stop by and say "hi" to Mandy. I remembered Mandy told me she was fond of this woman. I told her she would probably need a half hour, but she was welcome anytime.

"Terrific," the woman said. "I'll come by then; in the meantime I'll take my dog for his walk."

I closed and locked the door, then turned when I heard Mandy coming in to find Stanton behind her, gun in hand.

He pointed the gun at me. Mine was across the room with my wallet, phone, and keys. Fear engulfed me. I was afraid for Mandy, afraid I would never see her again. The hatred and crazy in his eyes indicated he was preparing to pop the cork. I put it in my head I was going to move on him, and it didn't matter how many times he shot me. Even if he shot me in the head, I'd get to him and rip his fucking throat out.

He'd get at least one round off, but I couldn't let it stop me. He held a Sig Sauer nine. It would go through me and leave a small hole, if it wasn't a hollow point. Fuck that. It wasn't a hollow point. It was a fast round, and a hollow point might not open. I needed a break here, but I'd get to him. I won't stop, I won't stop. I tensed. Nothing would stop me. It didn't matter what happened. If I got to him, she'd be okay. She *would* be okay. That's all that mattered.

If it was just him shooting me, I'd take the round. I had no idea what he would do after that. If I knew she'd live, I'd take the round.

"You get to watch this motherfucker die," he told her.

She was crying, but her voice was clear. "Please, I'll do whatever you want, don't hurt him."

"No, he's dead. Fuck him. Everything I've built is destroyed. Fuck both of you. I kept enough cash. By tomorrow I'll be in another country with a new name."

He held the gun with one hand at chest level. One handed, that was good. He extended it away from his body and didn't hold it in close, which was also good. He moved a little closer while he talked. I moved too, and she moved in front of me. I wasn't ready for it, but she moved fast. She stood in front of me, shielding me.

"No!" she screamed, and lunged for him.

The gun went off. I felt the burning sensation of the round tear through my right shoulder. I felt no pain at first, then it hurt like hell, but I kept moving. She lost her balance. I managed to push her to the floor and kept going. I crashed into him and the gun went off again. I moved the gun away from me and kept my momentum, although it felt awkward. I kept us moving toward the wall as fast as I could, and using my hands to push, smashed his head into the wall. He collapsed halfway before I grabbed him. The gun careened across the room. I spun him around, took his neck over my shoulder, and bridged it. I dropped all of my weight and snapped it as hard as I could. It doesn't happen like in the movies. The strength of the neck muscles and the vertebrae were stronger than people realized. It wasn't the effortless snap you see the hero execute.

He was out from me smashing his head into the wall. I twisted as I bridged his neck and put my full strength, weight, and adrenaline fueled rage into it. Scream would be the wrong word. I roared as I broke his neck and it came from deep down inside, from thousands of years ago.

Stanton hit the floor when I let go, but I didn't bother looking. The acrid smell and taste of gunpowder hung in the room. I tasted metal and felt the heat in my nose. My ears rang a bit. She was still on the floor. I went to help her up, and saw the blood on her shirt.

I knelt beside her. She was breathing. I jumped up, snatched the phone, and grabbed a sheet from the laundry basket.

I dialed 911. I spoke quickly but clearly. I gave the address, then cradled the phone to my ear with my shoulder. I saw stars, little flickers of metallic light dancing in front of my eyes, my first real physical pain. I felt blood under my shirt, and I thought back. The bullet went through. I opened her shirt. The hole was below and between her breasts.

I held the sheet over it and pressed gently. She opened her eyes. I brushed her hair back and smiled. She smiled back. Her eyes looked at my shoulder.

"An ambulance is coming, baby girl. Just lie still."

"Your shoulder ..."

"It's okay." I felt tears, but also felt numb.

"I don't want you to be hurt."

"You saved me. The bullet went through you first. The wound isn't bad."

"I thought it would hurt more," she said.

"That's how you know it's not bad."

"Shane," she said.

"I'll call your ex as soon as we get to the hospital." A red stain blossomed on the sheet, but she seemed to be breathing okay. Blood pooled on the floor around her shoulder. The bullet went in low, and exited higher.

"You're going to be fine."

"I love you. I waited my whole life for you."

"Now you're stuck with me," I whispered. Her voice weakened. "I've never loved anyone as much as I love you."

"I'm still not sleeping with Jennifer Aniston for your birthday."

"Never say never."

"Well, maybe just once."

"That's my girl."

"I'm cold, baby."

There was a cover on the couch. I reached over, yanked it off, and before I covered her, saw the red stain on the sheet had spread. I pressed a little harder and managed to cover her.

"Okay?"

She nodded, and when she coughed, blood appeared on her lips. She coughed again, and struggled to catch her breath. Her head was on my lap, and I helped her raise up, which allowed her to breathe easier. More blood was on the floor, but it didn't seem like much.

"It's okay, baby. If you fall asleep, when you wake up, I'll be in the hospital. Shane will be there, too," I said, so she wouldn't be afraid. She nodded slightly and closed her eyes.

"I love you."

"I love you," she said back.

She opened her eyes and said, "Shane."

"He'll be at the hospital when you wake up."

Some of her blood was on my hands and arms. I brushed her hair back with my left hand. She was talking to me about Shane again, and I told her she would be okay. She was repeating things. "Please don't do this!" a voice screamed in my head. I gently told her to stay with me. She was coughing, but smiled at me. I told her it would be okay, *she* would be okay. It would *all* be okay. The ambulance would be here soon. She insisted she was okay and smiled at me. The light left her eyes with the smile on her face. I moved her to the floor and tried mouth to mouth and CPR, but it didn't work. I looked at her. I didn't feel pain yet, but felt detached. I stood and looked down at her.

The bullet which passed through her and then through me, ripped a hole in the wall behind me. I turned to look at it. I had no fucking idea why. Then I heard sirens. I felt hot, the way you do when it's winter and you're wearing too many clothes inside. I kept staring at the hole until the gurgling sound forced its way in. I don't know how long it continued before I noticed it. I turned and saw Stanton was conscious. I walked over and looked down at him. I didn't need to see his head at the weird angle to know his neck was broken. I had broken it.

His eyes were wide and fixed on me. He was trying to breathe and move, but unsuccessfully. His hands moved a little. It wasn't a clean break if he could move his hands, but that could change. Despite his distress, our eyes met and radiated mutual hatred. The intensity of it connected us, and I felt it burn. I felt his hate and anger that he lost, and I bathed in it. This part would end, but he would wait for me in the anteroom of hell, and I'd be happy to oblige him when I got there. Tears streamed down my face, and the pain gave way to rage.

I roared again. I kicked him in his head as hard as I could, with every bit of energy I had left. His body lifted and slid away a few feet. The impact jarred my leg and knee. I thought I might have broken something in my foot, but didn't care. The gurgling stopped. It was a full break now. I dropped next to him, hoping there was something to finish off, but there wasn't.

26

I went back and sat with my back to the couch. The shoulder and back were still bleeding, but I didn't care. I just sat and looked at her. The cops came first. I heard them knocking on the unlocked door. I answered their questions. The ambulance came. Mariano walked in as the ambulance people went to work on Mandy. It was a lost cause. One of the cops kept trying to talk to me. Mariano came and sat next to me on the floor, and waved the cop off. A second ambulance arrived, and they took care of Stanton.

They put her on the gurney, working on her as they did. I knew she was dead. I was dead, too, part of me at least, the part that loved her, the part that counted. She was gone. Another ambulance arrived. I told Mariano I was going to get up. He helped me to the couch and I told him what happened as a detective wrote it down. He jumped out at us, fired the shot, I went after him, and we fought. I don't remember, it was a haze, but I knew what happened. I wouldn't let this pain leak. I had two things in my heart, loss and hate. The latter would keep the former at bay. I would relive this and kill this motherfucker again ... and again, but she was gone. "She can't be gone!" my mind screamed, but she was. She was gone.

She was gone.

She took a bullet for me because I didn't move fast enough, and her blood was still on me. The ambulance people cut away my shirt and bandaged the front and back of my shoulder. It wasn't bleeding too badly anymore. I couldn't raise my arm, maybe a severed tendon. The pain was almost bad enough for me to care about. She was gone. They wanted to put me on the gurney, but for some reason I resisted. I told them I walk out of here or I don't go. I have no idea why that was important.

Mariano spoke with them, and at some point, he insisted. He knew I would fight. He walked me outside, where a crowd of people and news crew were gathered. Her neighbor I met earlier was crying and trying to talk to the news people. I walked to the ambulance. Mariano kept his hand on my arm to make sure I kept my balance, then helped me into the ambulance and sat with me. I felt like my face was a plastic mask. And I felt tired.

How many times have I have heard the term broken heart before? How many times have I used it? I had no idea what it meant until now, until I sat with her and watched the light leave her eyes, and the life leave her body. A little longer than an hour ago, I was with her, felt the warmth of her skin, the smell of her perfume. For the first time in my life, I was a part of someone – her. We fit in every way. That was gone now. I mentioned Shane to Mariano again.

"I'll take care of it, Jimmy."

I wanted the rage to stay because I knew what was coming after. The rage would keep the loss at bay, but I was getting tired, and must have dropped off. Mariano had my arm, and said I almost fell. I needed to lie down and rest. He helped me on the gurney. I closed my eyes.

"She took a bullet for me," I told him.

"She did, Jimmy. She loved you. She'd want you to stick around."

The tears almost flowed when he said that. I thought they would for a second, and didn't care, but they didn't come.

I felt the pain. Nothing compared to what I felt inside, but it made itself known. "I'd rather go where she was, Chief," was what I thought, but didn't say anything. I was very tired.

"I'm going to close my eyes and rest a bit," I said.

"Is it okay if he sleeps?" Mariano asked the ambulance attendant.

"His vitals are steady," the girl said. "He doesn't appear to be bleeding inside. If he can, it shouldn't hurt him."

"I don't need to sleep. I'm just going to rest my eyes a bit."

I was in the hospital when I woke up. There was a lot of noise around me. Mariano was standing off to the side. A doctor or a P.A. walked over to me.

"Mr. Creed, do you know where you are and what happened?"

"Yes."

"Please tell me where you are."

"The hospital."

"Okay. Can you tell me about the pain?"

"Yeah, excruciating. Right shoulder feels like an electrical cord going down my arm and up my neck. I'm guessing severed tendons, at least one. After a while, I couldn't lift my arm, but not because of the pain."

"Okay, we're sending you for X-rays and an MRI, then probably to surgery. We have a great orthopedic surgeon. If a tendon was severed, it won't be arthroscopic surgery."

"I understand. Do what you need to get it over with. I need to be out of here in time for the wake and funeral."

"I'm so sorry for your loss," she said.

I looked at her and tried to smile. I wanted to say thank you, but the gravity of her death slammed me again. I nodded. She put her hand on mine for a moment, and then moved off.

I felt exhausted. I didn't realize killing someone would take so much out of me. Maybe getting shot had something to do with it too. I remembered it, I went over it. If she wasn't dead, I'd be smiling ear to ear.

It was hard not to scream when they positioned my arm for the X-rays, and it took everything I had not to scream when they positioned my arm over my head for the MRI. The two girls encouraged me, insisting it wouldn't be much longer. I didn't mind the pain, because it distracted me from a far worse pain. I'm guessing they could tell by the sweat pouring off me and my lovely shade of gray.

After the MRI, I fell asleep again, then awoke in what I assumed was a pre-surgery room. Everything seemed to be happening fast. I'm guessing Mariano had something to do with that.

When I woke up, I saw three people standing looking down at me. Two I didn't know, the third was Kenny Testa. He looked down at me and smiled. Despite the pain, I raised my eyebrows.

"Doc, what are you doing here?"

"Hey, Jimmy. Marilyn, the girl that used to work for me, is now working in the ER. She called me. My mom and dad are here, too."

The man with the stethoscope said, "Mr. Creed, Dr. Testa told us he's your personal physician, and we discussed your condition with him."

Using my finely honed powers of deduction, I surmised he was another doctor. He stood there with the woman, who I surmised was also a doctor, since someone called her 'Doctor.'

"He is, and that's fine."

"I'll let him fill you in, and if you give the go ahead, we'll take you into surgery."

"Will I be out in time for the wake and the funeral?"

"Yes. You won't be able to move your arm much for a while, but you're in no real danger. Overnight and tomorrow, or the day after, you'll be good to go."

I nodded. She smiled and they walked away. "What's the scoop, Doc?"

"Bullet went through, no broken bones, no major veins or arteries. A tendon is severed, another badly torn."

"I figured when I couldn't lift my arm anymore." I figured it was already torn, and I finished the job when I broke his neck. It was worth it.

"It won't be arthroscopic surgery. They'll punch a hole in the bone, put the tendon in, and plug it up. You'll be back to normal but it will take time. They can either repair the torn one, or will cut it and do the same thing."

"Well, I'm guessing the tendon won't reattach itself."

"No," Ken said. "It will be a long recovery. You won't be able to move the arm for a couple of months, then you'll need therapy. You'll come back from it, but it will take time."

I nodded but didn't really care. "I keep falling asleep."

"Massive adrenaline burst, and your body devoting energy to the wound."

"Seems reasonable. Can I sit up a little? I'm tired of lying down."

Ken reached behind the bed, moved things around, and raised the portion of the bed behind the top half of me. He grabbed a pillow and gently positioned it behind my head.

"Thanks," I said. He smiled.

"My dad wants to say, 'Hi.'"

"Sure."

In whatever group I was in at the time, from early on, I was the Joker. Every crew had at least one Joker. It wasn't because I didn't take things seriously, I just didn't take *myself* seriously. The Joker would, if the other people in the group knew him, put everyone else at ease. I often found humor in the darkest of places, but not now. I don't think I've ever been in a darker place than this.

Smitty walked in. Except for the white hair, he looked the same as he did when I first met him around thirty years ago. Scar tissue and a more or less flat nose. He was a big man, but moved as if he was much smaller.

He rested his hand on mine, "Is there anything I can do?"

"I wish there was," I said.

"I'm sorry."

I nodded. I remembered how concerned she was about Shane. I looked down at my shirt. Her blood was still there, but was dry now. I touched it.

"There is something, her son. She was worried about her son. He was interested in lessons. I was going to bring him by."

"Done. No charge. Ever."

I smiled. "You did that for us. For my family."

"Best thing I ever did. I love you, son. Get better."

I squeezed his hand, and he left. I was alone for a while. I don't think I've ever been alone to that degree in my life, and was looking forward to the anesthesia.

They were prepping me for surgery. They removed my clothes and put a gown on me. I knew it was rare these days, but there was always the chance I wouldn't make it. Surgery was always risky.

It would suit me fine if I didn't wake up.